THE
BABYSITTERS
COVEN

THE
BABYSITTERS
COVEN

KATE
WILLIAMS

DELACORTE PRESS

Visit us on the web! GetUnderlined.com

Educators and librarians, for a variety of teaching tools, visit us at RHTeachersLibrarians.com

Library of Congress Cataloging-in-Publication Data
Names: Williams, Kate, author.
Title: The babysitters coven / Kate Williams.
Description: First edition. | New York : Delacorte Press, [2019] | Summary: After new student Cassandra Heaven joins seventeen-year-old Esme Pearl's babysitters club, the girls learn that being a babysitter really means a heroic lineage of superpowers, magic rituals, and saving the innocent from evil.
Identifiers: LCCN 2018059287 (print) | LCCN 2019003475 (ebook) |
ISBN 978-0-525-70739-4 (el) | ISBN 978-0-525-70737-0 (hc) |
ISBN 978-0-525-70738-7 (glb) | ISBN 978-0-593-12380-5 (intl. tr. pbk.)
Subjects: | CYAC: Babysitters—Fiction. | Clubs—Fiction. | Witchcraft—Fiction.
Classification: LCC PZ7.1.W5465 (ebook) | LCC PZ7.1.W5465 Bab 2019 (print) |
DDC [Fic] — dc23

The text of this book is set in 12-point Baskerville MT.
Interior design by Ken Crossland

Printed in the United States of America
10 9 8 7 6 5 4 3 2 1
First Edition

To all the badass babysitters—

past, present, and future

CHAPTER 1

The devil was an artist. Her medium varied, from crayons to Magic Markers to finger paints, and she had coloring books, construction paper, giant pads of newsprint on a tiny plastic easel. But today she'd ignored it all, in favor of the hallway and a marker. Previously pristine white, the wall was now permanently adorned with black squiggles, dots, shapes, and lines, all drawn at eye level. Well, *her* eye level—a little less than three feet off the ground.

How did I know this art was permanent and not the water-soluble kind? Because Baby Satan—known by some as Kaitlyn—was still holding the Sharpie in her hand. As I surveyed her work—which was impressive in its own way, because she'd done all of this damage in only the time it had taken me to pee—she smiled sweetly up at me, topless underneath a pair of very dirty OshKosh overalls. She held the Sharpie up to her nose and inhaled deeply, a look of intense contentment on her face. "Give me that," I said, grabbing it from her. Two years old, and already into graffiti and huffing.

She was on one tonight. It had started with dinner, which was dinosaur-shaped chicken nuggets and bunny-shaped mac-n-cheese. She wouldn't eat any of it, not even when I insisted that the nuggets were actually made from real tri- ceratops. When I got up to go get a paper towel, she man- aged to transfer most of the mac-n-cheese to her seat and sit on it.

She thought this was hilarious and wiggled around, etch- ing orange cheese stains that would probably never come out into the butt of her overalls. "Squishy!" she squealed with de- light, and I was sorry that I'd taught her that word last week. After dinner, we played with blocks, which mainly consisted of me building the tallest stack I could and then cheering as she ran at them, full speed, from across the room to knock them down. It was right after this that I made that fateful decision to use the bathroom. I should have known better.

Now I placed the cap back on the Sharpie and put it on the kitchen counter, far back against the wall and safely out of her reach. "All right!" I said. "It's bedtime."

Bedtime started with a bath, complete with fizzy dye pods—two blue and one yellow—to make turquoise "mer- maid water." She drank some of it. Teeth were brushed, sorta, and pajamas were donned. I usually allotted the devil three bedtime stories, which was enough to have her nod- ding off, her chin coming down to her chest, but tonight her blue eyes were still wide open and alert. Each time I'd finish a story, she'd climb out of bed, run across the room, and come back with a new stack. "More!" she'd scream, slamming them into my lap with a surprising, and almost impressive, violence.

In this moment, I saw my future stretching out before me.

Kaitlyn never goes to sleep.

Her mom never comes home.

I read bedtime stories until the world ends.

It was times like these that I wished I could tap out and have another babysitter come in and take over. Baby Satan had a million stuffed animals, and my eyes settled on a floppy dog that was nearly life-sized. Couldn't he read a story for once?

His ears twitched, as if he were responding to my mental plea.

I blinked and rubbed my eyes.

Babysitting was making me hallucinate.

I sighed. Kaitlyn was still wide-awake. Not a hint of sleepiness anywhere on her admittedly cute face.

I picked up another book. "Okay," I said. "This one's about a bunny who runs away. It's called *The Runaway Bunny.*" She smiled, all cherub cheeks and dimples, and something in me softened. "See what they did with the title there?" I said. "The people who wrote this book must be pretty clever, huh? I bet they were geniuses."

"Smart bunny," she said.

I nodded, reaching over to tuck a strand of hair behind her ear. "A very smart bunny. You ready?"

It took seven stories before she finally fell asleep, her

blankie pressed against her cheek. I gave the wall a few half-hearted scrubs, but the thing about permanent markers is that they're permanent, so I admitted defeat and went into the kitchen. After everything I'd had to endure tonight, I deserved a snack. I mean, the number one perk of babysitting is OPP—other people's pantries.

I opened the pantry to what could have stocked a vending machine: potato chips, Chex Mix, Cheez-Its (Kaitlyn's mom, Sharon, had even started buying the white cheddar ones, just for me), pretzels, Doritos, jumbo-sized bags of M&M's, Twizzlers, gummy bears, you name it. None of this had anything to do with the fact that it was almost Halloween—this was just what Sharon ate all year round.

I grabbed what I wanted, found a big bowl, and poured in a layer of Frosted Flakes. I smashed up a few pretzels and added them, then a handful of Corn Chex, some potato chips, and a generous layer of M&M's. Then I sprinkled the whole thing with sugar, poured some milk on it, and stood back to admire my specialty: Babysitter's Crunch, the perfect mixture of salty and sweet. Kellogg's should market this stuff.

It looked so pretty and delicious that I thought for a second about posting it, then remembered that would just announce to the world (or at least my 67 followers) that I was spending yet another night with Tony the Tiger and a human who thought "potty" was a dirty word. I'm not ashamed of babysitting, but I know it's not what most people think of as a "cool job."

I took my crunch and sank into the couch in front of the

TV. OPTVs are also serious babysitting perkage, and Sharon had every channel and subscription imaginable. I finally settled on a reality show where a girl with breast implants, hair extensions, acrylic nails, and a spray tan cried to the camera about how she couldn't stand fake people.

A loud *thunk* sounded from the second floor of the condo, and I bolted up off the couch, my bowl tumbling from my lap and spilling the last of its sugar milk out onto the rug. Nervous reaction aside, I was sure it was nothing—a book falling onto its side or closet junk settling—but it is my babysitterly duty to investigate things that go *thunk* in the nightish. I inched a few steps up the stairs and called Kaitlyn's name, not wanting to wake her if she wasn't already up. I waited a few seconds but didn't get a response, so I tiptoed the rest of the way up to her room. I figured I'd peek in just to make sure she was okay. I mean, I was sure she'd be heard halfway to Egypt if she wasn't, but better safe than sorry.

I grabbed the door handle and turned, but nothing. It wouldn't budge. WTF? How did her door get locked? I turned again, harder this time, but it still didn't move. This wasn't Kaitlyn's MO at all—she loved an audience. If she was going to lock the door from the inside, she would have made sure I was standing right outside, begging her not to do it.

I got down on my knees and peered under the door into the room. I could see the soft cast of Kaitlyn's night-light change from red to purple, but that was it, and the room was silent. As I stood back up, blue and green bathed the toes of my Chelsea boots.

"Kaitlyn," I said quietly. "Open the door, okay, munch-kin?" I tried the handle again. I was starting to get that feeling a babysitter never wants to experience: Oh crap, oh crap, oh crap. Aka panic.

"Kaitlyn?"

I was full-on yelling now, and still getting nothing, not even a peep, from the bedroom. I grabbed the door handle with both hands and jiggled it frantically. Then I was falling into the room, the door swinging open and slamming into the wall. The window was wide open, screen and all; the curtains billowed gently. And the room was empty.

The blood rushing to my head sounded like a freeway in my ears, and the floor tilted under my feet. It was like every-thing was spinning. I stumbled to the window and stuck my head outside, and froze when I saw Kaitlyn standing on the roof of the porch. At the edge. One story up over the paved driveway.

She was clutching her blankie, tears running down her face.

"Mesme! Mesme!" she yelled when she saw me, and my heart stopped as she started to take a step forward, and wobbled.

"Kaitlyn, don't move!" I yelled as calmly as I could. "It's okay. I'm coming to get you! Just stay right there." I hated heights. I couldn't even stand on a chair without get-ting dizzy, but I hauled myself through the window and out onto the roof. Carefully, on my hands and knees, I crawled toward her, telling myself not to look down. The rough shingles scraped my palms and the tops of my boots, and I could feel the sweat dripping from my pits and rolling down the inside of my arms. I crawled until I was right next to her, then shifted onto my butt and pulled her into my lap. She had snot streaking her face, and she buried it into my neck with a sob.

"The man, Mesme," she burbled. "He not nice. He not nice at all." It made me shiver. A man? What was she talking about?

"It's okay, honey. Don't be scared, booger," I said, rubbing the back of her head and using every nickname I'd ever called her. "Pumpkin, you just had a nightmare, that's all. It's over now, turtle." I scooted us back toward the window, straining to see or hear any sign of someone else.

All I heard was the rustling of dry leaves as a gust of wind swept by.

Kaitlyn wouldn't let me put her down, so I climbed back in through the window with her in my arms, then held her as I peered out again and looked up and down the street. It was empty. I slammed the window shut and locked it, then steeled myself to look in the closet. Nothing but broken toys and dirty laundry. Kaitlyn blubbered into my shoulder, and I rubbed her back and softly rocked side to side, hoping she couldn't feel how badly I was shaking. The night-light had faded into a warm orange, and I walked over and sat down on her bed.

"What happened, sweetie?" I asked, barely able to get the words out. My brain was screaming at me to call the cops, but my body wasn't reaching for my phone. My hands kept stroking Kaitlyn's hair, and my butt was staying right where it was planted.

"Not nice," she said again, still talking about the man.

"What'd he look like?" I pressed.

"He got fountain hair and marker eyes."

Great. What the hell did that mean?

"What color was his fountain hair?" I asked.

"Sunshine."

"Okay," I said, rocking her back and forth. "What kind of clothes did he have on?"

She sniffed. "Ruffles. Pretty and sparkly."

Okay, so a man with sunshine fountain hair and marker eyes, in pretty sparkly clothes with ruffles . . . Oh my God, she was describing David Bowie. From *Labyrinth*. I was so relieved, I almost laughed.

"Did he have a pretty bubble too?" I asked. She nodded again. My heart slowed. "Does mama let you watch movies?"

"I like movies," she said.

"I know you do, kitten." My knees seemed like they could hold weight again, so I stood up and turned to put Kaitlyn back to bed. It sounded just like Sharon to let Kaitlyn watch movies that were way too old for her. But hey, I was only seventeen. Who was I to neg on someone's parenting?

"How did you get out on the roof, tiny girl?" I asked.

"I didn't do it, Mesme," she said, and I sighed. I'd heard those exact words just a few hours earlier, when I'd confronted her about her hallway art.

"Okay," I said. "Just don't ever not do it again, all right? That was very dangerous."

I pulled the covers up to her chin and pulled out *Goodnight Moon* again. This was going to be a long night.

It took two more stories after Goodnight Moon to get Kaitlyn calmed down, but she finally drifted off to sleep, a stuffed pig tucked under one arm and a sloth under the other. It was just another hiccup in a normal night of babysitting, so as I sopped the remnants of my crunch up off the rug downstairs, I was surprised to see that my hands were trembling.

She'd seen a movie. She'd had a nightmare. Maybe she'd started sleepwalking. That had to be it, right? Except . . .

In all the times I'd babysat for Kaitlyn, she'd never gotten out of bed, no matter how much time it had taken for her to go to sleep. Forget climbing out the window—how had she even done that? The whole thing was freaky, and despite a handful of yogurt-covered pretzels I consumed in one swallow, I was still jittery when Sharon got home. Being a babysitter meant that you were supposed to keep your cool in tough situations, no matter what kind of torture your charges dreamed up for you. What you were not supposed to do was immediately panic and forget how to open a door.

I'd been debating how much to tell Sharon, and the second she came in, I decided as little as possible. She seemed upset and distracted, and kept writing and then deleting a text from her phone.

I tried to act casual as I gathered up my stuff. "Has Kaitlyn ever sleepwalked before?" I asked.

Without looking up from her phone, she grabbed a Diet Coke from the fridge and opened it one-handed. "No," she said, frowning at her screen. "Why?"

"I think she had a bad dream tonight," I said, feeling out how much I should reveal. "And she got out of bed and seemed really upset and she kept talking about a man who opened the window."

Sharon looked up and set the phone down on the counter. "Oh dear," she said, her face equal parts worry and annoyance. "It's my fault. I'm going to have to stop letting her watch all those movies. It's the only way to get her to sit still, but she has such an imagination that it'd be no surprise if they're giving her nightmares. She went back to sleep, though?"

The cobra in my stomach uncoiled—I'd been right. It was the movies, and it had just been a nightmare.

Sharon opened her wallet and thrust some bills into my hand. "Thanks again, Esme," she said. "You're a lifesaver. I don't know what I'd do without you."

I'd worked my ass off, as I always did with Kaitlyn, but I felt weird taking Sharon's money. Maybe it had been just a nightmare, but maybe it had been . . . I don't know. There was something tugging at the edge of my mind that wouldn't let go, something that didn't respond to reasonable explanations. I couldn't stop thinking, what if I hadn't gotten to Kaitlyn in time? I knew I should tell Sharon everything, but I couldn't get the words to my tongue.

"Esme?"

Sharon's voice snapped me back to where I was, and she

was still standing there, her arm out with several bills in her hand.

I took the money. "Thanks a lot," I said, "She's a great kid." I shoved the bills into my pocket. "Oh, uh, the wall," I said, suddenly remembering. "She got a marker and, in the hallway . . ." I looked up, and Sharon had her phone again, the blue light reflecting off her face as her thumbs furiously typed away. Oh well. She'd figure it out as soon as she saw it. And maybe she'd even be proud—after all, it looked like Kaitlyn was halfway to figuring out how to spell her own name.

I walked home alone in the dark because, yes, even though I'd turned seventeen in August, which meant I'd turned sixteen over a year before, I still didn't drive. Sharon always forgot, and it was easier to just get out of the house and hurry home alone than it was to remind her that I didn't have a license, and then spend fifteen minutes making small talk in her kitchen while I waited for a ride. Sharon was a single mom—like, really single. As in, it was all she talked about. And while she was a good client who paid well, the last thing on earth I wanted was for her to open up her dating apps and ask for my opinion on her profile pics again. And tonight, I just wanted to get out of there.

I thought I was pretty unflappable as a babysitter. I'd dealt with poop, projectile vomits, siblings that went all UFC on each other, and a klepto kindergartner who stole my phone and my house keys. I should have been able to take a little sleepwalking in stride. All in a day's work, right? Yet I couldn't get the image of Kaitlyn on the ledge out of my head. It was a nightmare, all right. But mine, not hers. Something happening to the kid you were in charge of was the worst thing a babysitter could imagine. I couldn't even begin to think about what would have happened if Sharon had come home to find Kaitlyn perched on the roof and me watching reality TV while eating junk food out of a mixing bowl. Or worse . . . I stopped thinking and forced myself to take a deep breath. I wasn't letting my mind spiral there. Not tonight, not ever.

Deep down, I know I'm a good babysitter, and it's a job I want to hold on to. Babysitting is about the only thing standing between me and a job that requires me to wear an embroidered polo, and nothing good ever came out of a job with a uniform. David Gibson worked at Target, and Mark Malloy had told everyone at school that he'd once seen David get a boner while restocking the super plus tampons. The boner in question was probably no more than a pleat-front khaki malfunction, but still, gossip like that was exactly why I liked to stay out of sight, locked away in someone's family room, far away from the prying eyes of people my own age.

Other teenagers?

Thanks, but no.

Still, I had to admit that the stakes were way higher with babysitting. If I screwed up, someone small and innocent could get hurt. If David Gibson made a mistake, he accidentally shelved the tampons next to the tennis balls.

My major screwup left me feeling like I'd downed three bottles of cold brew—I jumped every time a leaf rustled, and I double-timed it to put some distance between me and the family of ghosts swinging from an oak tree. God, I swear the Halloween decorations around here get more elaborate every year.

I stopped at a crosswalk and waited for the light to change, with a flower bed full of dismembered limbs to my right, and a psychopathic-killer-themed driveway to my left, complete with bloody boot prints leading into the garage. It was a sign of just how twisted small-town life really was. This was one of those nothing-ever-happens places where fender benders made the paper, but still, if Yankee Candle ever introduced a Moonbeams on Rotting Flesh scent, it would sell out in Spring River. There was no place like suburbia for repressing a dark side, and now it came out earlier every year. This year, I'd started seeing skeletons in July.

The light finally changed, and I stepped into the street. Starting to cross, I couldn't help but think how the night's events were just a few more things to add to my list of stuff I wished I could talk to my mom about. I mean, I could definitely talk to her about it. She just wouldn't say anything in response.

So, I'd do what I always did when something bothered me.

Step one: Shake it off.

Step two: Pretend it hadn't happened.

Step three: Never think about it again.

It had gotten me this far.

CHAPTER 2

When my alarm went off the next morning, I felt like a bag of wet cement.

Which had nothing to do with what had happened the night before.

"Wet cement" was pretty much how I felt every morning, especially Mondays, because high school. Errrrgghh. Gag me with a spoon and tell me it's dessert. I've heard that Rimbaud wrote "A Season in Hell" about high school. Okay, maybe he didn't. Maybe that was just my interpretation—because it made sense. No one knew about misery and hatred like an assistant principal with an associate's degree and a God complex. Drown *me* in sand and blood. No, really, *please.*

Life as a Spring River Bog Lemming made me want to run off a cliff. Yes, I said that right. We were the Bog Lemmings. Apparently, by the time they'd gotten to Spring River, all the good mascots had been taken, which is all you need to know about this town and its pantheons of education.

The best thing about school was that it meant I got to see Janis every day. Janis was my best friend and the best-dressed person I knew IRL. Actually, one of the best-dressed people I'd seen, period. She'd moved to Spring River in seventh grade, and I still remembered what she wore the first day she came to school: bright yellow leggings, a long gray sweater covered with multicolored pom-poms, pom-pom socks, and papier-mâché earrings, and her hair had been pulled into two afro puffs secured with those ponytail holders that had round plastic beads. Janis somehow made them look retro-cool, and not kindergarten. She told me later that her theme for that day had been "gumball machine."

I thought she was the bravest person I'd ever met in my life—who else would show up for their first day at a new school in a themed outfit? We'd been best friends from the minute she'd plopped down next to me at lunch and com-plimented the vintage Fiorucci stickers on my binder. We lived in a town that considered Fruit of the Loom to be the height of fashion, so Janis was my lifeline. I didn't want to know where I'd be without her in my life—probably wearing things because they were "practical."

Every night we texted each other what the next day's look was going to be. Today Janis was "Denise gets a step-daughter," and I was "Sylvia Plath goes to prom."

I had on a vintage knee skirt and a sequined sweater set, which contrasted nicely with the Jean Seberg *Breathless* hair and silver nose stud that I considered my signatures. I'd gone for a lipstick that was matte pink, swapped my normal tortoiseshell glasses for rhinestone cat-eyes, and added the pièce de résistance of my themed outfit: pewter bell jar earrings I found at the antiques mall.

If I'd gotten to school early, I could have seen Janis before class, but I did not generally get to school early. I usually got to campus right before—and occasionally right after—the first bell, so most days I didn't see her until lunch. And because of our sucky schedules, that was actually at eleven a.m., which—if you ask me—was too early to brave the mysteries of the Spring River High cafeteria. No matter what the cafeteria menu claimed to be serving (Spinach salad! Chicken parmesan! Steak tacos!), the food in the buffet line always resembled something you could buy at Petco. In my time as a student there, I'd never seen a food that wasn't brown. It was disgusting, but the only other option was to bring your lunch, and that would require planning. And Dad actually going to the grocery store. So brown it was.

Today, the morning was pretty uneventful. I eased through my first three periods as well as one can and headed to the cafeteria, where I found Janis in the lunch line and slipped in behind her. "Denise gets a step-daughter" was right when Lisa Bonet was going boho but wasn't yet full earth mama. Janis had on baggy shibori-dyed pants, leather slippers, a gauzy silver shirt, and an oversized men's blazer. Even without dreads down to her waist, she looked Huxtable as hell.

We inched through the line, collecting our browns, and I

followed Janis to our table, over in the corner farthest away from the main wall of doors, and sat down next to her. We always sat on the same side with our backs up against the wall, like mobsters, because the cafeteria was one place where you definitely never wanted anyone coming up behind you. They could be carrying gravy. Or worse, marinara.

Today's browns were a slice of pepperoni pizza (orange-brown with red-brown spots) and a side of french fries (crispy brown). "So, how was last night?" Janis asked, dabbing her pizza with a paper napkin in a futile attempt to sop up the grease.

Even though we had been texting all night and throughout the morning, I hadn't mentioned anything about what had happened with Kaitlyn, and now that we were together in person, I still felt weird bringing it up. There was something that kept the words from forming on my tongue. Somehow saying it out loud made it more terrifying. And real.

"Fine," I said finally, adding what I could only hope was a normal smile. "The usual." I was wondering how I could change the subject, but I didn't have to: Janis changed it herself.

"There she is!" she said, slapping my arm as if she'd just seen a celebrity.

"Who are you talking about?"

"The new girl," she said, then shot me a look. "You didn't hear about the new girl?"

I shook my head and rolled my eyes. Janis always seemed to forget that she was my one and only friend, and therefore my one and only source of gossip. "Some guy dropped her off this morning," she continued. "I saw her get out of his car, which was a real POS, but he was hot AF."

I raised my eyebrows, interested in the development. Most of the males in Spring River were disgusting AF, so anyone who wasn't—even if it was someone else's boyfriend—was worth a mention. This was enough info to pique my interest, so I slowly turned like I was trying to stretch, and there was the new girl, standing right past the cashier, poised with a tray of browns and surveying the complex geography of available seats. The lunchroom was like Spring River's own sorting hat, but instead of houses, it separated you into castes. Usually you could look at someone and immediately know if they were going to be a plebe or an aristo, but with the new girl, it was hard to tell.

She certainly was pretty enough to fall right in with the ruling class. She looked dewy, like she'd just been dipped in olive oil—in a healthy, glowy way. Her black hair hung pin-straight to the middle of her back, so shiny that you could probably have seen yourself in it if you'd tried hard enough, and she looked like she'd been sucking on a lollipop, or at least had really good Korean lip gloss. She'd also clearly won some genetic lottery, because she was skinny—*with boobs.*

But her clothes looked like they'd been pulled out of a trash can: scuffed Converse that had once been white, *maybe,* and jeans that were distressed in a didn't-come-this-way-but-are-this-way-because-they're-old way. She wore a flannel that was at least three sizes too big over a baby tee that was short enough to reveal a strip of taut stomach.

That strip of stomach was enough to get the guys' attention, which meant she also got the girls' attention—the guys wondering how long it'd take to get a bite out of this piece, the girls wondering how long it would take to make her cry and lock herself in the bathroom. But there was something about the new girl that suggested she wasn't the crying type. And that she bit back.

As she stood there, more and more people noticed her, and a hush rippled through the cafeteria. She had everyone's attention. We waited with collectively bated breath. The most exciting event of the year! Everyone was dying to know! Who would she pick? Would they accept her or reject her— for all the world to see?

But instead of coming to sit at a table, she turned around, dumped her lunch into the trash, tray and all, and walked out.

"Bold," Janis said, sopping up the last of her ketchup with a pitiful excuse for a fry. "I like it."

Cassandra Heaven.

By the time the bell rang for next period, I knew her name, because the table of cretins next to us couldn't stop joking about who was going to be the first to spend "seven minutes in Heaven."

Janis and I got up and cleared our trays as Craig Lugweather said something disgusting about how he was going to "open up those pearly gates and come right on inside."

Craig Lugweather had been my chem partner the previous year, and had spent all class watching bouncing-boob GIFs on his phone under the table. And when I say "all class," I don't mean just one day—I mean all semester. A different boob GIF every day, like he had some sort of Google alert set up that zapped them right to his phone. He did nothing while I tried to mix various -ides and -iums without blowing us up. By the end of the semester, I wished I *had* blown us up. Taking myself out would have been worth it if I'd taken him with me.

As Janis and I headed toward the trash bins, an explosion of laughter erupted at his table, and I couldn't help but look back. Immediately I wished I hadn't, because Craig's hands were formed in an obscene gesture that left nothing to the imagination. He was the Harvey Weinstein of the junior class, and if there was any justice in this world, the Humane Society would have neutered him a long time ago. Just looking at him now made me feel kind of pukey.

I shook my head, and as I turned away, something caught my eye. An almost-full bottle of Hawaiian Punch on his lunch tray wobbled ever so slightly, then tipped over so that it dumped sticky red directly into his lap and interrupted his pantomime.

"Dude, what the?" Craig screamed, immediately punching Dane Kirball in the shoulder.

Dane punched him back. "I didn't touch it, bro!" he said. "You did that yourself."

The whole thing made my body feel like it had collided with an electric fence. Because I could swear that somehow I'd done that. Even though I hadn't. Because I couldn't. Because that would have been impossible.

Right?

CHAPTER 3

Janis and I walked toward our lockers in silence, and I felt the dread mounting with each step. Lunch with Janis was definitely the highlight of my day. After that it just got suckier and suckier. I dropped off the books I didn't need and made my way to my next class. Driver's ed.

The fact that I still didn't have a driver's license was one of my most epic fails, and it made me want to bury my head in my locker like an adolescent ostrich. Granted, there weren't many places I needed to go where Janis wasn't also going, but someday I was going to have to take the wheel. *Passenger for Life: The Esme Pearl Story* did not sound like a page-turning bio. It would just be page after page of me sending the same text: "Hey, do you think you could pick me up?" Ugh.

Dad had had big plans to teach me how to drive as soon as I'd turned sixteen last year, but after a few months of "next weekend," combined with neither of us rushing to get me into the driver's seat (aka hanging out, just the two of us), we'd finally decided that driver's ed was the best option. Lower insurance rates too, Dad reasoned, probably more as a way to make him feel better about it.

I'd been too late sophomore year, so all the classes had been full, so I'd tried to sign up for the summer school session, but that had cost extra. That was how I now found myself, lunch congealing in my belly, a junior on my way into a class with a bunch of sophomores and one freshman who looked like he was actually about thirty-five and out on parole.

The driver's ed room was full of driving simulators that had probably been considered pretty high-tech back when the school had first bought them in, oh, I don't know, 1963? In all the instructional videos, the women wore gloves and the men wore hats, and everyone stopped at all the stop signs and used their blinker when changing lanes.

Don't get me wrong. I loved the retro fashion, but I wasn't sure that the era represented a realistic depiction of driving anymore. Shouldn't this class have been getting us prepped for how to deal when a guy in a jacked-up Chevy with truck balls dangling off the back made a right turn from the left lane into a Buffalo Wild Wings parking lot and cut you off in the process? I mean, that was what happened to Dad when he was driving me to school this morning. It made him spill coffee on his cargo slacks, and he was not happy about it.

I took my seat in the back of the room, and zoned, staring out the window at a crow picking at a Burger King bag in the parking lot. He was really going for it, and I was starting to get into it. Like, I was emotionally invested in whether or not there were any fry crumbs left in that ball of greasy paper, and if so, was—

"Esme Pearl."

Hearing my name snapped me out of the drama happening outside, and it took a second to realize that I wasn't just getting called on to answer a question.

Crap. I'd forgotten that today was my day to actually drive. Not in a simulator but in a real, three-dimensional vehicle, outside in the world. I gathered my stuff back up and started to head to the front of the room, and stifled a groan when I saw the three students I'd be sharing said vehicle with.

All three guys, all three football players, all three grinning like they'd somehow rigged this so that they could be together. They probably had, which made me anxious about whatever was coming next. I was sure it wouldn't be good.

The four of us made our way out to the back of the school, the three of them laughing and talking and me trailing behind, alone and quiet. Our driving instructor led us to the car that was waiting for us in the parking lot.

The car was a Toyota Corolla, shiny beige and one step up from a tuna can on wheels. The instructor was Mr. Dekalb, who was about ninety years old and as deaf as a concrete block. He had gray hairs sprouting out of the pores on his nose, and his eyebrows could have used a good sesh with a weed whacker. He smiled and gave us a speech that was pretty much unintelligible but which I gathered from facial cues and hand gestures was about safety and respect for the road. Then he consulted the clipboard he was holding, and cleared his throat.

"Miss Pearl," he said, before being seized by a mucusy cough. "Ladies first."

He stepped aside and opened the driver's-side door, then looked at me expectantly.

Oh, hell. His outdated chivalry meant it was my turn to drive.

Mr. Dekalb sat shotgun, and the three guys crammed into the back. Their knees butted up against the front seat, and they made lots of gay jokes about accidentally touching each other's legs. Since Mr. Dekalb couldn't hear anything quieter than a honking horn, he had no idea what they were saying, and I tried to ignore them as I adjusted my mirrors and buckled my seat belt.

The gay jokes progressed, or regressed, to dick jokes, and I cleared my throat loudly, but none of them paid me any attention. Mr. Dekalb scribbled something on his clipboard; then he told me to start the car. I turned the key, and the Corolla whined to life just as there was a sound like splitting fabric from the back seat.

The bros dissolved into giggles that quickly turned to gags.

One of them had just ripped a massive fart.

We were hot-boxed by a flatulent cloud of eggs, kimchi,

and old burritos. My eyes were watering, and I gagged, grabbing the steering wheel and leaning forward as if I could somehow get away from it. Next to me, Mr. Dekalb still hadn't heard a thing, but boy, could he smell it.

"Maybe some fresh air?" he said, beginning to press a button on his door, trying to roll his window down, but it wouldn't budge. In the back seat, the boys were punching each other and pretending to vomit. We were all mashing at the window buttons, but none of them opened so much as a crack.

"The child lock, Esme," Mr. Dekalb said. "The child lock . . ." He was holding his hand over his nose.

I had no idea what the child lock was. I pressed something on my armrest, but it just locked the doors. The guys in the back seat were now yelling at me to open the doors or roll down the windows. I kept pressing buttons, on the door, on the steering wheel, on the console, and the windshield wipers flipped on, then the AM radio. Nothing happened, and I was starting to panic.

I dropped my hands from the wheel and sat back to catch my breath, except breathing was the last thing I wanted to do.

That was when it happened.

With a jerk, we were zooming backward. Only, I wasn't touching anything! My stomach lurched as the gas pedal pressed to the floor. The steering wheel was rocking back and forth like it was being controlled by an invisible toddler, and the Corolla cut a wild squiggle through the parking lot, then jumped the curb and stopped only when it plowed right into a baby birch tree that had been planted with much ceremony by the graduating seniors of last year's environmental club.

For a split second, we all sat there in shocked silence, no one saying anything, nothing but the fuzz of static coming from the radio. I blinked back tears brought on half by noxious butt fumes, half by impending humiliation. What had happened?

I saw a different button. I pressed it. Everyone gasped for breath as the windows rolled down.

That was when the airbags deployed.

No one else ended up behind the wheel in driver's ed that day. Everyone knew that something was up when we were back in the classroom within fifteen minutes of leaving. The three bros couldn't keep their mouth shut for a second, and were barely in the door before they were recounting the tale like they were war heroes just back from the trenches.

I was slinking back to my chair when Mr. Dekalb cleared his throat. "Esme, please come with me," he said, and motioned for me to follow him out the door. Normally those are the last words you want to hear coming out of a teacher's mouth, but in that moment I would have taken any excuse to GTFO of that classroom, where half the eyes were on me, who was hating it, and the other half on my passengers, who were loving it. Every second of it.

Mr. Dekalb didn't say anything as we headed down the

hall to the office. He pushed open the swinging door and let me go first. I stood in the middle of the room, not sure what to do next. He walked past me to the counter.

"I need an accident report, Donna," he said to the school secretary, who was reptilian in features and had hair like a crash helmet.

"Oh jeez, Gary, again?" she said. "Was this one texting too?"

Mr. Dekalb ran his hand through his hair, dislodging a few flakes of dandruff that drifted down to settle with the others on the shoulder of his sweater. "Nope," he said, shaking his head. "Just can't drive worth a hoot." I was about to clear my throat, thinking that maybe he was so old and senile that he'd forgotten that I was standing right there, when he picked up a phone and turned toward me.

"Esme, what's your mother's number?"

"My mom, uh . . ." I stumbled on my words.

"Ah, yes," he said, nodding, because even freakin' Mr. Dekalb knew about Mom. "Your father's, then?"

I recited it, and he dialed as I held my breath. I could hear the phone ringing through the receiver, and he was just about to hang up when Dad answered.

"Hello, Mr. Pearl?" he said. "This is Gary Dekalb, your daughter's driver's ed teacher. I am, unfortunately, calling because there's been an accident." He paused for a second. "No, she's fine, but there has been significant vehicle damage, and property damage as well." I tuned out right after I heard him say, "You see, she ran over a tree. A baby tree."

The next thing I knew, he was holding the phone out to me. I would have preferred to have this conversation never, but no such luck. I took the phone from Mr. Dekalb and held it up to my ear, keeping it an inch away from my skin since I had no idea where this phone had been. Today was shaping up badly enough without a case of ear herpes.

"Hello?" I said.

Dad answered with a sigh. A looong sigh, like a slowly deflating air mattress. Just when I thought he couldn't possibly have any air left in his lungs, he took a breath and sighed again.

"Esme, I'm not mad," he said, finally. "I'm just glad no one was hurt."

"Okay," I responded, because I wasn't sure what he wanted me to say.

"And I take half the blame," he continued.

"Okay."

"We should have been practicing. If my seventeen-year-old daughter doesn't know the difference between the brake and the gas pedal, I can't blame anyone but myself."

A flame of anger flickered in my chest. Did he really think I was that dumb? But just as quickly, I extinguished it. Because I didn't have an excuse. I didn't even really know what had happened. I swear I hadn't touched anything, but I couldn't say that, because it would just sound like I was trying to say it wasn't my fault.

Besides, it sounded nuts, and I knew all about that.

"We'll have to put the money we were saving to buy you a

car toward the damages," Dad continued. "And you'll probably have to contribute some of your babysitting money as well. I hate to do this, but you've got to take responsibility for your actions, and the sooner you learn that, the better."

I told him "Okay" again, we exchanged a few more words, and then he hung up and I handed the phone back. Mr. Dekalb, who displayed a sense of intuition that was totally surprising, wrote me a bathroom pass and excused me from the remainder of class.

I gratefully took it and headed to the girls' bathroom, where I sat on the toilet fully clothed, my knees tucked up under my chin, and tried to steel myself for my next port of call on this humiliation cruise. It awaited me right after the next bell.

CHAPTER 4

Gym. I hate it. I despise it, I abhor it. If it were a person, I would speed up if I saw it crossing the street. If it were a building, I would set it on fire. But it's a class, so I take it. Because I have to.

I thought I was so smart, getting out of gym freshman and sophomore year. Freshman year was the year everyone was supposed to take it. Unless you were in band. So a crappy piccolo player I became. I could barely blow my way through "Twinkle, Twinkle, Little Star" without spit pooling and dribbling out of the end of my petite wand. Gross it most definitely was, and after a full year of placing paper towels around my chair, I had to admit—and the band teacher readily agreed—that perhaps music was not for me.

At the beginning of sophomore year, I was lucky enough to get mono. That came with a doctor's note that got me out of gym for the whole first semester, and a computer glitch meant that gym didn't show up on my schedule for the second semester either.

So of course it came around to bite me in the butt junior year, when it was me and a bunch of freshmen who were all still bigger and stronger and better at sports than me. And fellow junior Stacey Wasser, who took gym because she *liked* it.

I couldn't even wrap my head around that—it was like liking the norovirus, or the longest, slowest line at the checkout counter. She was the biggest bully the school had ever had. Even the teachers ducked when they saw her coming. Also, she'd hated me ever since we'd had art class together freshman year. I made a turtle flute out of clay, and it pissed her off because I guess she'd had a bad experience with a turtle when she was little. IDK, and I didn't really care either. All I knew was that my turtle came out of the kiln with a fist print right in the middle of it, and that really made her laugh. I gave all gym activities about an 8 percent effort, but I did burn a lot of calories trying to stay as far away from Stacey Wasser as I possibly could.

The only thing worse than actual gym class were the few minutes leading up to it, in the locker room. The locker room was a steamy armpit. Walking into it felt like heading into the bathroom right after someone else had taken a too-long shower that had used up all the hot water and left filmy puddles on the floor.

And the hair—oh God, the hair. Long brown hairs, long blond hairs, long red hairs, long black hairs . . . curly, short hairs that *did not* come from someone's head, if you know what I mean. Rodent-sized clumps of hair that had been pulled from hairbrushes and tossed into corners, only to escape and attach themselves to the butt of your shorts as soon as you made the mistake of sitting on a bench, or stuck between your toes if you ever chanced to touch a bare foot to the ground.

And don't even get me started on the gym uniforms.

They looked like they'd been designed by the fashion team at Depends. The front and the back of the shorts were indistinguishable, and they were the highest of high-waisted. You could pull them up to your armpits and look like a grandpa out for his regular mall walk, or you could roll them down until you had a good three inches of thick fabric orbiting your belly button. Some of the curvier girls had managed to make them look awkward-sexy in that seventies way, but I didn't even try. I was just a stick figure in incontinence pants.

I changed out of Sylvia Plath and into my diaper wear as quickly I could and kept my tank on under my T-shirt. Any time you can do a thing to avoid getting naked at school, you should definitely do that thing.

I looked up long enough to notice the new girl, Cassandra Heaven, standing at the end of a row of lockers, her gym uniform crumpled in her hand and a look of total dismay on her face. In any other environment, I would have said hello, made a joke, done something to try to make her feel like the hellhole she was in wasn't going to be so hellish.

But this was gym. It was every girl for herself.

I shut my locker, locked it, and walked out to the gymnasium, where I leaned up against the wall, wishing I could just blend in with the tile. I jumped when I heard an adult male voice say my name, and then groaned silently to myself.

"Hi, Brian. Er, I mean Coach Davis," I said, forcing a smile. Coach Davis was in his early forties and wore a nylon tracksuit every day. He wore a gold chain tucked into his T-shirt, and in all the years that I'd known him, I'd never managed to figure out what was on it. He was the head of the school's athletic department, the football coach, and also my dad's best friend. In fact, he was basically Dad's only friend, and it was a friendship that had always puzzled me. I mean, my dad was a dork. Like, he was a legit Tom Cruise fan, and his favorite musician was Dave Matthews. And Coach Davis was kinda cool. Like, not cool in an I'd-want-to-hang-out-with-him way but in a top-of-the-Spring-River-food-chain kinda way. There was something about him that made people pay attention—I'd once seen a grown woman lose her mind in a 7-Eleven because she mistook Brian for Ludacris. Like any celebrity had ever set foot in Spring River.

I didn't even really know how he and Dad knew each other—I thought it dated back to being on the same team, somewhere, doing something that involved a ball—but Brian had been around for as long as I could remember, and, truth be told, I always got the vibe from him that it was more obligation than fun times. Obligation to what, though, I had no clue, but it did lead to plenty of awkward interactions for me. Like this one.

"How's it going?" I asked, forcing myself to stand up straight and not look miserable.

"Good, Esme," he said. "Glad to see you out here getting some physical activity."

"Well, it is physical education, right? Haha. Gotta kick some balls, you know?" Oh my God. Could this small talk be any worse? Thankfully, I was saved by the whistle, and Coach Davis flashed me a thumbs-up and walked away. I breathed a sigh of relief, and then immediately felt guilty about it. He was really nice—to me, and especially to Dad. But still, there was just something about Brian that I couldn't quite put my finger on, like he was always about to say something serious and then decided not to. It always made me feel weird. I didn't want to have a heart-to-heart with any adult, but especially not a male gym teacher.

The door swung shut behind him, and I turned my attention back to the whistle blower, who was my bad perm of a gym teacher and the cheerleading sponsor. Three more short tweets, and then she announced that we were going to have fun today and play dodgeball.

I actually LOL'd.

Surely there were United Nations accords against dodgeball by now, right? No one had played dodgeball IRL since the eighties. It was like smoking—people had finally realized it was bad for you.

Right?

Right?

Wrong.

Coach Perm was busy emptying out a big bag of red rubber balls, and they poured, bouncing, onto the floor. "All right. Count off into teams!" *Tweet, tweet.* "One!" she yelled, pointing at a gangly freshman, who shuffled off to one side of the room. *Tweet, tweet.* "Two!" yelled a redhead, bounding off to the other.

"One!"

"Two!" The counting-off continued, with people yelling out their numbers like they were super stoked (sadists, probably) or mumbling them like they were heading off to the executioner's chamber. Before I knew it, it was my turn. "Two," I groaned. As I walked over to join my teammates/fellow denizens of hell, I surveyed our opponents, wondering which one of them was likely to hurl a ball straight at my face in an attempt to break my glasses.

I didn't have to wonder for too long, because guess whose team I was not on? Yep, Stacey Wasser's, and there was no doubt she had it in for me. She was already eyeing me with a look that I usually saw on the faces of kids who were busy picking the wings off butterflies.

I shuffled to the middle of the gym with everyone else, planning to do what I always did: get myself eliminated as soon as possible and go back to standing on the sidelines. Coach blew her whistle yet again to signal the start of the game, and everyone ran for the balls except me. Stacey Wasser elbowed two of her own teammates out of the way to get one. As soon as it was in her paws, she stood up, looked at me, and used all of her strength to launch it straight at my face.

Oh my God, I thought, this is going to hurt.

Instead of ducking, though, I froze, staring at the ball . . . and then I watched in shock as it changed directions mid-flight and zoomed right back the way it had come. The thing that finally stopped it was Stacey Wasser's nose, and when it made contact, all I could hear was the *thwack*, like rubber on a watermelon. I couldn't move. Stacey Wasser was as shocked and confused as I was. She held a hand up to her face to feel where the ball had hit her, and she looked like a hippo about to charge. I was staring death in the eyes.

"You're out!" Coach yelled, pointing at Stacey Wasser and giving her no choice but to leave the floor.

All around me, the game kept going. Balls flying through the air, the squeak of rubber soles on wood, grunts and whistles as people got hit. It was chaos, but as she made her way to the side of the gym, Stacey Wasser never stopped staring at me. What was going on? It was like I'd sent her ball flying right back at her. And from the look on her face, I could tell she thought so too, because her bovine eyes were drilling into me, as hard as onyx.

I had a sudden overwhelming urge to run up to her and beg her forgiveness, to swear that I hadn't meant to do it. Except, what the hell did that mean? How could I have not meant to do something if I hadn't *done* anything?

I felt dizzy, like the room was turning around me. It was

all I could do to keep standing up. When a ball smacked me in the ass and Coach Watson tweeted her whistle again, I was out. Normally I was grateful to be out of any game, but this out just brought me one step closer to Stacey, who was standing on the sidelines, frothing to get back in.

Gulp. The only thing stopping me from crawling into the trash can to hide was the knowledge that all the guys spit in it. Though at this point, globs of phlegm might be preferable to spending one more minute with my nemesis's side-eye.

After what felt like three lifetimes and a school assembly, the game ended and everyone was supposed to divide into new teams. This was my chance, so I was going to take it. I walked backward until I was standing right in front of the gym door. Then, as soon as Coach was distracted by two freshmen who didn't seem to get the "one-two" concept of counting off, I pushed through it and ran down the hall to get back into the locker room. I grabbed my clothes and changed in a bathroom stall, then shoved my gym uniform into my backpack and left. The whole thing probably took me thirty seconds. I'd never moved so fast in my life. On the way out the door, I smashed into Cassandra Heaven and practically knocked her over. I mumbled some very sincere apologies and looked back to see her staring me down with a look straight out of a mug shot. In one gym class, I'd managed to rack up two enemies. Go, me.

The afternoon had been chaos. Humiliating, unexplainable chaos. All around me, things were falling apart, though I wasn't actually doing anything to cause it. That was the weird part, the part that made my heart race and my feet start sweating in my shoes.

There was no way I'd thrown a ball at Stacey Wasser, no way I'd driven the car up over the curb, no way I'd dumped a drink into Craig Lugweather's lap. I'd been halfway across the lunchroom when Craig's drink had spilled, and I didn't have enough aim to hit the side of a bus with a ball, much less someone's face. Even if it was a very wide, flat face.

Still, something deep down in me knew I was responsible. I'd done it, even if I had no idea how.

CHAPTER 5

There was only one place I wanted to go: home. So I just started walking. I was halfway across the bridge when my phone dinged. Janis, texting me from Earth Sciences, the only class we had together.

> where r u?
>> going home sick
> lucky. winchester's trying to crack a geode with a mallet
> she's been working on it for 15 min
> she has the strength of a toy poodle
> . . .

Then the dancing ellipsis hung there for a minute, like Janis was thinking about what to say next. I groaned. Janis was rarely at a loss for words, which meant . . .

i heard about driver's ed

u ok?

u have to pay?

> i hate my life

aside from that

look on the bright side

> wut bright side?

there's no such thing as bad pr

> maybe if you're a kardashian. not a high
> school junior

tru. you still want to have club 2day?

> sure. i mean, what else do either one of us
> have to do?

c u soon

Everything in my life came back to babysitting.

Our "club" was a babysitting club. Janis and I had started it in seventh grade, and though things had changed over the years, we'd taken it seriously from day one. Dad had gotten us a burner phone to use for appointments (we still had it, even though it now probably belonged in a RadioShack museum), and Janis's mom had photocopied our flyer and hung it up in all the faculty lounges on the university campus. "Call one number + reach four qualified babysitters!" it said. We were in business.

If it sounds just like "The Baby-Sitters Club" books, that's because it was exactly like the books.

As the only person of color, Janis claimed Claudia, and there was no arguing that Janis also had the best outfits.

Chelsea Chatsworth was Stacey because she was from Ohio, which was closer to New York than the rest of us had ever been.

I should have been Kristy because the club had been my idea and we met in my bedroom, but the Kristy title went to Lacey Durbin, who played volleyball and had once been in a fight.

I was stuck with Mary Anne, even though my handwriting was atrocious and spelling had never been my strong suit.

But that was then, and this was now, and the club wasn't much of a club anymore. Chelsea had gotten a job at the tanning salon so that she could meet the guys who worked at the sub shop across the street. (She was now orange and had a boyfriend who smelled like Havarti and Dijonnaise.) And Lacey played so much volleyball that her kneepads had permanently fused to her skin. They didn't have time for babysitting anymore, so now it was just Janis and me. Though not for Janis's lack of trying. She'd had regular jobs twice.

Her first go was at one of those places that made pizza-sized cookies, and she had to wear a white button-down, a brown visor, and a brown apron—which, let's face it, was dressing like a cookie. Janis lasted about four days before she started writing Jenny Holzer quotes on all the demo cookies, and she finally got fired, because no one wanted to buy an M&M cookie cake that said "Men Don't Protect You Anymore," no matter how perfect the curlicue frosting.

Her second try was at Jammin Juice, where she got fired for listing the daily smoothie as a "white girl special with an extra entitlement boost." Neither one of these firings was Janis's fault. She was just too woke for corporate America.

Last summer, I picked up a couple of applications from around town, but I never got around to filling them out. Being a babysitter suited me, so I'd decided I was sticking with it. Besides, it was one of the few things that made me feel closer to my mom.

I didn't talk about Mom that much, even though she was the storm cloud that hung over my head, the looming blackness that threatened to darken even my sunniest days. In short, Mom was crazy. I know. I know. You aren't supposed to call people crazy. It's insensitive. It sounds mean. But that's the word that had been lodged in my head ever since I'd been in third grade, when Emily Sussman had come up to me on the playground, climbed into the swing next to me, and said "My mom said that your mom went crazy."

"Oh," I said, dragging the toes of my glitter oxfords in the dirt.

"And she also said that you can't come over," Emily continued, "because crazy runs in the family, and she doesn't want any cuckoo kids in her house." She laughed as she ran off.

Ever since then I'd lived by the belief that if I said "crazy" enough, maybe it wouldn't hurt as much when other people did.

When I was three, things changed almost overnight. And

by "things," I mean Mom. I was too young to remember everything, but certain events are imprinted in my mind. She painted the living room windows black to keep "them" out. She got caught shoplifting small things—like plastic toys and jars of spices—when I was with her.

Emily Sussman's mom was clearly a bitch, but what if what she'd said was true? Maybe crazy really did run in the family, and Mom's present was my future. I didn't want that. I wanted to keep my mind clear, my thoughts sane, and all signs of craziness—like thinking that objects moved by themselves—to myself.

There were a lot of ways I didn't want to be like Mom, and there was a lot I didn't know about her. But one thing I knew, and one way I wouldn't mind following in her footsteps, was that Mom had been a babysitter. We had pics of her as a teenager, standing on a playground and holding a toddler upside down, his fat belly exposed, both of them laughing. She was wearing a badass outfit that included a denim motorcycle jacket covered with patches. She'd even had her own babysitting club, or at least, that's what I thought Dad was talking about when he said she "had some group of women she always met with, and I know they did something with kids."

I'd never get to ask her about it, because after one final incident, all traces of Mom's momminess went away. Mom and me barricaded in the kitchen, and almost all of Spring River's meager police force outside because they thought she had a gun, even though it was really just a banana wrapped in duct tape. The write-up in the newspaper quoted one of her old babysitting clients. "I can't believe we ever trusted her with our children," said a Mrs. Susan Gilliangham. Mom hasn't lived with us since.

If I ever met Mrs. Susan Gilliangham, I would punch her in the face.

I loved my father, but he wasn't exactly a pillar of emotional support, and I often wondered what it'd be like to have a mom I could talk to about real stuff. Like, if I told her about my super sucky day, would she say something to make me feel better? Would we laugh it off together? Maybe I wouldn't even have such sucky days if Mom were still around.

Also I wouldn't always be worried that I was going to go "crazy," too. I couldn't stop thinking about all this as I waited for Janis to come over, and when she finally appeared in my bedroom doorway, having let herself in like she always did, I was so grateful for the distraction that I practically jumped up and hugged her.

"Ready to get down to business?" she asked, which was 97 percent a joke, because our babysitters club meeting was really just me and Janis hanging out, which was what we did every day, whether we had a "meeting" or not. Janis flopped herself down next to me, dangled her shoes off the edge of my bed, and tossed the burner phone onto a pillow. "I think we should get rid of this thing," she said. "I was texting with Denise Arlington last night, and it took me so long that I think she thought I was drunk."

I grabbed the phone and flipped it open. "How would people book us for jobs?" I asked.

Janis rolled her eyes. "They'd text you or text me," she said. "You know, communicate like regular-ass people."

I flipped the phone closed and placed it back on the pillow. I didn't want to get rid of the phone. It made it seem like the club was still real, and I liked that Janis and I shared a number. "Let's keep it for a while longer," I said, "since it's paid up through the end of the year." Janis shrugged and then shoved it back into her backpack. She pulled out a copy of French *Vogue* and started to flip through it.

"Janis," I said, "do you ever think about how much responsibility babysitting really is? Like, you're in charge of a kid's life."

She looked up at me, an eyebrow arched. "Are you just now figuring that out?"

I shook my head. "No." I swallowed. "I was just wondering about it recently."

Janis flipped over onto her back so that she was staring at the ceiling. "I think about it all the time. I mean, can you imagine if a kid got kidnapped on your watch?" She licked her lips like she was relishing the thought. "It'd ruin your life, just like that *When a Stranger Calls Back* movie. You'd have to buy a gun and spend your whole college career looking for people painted like the wall. And then you'd have to go on all the talk shows to tell your horrifying story, and then write a bestselling book about it, and then in the movie version, the actress who played you wouldn't really look anything like you, and her entire wardrobe would come from Kmart because the director had some asinine idea that she needed to be approachable. Or something like that."

I sighed. Janis could be as extra as a side of guac, and that wasn't exactly the opening for a heartfelt discussion about how scared I'd been last night. Before I could say anything else, her phone dinged with a text, and reading the message put her in a mood. "Ugh," she said. "I have to go pick up my brother." She started stomping around the room and gathering her things. "Maybe tomorrow's look should be 'family chauffeur,' and I'll get one of those little black hats, and wear a suit. . . ."

"But isn't that how you convinced your parents to get you a car?" I pointed out. "By telling them you could help give Jason rides?"

She looked up from stuffing a sweatshirt into her backpack and rolled her eyes at me. "Don't take their side, Esme."

"Never," I said. "Text me later?"

She nodded and, with a scowl, headed back out the door.

It was still early, and I had no idea what I was going to do with myself for the rest of the night. I felt restless and anxious, and when scrolling for fashion inspo did nothing to settle my nerves, I got up and followed a trail of snores and snorts into the kitchen.

"Hi, Piggy," I said, squatting down at the source of the commotion. "Hello, beautiful girl. How are you?"

Pig was my pit bull. Seventy-five pounds and as hard as a rock but with the temperament of a bag of fuzzy mashed potatoes or a couch cushion full of vanilla pudding. Pig had lived with us for about five years. One morning when I was twelve, Dad and I were at Costco buying Popsicles. It was the middle of the summer, and we had the windows rolled down. "Look, Dad," I said. "A dog." There she was, sitting alone in an empty parking space, not an owner in sight.

Dad looked over at her, and she got up and started to trot toward us.

"It looks like it's coming over here," Dad said. "Oh my God," he said next, as she broke into a sprint. About six feet from the car, she launched herself into the air and sailed right into the back seat through the open window. I could have sworn she was smiling. Dad tried to cajole her out of the car, but she wouldn't budge, not even for a bite of the corn dog he'd bought himself for lunch. He finally gave up and just drove home.

He kept saying he was going to make some phone calls and take her to the shelter in the morning, but that night, when she started snoozing with her head on his foot, all three of us knew she wasn't going anywhere. I originally named her Marshmallow, but after a few nights of her snorts and snores reverberating through the house, she was redubbed Pig. I'd since learned to sleep through the snores, which meant I could now probably sleep through dynamite or an EDM fest outside my window.

I dumped some kibble into her bowl, and after she gulped that down, I put her leash on and took her for a walk. We only went around the block, because Pig was not especially athletic, and taking her for a walk was basically like dragging an RV down the sidewalk. When we got back to the house, Dad was standing in the kitchen, his face buried in an empty refrigerator.

I braced myself for an awkward conversation, knowing that our brief Mr. Dekalb–chaperoned phone call earlier was in no way the end of our driver's ed discussion. But Dad's phone started to ring. He grimaced at the caller, grabbed a beer from the fridge, and answered. "This is Dave."

As soon as his back was turned, I scooted up the stairs to my room, shut the door, and sent him a text saying I had cramps and was going to bed early. Period problems work on dads like garlic works on vampires, and this was a guaranteed way to make sure he stayed away for the rest of the night.

I kicked off my shoes and climbed into bed, then realized that it was only seven-thirty and I'd outsmarted myself. My empty stomach grumbled, my phone was in the red at 6 percent, and food and phone charger were both back in the kitchen, where Dad was certainly off the phone by now, warming up a can of chili and getting ready to settle in for his nightly *Law & Order* marathon.

I had just enough power left to text Janis my look for tomorrow—car crash survivor—before my phone died, leaving me to a night of very quiet activities and, for lack of anything better to do, actually going to bed early.

I fell asleep quickly enough but slept horribly. My night was filled with dream fragments that felt real, those little scene snippets that leave an icky residue behind in your waking life. Twice, I woke up feeling like I'd been electrocuted, convinced I'd heard a little kid outside my second-story window, and I dreamed that I was standing in the middle of the football field at school, unable to move from a chalk line as a car reversed right toward me. Thankfully, my eyes popped open right before it hit.

When my alarm started howling, it almost felt like a relief. There was a moment when I considered pretending to be sick, but Dad would have seen through that in an instant, and rather than making me go to school, he'd have humored me. Let me stay home, but then insisted on taking me out to breakfast so we could talk about things. Over, and over, and over. Thanks. But no. I'd go to school and hold my head high and show them that it would take more than a dented—like, majorly dented—Corolla to keep Esme Pearl down.

All I had to do was watch myself every hour, every minute, every second of the day, to make sure I didn't say too much about what had happened in that car, or do or say anything else that would reveal that I'd already bought a one-way ticket to crazy town.

The night before, I'd decided what I was going to wear

without even looking at my clothes, and I have to say, this was one of my most unique talents. If I were a superhero, I would be "girl who doesn't have to try something on to know if it will look good." Could you imagine the villains I could take down with that one? I'd save the prince while the evil queen was still at home trying to decide which shoe looked best with her gown—the leopard pony-hair stiletto or the red Lucite block heel?

As I pulled out the pieces I'd decided on, I tried to shake off the last twenty-four hours, and I started to feel a little calmer as I got dressed. Crash Test Dummies was a nineties band that had one hit, where basically all they did was *hmmm*. I'd never heard of them, but I had looked them up after I'd found one of their T-shirts at a garage sale. The T-shirt was super weird, with the band made out to look like they were part of a Renaissance painting, and I paired it with acid-washed jeans that I'd cut into shorts, my scuffed floral Doc Martens, and black tights from Target that I'd frayed with mid-aughts Rodarte-esque cobweb holes. The whole look was very "backstage at the first Lollapalooza," and I flashed my reflection a smile. The day might royally blow, but at least I could make sure my outfit kicked ass.

I got lucky. Dad talked about the wreck only for the first half of my ride to school. I apologized a lot, and made several promises to help pay for everything. This must have satisfied him, because then he switched to his favorite subject: Spring

River football. When Dad met someone new, he could barely last five minutes before name-dropping that his best friend was the football coach. And I didn't know which was lamer—that he expected this to impress people, or that some people actually were impressed. I couldn't have given two farts about football, but I humored him by saying "Yeah" and "Really?" at what seemed like appropriate times. He pulled up in front of the school, and as I got out of the car, I thought I was home free. Then he called me back just as I was about to cross the sidewalk.

"Listen, kid," he said, "I know you weren't in top form yesterday, so that's why I'm letting it slide this once, but no more skipping class."

I swallowed. "They called you?" He nodded. "What'd you tell them?"

"The truth," he said, then smiled. "That you had a doctor's appointment, and I'd forgotten to call in to excuse you."

Dad was a dweeb, but he really did come through sometimes, so I smiled and gave him a very genuine, sincere thanks. Then I took a deep breath and braced myself for what surely awaited me inside hell's hallowed halls. Dad flashed me a thumbs-up as he drove away.

I turned and made my way up the sidewalk, and sure enough, I'd barely made it through the door into the school when I caught people looking at me and snickering. No one bothered to pretend they weren't talking about me. Quite the opposite, in fact—their voices got louder as they saw me coming.

"I heard she got arrested because Mr. Dekalb forgot to fill out the paperwork, so she was driving without a permit!"

I pretended to text someone.

"I heard she already had to get a job to pay for all the damages and she's probably going to drop out. My sister saw her cleaning the bathroom at Chuck E. Cheese."

I pretended that my pretend text was really funny.

"I heard one of the guys got whiplash and is considering suing because he can't even play in this week's game. Anyway, the whole thing happened because she farted."

I pretended I was deaf.

When I finally saw Janis, it was like I had been shipwrecked and she was an island. My relief was short-lived.

"I have lunch detention," she said.

"Again?"

"Ugh, yes, again."

"Janis, you're kidding me, right? Who am I supposed to sit with at lunch now?"

"You can't be mad at me for getting lunch detention, Esme, because you're the whole reason I have it. I was texting you when I got caught. We can meet up as soon as I'm out, I promise."

It was NBD, really, but for some reason, as I watched Janis walk away, I felt like I was going to cry. The brave face I'd put on just minutes before was already gone. I'd spent most of my life carefully constructing an I-don't-care buffer between me and the rest of the world, but that had disappeared. It wasn't just that I was upset about the car or the dodgeball, or even Kaitlyn. There was something bigger, something darker, blooming and unfolding in my chest, that made me feel like I was going to lose control any second.

What the hell was wrong with me?

I had no idea. I just knew that I wanted it to go away ASAP.

I decided to skip the cafeteria at lunch altogether and just eat a bag of pretzels alone like the sad pile of human that I was. I headed out to the lawn and was so absorbed in trying to figure out where to sit so I could have the least contact possible with my schoolmates that I almost tripped over Cassandra Heaven, who I hadn't even noticed was sitting on the steps. I mumbled an apology, kept walking, and got almost to the end of the sidewalk before I realized that she was following me.

At least, that was what it seemed like, even though we were probably just going in the same direction. Then she spoke to me. Specifically, she said, "Hey." I turned around, startled, expecting her to ask some benign question about off-campus lunch policy or something, but instead she just stood there. She was at least half a head taller than me, and even more glowy up close, like one of those girls who's not lying when she says "I don't really wear makeup."

"So," she said finally, shoving her hands into the pockets of her jeans and shifting back and forth from foot to foot. There was something in her body language that made it seem like she was working up to something, though I hadn't the foggiest idea what that could be.

"I hear you have a babysitters club?" she finished, and I was so surprised, I LOL'd. No one in the history of high school had ever asked me about the babysitting club before, and I preferred it that way. Was this the beginning of a very elaborate way to make fun of me? Was this a joke and I was the punch line? But Cassandra Heaven had been at our school for two days—certainly she had no reason to pick on me. Besides, the look on her face was 100 percent serious. Earnest, even. Almost, if I dared to say it, excited?

"I guess," I said finally. "It's not so much a club as it is . . ." She crossed her arms, and I could see that there was a rip in the sleeve of her flannel. I stared at her elbow as I tried to think of a way to explain the club that wouldn't sound totally lame.

Except, that's the thing. It *was* lame. Janis and I were two high school juniors with a babysitting club, for freak's sake. "It's kind of a joke," I finally said. "It's really just my friend Janis and me hanging out."

"Well," she said, "can I join?"

> what do u mean u told cassandra heaven she could
> join tbsc?
>> exactly that. idk, i panicked.
> it's not even a club.
>> i know, j
>> no one has ever asked before, so i didn't
>> know what to say

ooooooooo-k, but i think she's gonna be
disappointed.
of course she's gonna be disappointed
i'm disappointed.
is that how people describe us to new kids?
like oh, there go the babysitters.
?????
there are worse things to be known for,
right?
sure. like lice.
anyway, CH is coming over tomorrow after
school
...
...
j?
i'll be there. i just have to decide what to wear.

I got through the whole next day of classes by keeping my head down, not crashing any cars, and volunteering to man the scoreboard in gym. After school, Janis gave me a ride home. As soon as we got to my house, I planned to clean my room, because that seemed like the thing to do when you have someone new coming over, but after ten minutes of standing in the middle of it, debating where to start, I just kicked some stuff under the bed and called that good enough. I also thought that maybe I should put out some snacks, but it had been a while since Dad had gone to the store, and all we had was some stale Smartfood and a few cans of Squirt, the soda with the grossest name ever. I put the popcorn in a bowl anyway and arranged the sodas in a clear spot on my desk.

"It's like you're trying to impress this new girl or something," Janis said, "shoving clothes under the bed and being all fancy." I threw a handful of popcorn at her, and when it scattered onto the floor, Pig gobbled it up.

I had told Cassandra to come at four-thirty, and there was a part of me—okay, more like all of me—that was hoping she wouldn't show.

But at 4:29, the doorbell rang. I went out and opened the front door and there she was, standing on my porch in a variation of what she'd been wearing every other time I'd seen her—clothes that would have been too tattered for Kurt Cobain.

"Hey," she said, stepping into the foyer. "Nice house."

"Thanks," I said, nodding and knowing that this was a lie, as the best thing that could be said about our house was that it had walls.

"We usually meet in my room," I explained, leading her down the hall.

"What do you guys do during meetings?" she asked.

The real answer was "Try on clothes and lurk on people on the internet," but that didn't seem professional.

"Talk about babysitting safety and strategize about how

to get new clients," I answered. I was glad Cassandra was behind me so that I couldn't see her face, because even I didn't believe my own BS.

When we got to my room, it hit me that I really hadn't thought this through. Janis had taken my only chair, and Pig was sprawled across my bed, eyeing Cassandra with just as much wariness as Janis. Cassandra stood in the middle of the room as I balanced the bowl of popcorn on a pillow and tried to shove Pig to the floor. It was like moving a sandbag, but eventually she groaned and lumbered down, and I motioned for Cassandra to take her place.

"Sorry it's so messy," I started, looking around like I would find some excuse in a corner, hiding. "I was gonna clean up, but then I remembered that I really hate cleaning."

"No worries," she said, flopping down onto the bed in the warm spot that Pig had just vacated. There was something about Cassandra's presence in my bedroom that I couldn't put my finger on. It wasn't like she made me nervous. It was just that there was something expectant about her, in the way she looked around the room and at me and Janis. I wasn't used to people expecting something from me, and I didn't quite know how to handle it. For one thing, I was about 110 percent sure that whatever she expected was not going to be happening, and that she was going to be pretty dang disappointed when she realized that this baby-sitting club was just a couple of babysitters, and barely a club at all.

I passed her the bowl. She picked up a kernel and

squeezed it between her fingers, then dropped it back into the bowl and passed the bowl to Janis. Janis didn't even pretend she was going to eat anything, and just set the bowl on my desk. Still, none of us had said a word since Cassandra sat down.

Finally I cleared my throat. "I, uh, guess I'll call this meeting to order."

Janis guffawed, and Squirt squirted out of her nose.

I shot her a look, my eyebrows raised. "Janis, if you want to run this meeting, you're more than welcome to."

She shook her head, her eyebrows halfway up her forehead. "Oh please, do go on," she said, wiping her nose with the back of her hand. "I can't wait to see where you're going with this."

I looked at Cassandra, and decided to be straight with her. "Look, it's true that we have a babysitting club, but it's not like we have a president or a secretary, or dues, or even meetings. . . ." I was rambling. "Janis and I just hang out. And yeah, we babysit, but that's kind of just like, I don't know . . . our jobs?"

Cassandra nodded, slightly biting her lower lip. "I know. That's why I want to join."

Janis arched an eyebrow at her. "So, you babysit?" she asked. "You don't look like a babysitter."

"Of course," Cassandra said. "I love kids." She flashed Janis a thousand-watt smile. "And you don't look like a babysitter either." Janis was wearing leopard-print paper-bag pants, a black cropped turtleneck, and a lipstick-red blazer, with oversized tortoiseshell glasses that didn't have lenses. It was her eighties art-gallerist look. Cassandra had a point.

"So, Esme, have you ever had another job?" Cassandra turned her smile on me, like I was there for an interview or something.

I shook my head.

"I worked at Jammin Juice for like a week," Janis offered. "And before that, this big cookie place in a strip mall. Both were awful, but there's a rumor that we're going to get an Urban Outfitters over by the university, and . . ."

Janis stopped talking when she realized that Cassandra wasn't listening and was still just staring at me. "How old were you when you started sitting?"

"Like, twelve?" I answered. It kind of made me uncomfortable, how much Cassandra was focused on me and ignoring Janis, which was not the way I had hoped this would go. I wondered if Janis was picking up on it as much as I was. I wanted to steer the conversation back to Cassandra, but she kept at me with the rapid-fire questions.

"And what made you want to do it?"

I shrugged. "I don't know. Money?"

"Did anyone ever teach you how to babysit?"

"I took a child CPR class, if that's what you mean?"

"It's not," she said, but didn't clarify. "How do people find you for jobs?"

"I don't know," I said. "Word of mouth? Mom gossip? People just know that we're the babysitters, so they call us."

"How do they call you?"

Janis jumped in. "There's a big light in the center of town," she said. "And so when someone needs a babysitter, they flip it on, and it projects a giant pacifier into the sky."

Cassandra's eyes widened. "Seriously?"

"No," Janis said. "They use a phone. Or sometimes they send what is called a 'text message.'"

She pulled the burner phone out of her backpack and waved it back and forth in front of Cassandra's face. All three of us sat there looking at it, and everyone jumped when it started to ring. It felt, weirdly, like we'd willed the sound into being. After five rings, Janis finally answered it.

"Hello?" Her voice was hesitant, like the ringing phone was some sort of haunting trick on Cassandra's part, but whatever she heard on the other end made her relax, and her gaze flicked up and met mine.

"Oh, hi, Carolyn! It's Janis. Great to hear from you. It's been a while!" Then she nodded and mm-hmmd. "I can't tomorrow, but let me check with Esme." She put her hand over the mouthpiece.

"It's Carolyn Harrison," she said. "Steve's out of town and she has to work late, so she needs someone to babysit tomorrow night."

This was good news, as the Harrisons were some of our favorite people to babysit for. Their son was perfectly be-haved, and their fridge had every beverage imaginable. I'd babysat for them almost a month before, but they hadn't called since, and I'd been slightly paranoid that it was be-cause I'd gone overboard on the snack raid and had drunk three blood orange San Pellegrinos in one night. I'd put two of the empty bottles in my backpack to take home, but they still might have noticed.

Now it pained me to say no—since it would be a chance to demonstrate my restraint and drink nothing but tap water and maybe a diet ginger ale—but I shook my head. "I have to go visit my mom," I said.

Janis nodded and put the phone back to her ear. "I'm sorry, Carolyn," she said. "It looks like she's boo . . ." Cassandra cleared her throat, but Janis kept talking, making apologies into the phone and pretending like she didn't hear Cassandra, who was clearing her throat just two feet away.

"I can do it," Cassandra finally said, loudly enough that Janis couldn't ignore her. "I can babysit tomorrow."

Janis stopped talking, and a beat passed in silence. Then she let out a sigh that sounded like air slowly escaping from a balloon. "Actually, we have a new babysitter we're working with. Her name's Cassandra, and she said she can be there tomorrow, if that works. . . . Mm-hmmm. . . . I'll give her your info. Okay, great. . . . No problem."

Janis clicked the phone off and looked at Cassandra with a concrete expression on her face.

"They're some of our best clients," Janis said. "And they haven't called us in forever. You'd better not mess this up."

"I won't." Cassandra smiled. "Like I said, I love kids."

After that, I wasn't really sure what to do with the rest of the meeting. If we'd been a real babysitters club, I'm sure we'd have reviewed payment protocol and disciplinary philosophies or something like that, but since we weren't, we just sat in silence, looking at each other awkwardly. Janis was waiting for Cassandra to speak, and Cassandra was waiting for me to speak.

"Um, this meeting is adjourned, I guess?" I said finally. I was feeling pretty uncomfortable with the shred of authority that had fallen on me, so maybe I really did deserve the Mary Anne title.

I wanted to talk to Janis and ask her what she'd thought of Cassandra, but they left at the same time and I didn't get a chance. For the rest of the night, I couldn't concentrate on anything, not even an Alexander McQueen documentary that I'd been dying to watch. I painted my nails a shade of metallic pistachio but immediately messed them up trying to find a pack of gum at the bottom of my backpack. When Dad came home late from work, as usual, I was almost excited to have someone to talk to, and when he asked if I wanted to go out for Thai, I jumped at the chance.

My distracted feeling continued all through school the next day too. I kept looking for Cassandra, but I didn't see her once, not even in gym, where there was no need for someone to keep score, so I spent the whole hour trying to stay out of Stacey Wasser's way by standing about ten feet behind her, since I wasn't sure her neck turned enough for her to look over her shoulder.

I wanted to talk to Cassandra. About what, exactly, I wasn't sure, but I felt like talking to her would be reassuring. Because I had to admit—I was second-guessing myself about letting her join the club. Now that I'd had time to think about it, like a whole-night-of-lying-in-bed-not-being-able-to-sleep amount of time, something seemed off. Like, a new girl—a new, hot girl—shows up at school, and the first thing she does is try to get in with a couple of babysitters? And babysit?

I wanted to talk to Janis, so when she slid into her seat late in Earth Sciences, I snuck my phone out of my backpack and risked getting us both detention to send her a furtive text. From the back of the classroom, I could see her drop a pencil to the floor, then palm her phone into her lap and respond without even appearing to look down. Janis was good.

> **U seen Cassandra?**
>> nope
> **i'm worried maybe we shouldn't have let her join the club**
>> ha, you're just now thinking that?
> **you already thought that?**
>> ya.
> **y?**
>> because it's weird. we don't know anything about her.

I didn't know how to respond. She was right. Clients like the Harrisons weren't easy to come by, but what bothered me was something bigger than that, even though I couldn't even begin to identify or articulate it. Something was giving me major anxiety, and I had the destroyed cuticles to prove it.

When the bell finally rang, ending the day, I said goodbye to Janis and walked to the corner of the grounds to wait for Dad, since he picked me up on days when we were going to visit Mom. I leaned up against the street sign and tried to shake off my funk for my family's sake. Dad could rarely be counted on to maintain a smile through a visit to Mom, and Mom was hard to predict. Some days she was bouncy and all over the place. Others, she was sullen, but either way she couldn't really hold a conversation. Sometimes it seemed like she was really trying, but the words were bubbles that popped and disappeared as soon as she got close. It was like her mind gave orders that her body refused to obey. It was hard to watch.

I always tried to dress in my most cheerful attire for these occasions. Nothing goth, death metal, or grunge, and all rainbows and light. Today I was wearing a pair of vintage Guess jeans with zippers at the ankles and an oversized pink fuzzy sweater that hung off one shoulder to reveal the neon lavender straps of my bralette. I finished the look with platform black leather Sk8-Hi shoes and a silver faux-leather motorcycle jacket with a rose, hand-painted by Janis, on the back.

It was one of those perfect Kansas fall days, when the air was candy-apple crisp and the sun made everything golden. Across the street, a woman walked a fluffy puppy that barked at every blowing leaf. I tried to look away from such a scene of happiness, only to see a freshman couple taking selfies with their hands wrapped around the same cup. I could practically smell the pumpkin spice and whipped cream.

Everyone else seemed so happy that it made my teeth ache.

I squinted, and at the other end of campus saw a flash of dark hair coming out the side doors and walking down the sidewalk. *Cassandra.* I'd given her my phone number, but I realized that I stupidly hadn't gotten hers, and there were so many last-minute instructions I wanted to pass on. Like stay away from the San Pellegrino, and how Brandon liked "Row, Row, Row Your Boat" but "The Itsy-Bitsy Spider" sometimes made him cry. How, unless she wanted to clean up a puddle of pee, she should just put the dog outside as soon as she got there and not let him back in until the parents got home.

Cassandra was too far away to yell to, so I turned to check on my dad, and sure enough, his red Ford was rounding the corner right at that moment. He pulled up, and I opened the passenger door. Before I climbed in, I glanced over my shoulder again, but she was gone.

Dad and I went to visit Mom at her facility twice a week. Over the years we'd realized that we needed to have a schedule, and also needed to treat said schedule as if it were carved in stone. If we didn't, we'd never go. Dad pulled away from the curb, and I could tell he was grinding his teeth by the way his mouth was pulled into a straight line.

"So, um, kid," he started, "when we get there, you can go straight in to see your mom, okay?"

"Okay," I said, knowing there was no way the need to

strategize was a sign of something good. "Is everything okay?"

"Not exactly," he said. "She's being moved to a locked ward, and there's some paperwork I need to fill out."

"You mean to lock her in?" I asked, surprised.

He must have picked up on the note of panic in my voice, the panic I tried so hard to control every time there was some sort of new development with Mom, and he sighed. "She'll be able to move freely in the ward but will need a chaperone to go farther." I nodded, and swallowed around the lump in my throat. "She got out again, and they found her trying to cross the highway."

I sucked in a breath sharply and bit down on my lip. The highway was six lanes of traffic with a seventy-miles-per-hour speed limit.

"Where was she going?"

"I wish I knew," he said. "But I spoke to one of the doctors this morning, and we agreed that because her condition is so unpredictable, it's best not to take chances." Dad flipped on his turn signal, and I stared out the window, giving a nearby McDonald's sign a long, hard study as he pulled into the lot and parked in the same spot he always parked in. He looked up at the building in front of us for a second before he turned off the engine, like maybe he was going to change his mind, throw the car into reverse, and drive straight to a sports bar instead.

In these moments, I always wondered if he was thinking about how he'd never imagined that this would be his life, that he would buy his daughter her first bra or leave a *So, You Got Your Period?* pamphlet on her pillow. (Yeah, he really did that.) That most of his money would go to pay for his wife to live somewhere where she was (mostly) safe from herself, that he'd be married to someone who didn't know that putting your hand on a hot stove would blister the skin, it wasn't okay to eat plastic fruit, and interstates weren't for strolling.

I followed Dad across the parking lot to the glass double doors that were always seasonally decorated, as though a few construction-paper pastel eggs or glitter elves could make you forget where you were headed. Today the doors were covered with ghosts and zombies, and it looked like someone had tried to take a bite out of one of the oversized cardboard pumpkins. As soon as we were inside, the chemical-cleaner-and-cinnamon-potpourri smell hit me in the face like it always did, a surprise no matter how many times I'd smelled it before. I still don't think Mom should be in here, and I don't think Dad does either, but there's no place else for her to go.

Dad disappeared into the office, and I made my way down the hall to Mom's room, a path I could walk in my sleep. At her door, I knocked softly, and when there was no answer, I let myself in. Today Mom sat with her knees pulled up to her chest and her arms wrapped around them, her head leaning dejectedly against the back of her chair. Despite everything—the escape attempts and the freak-outs, and the pharmaceutical cocktails that were introduced to try to prevent them—Mom was still gorgeous. Her skin was milky moon pale, and her cheeks were always rosy. Her slate-blue eyes were made even more startling by her midnight-black hair, which didn't come from a box and still wasn't streaked with strands of silver. I had not inherited her good looks, which made me happy. If I hadn't inherited her looks, then maybe I hadn't inherited her mind either.

I threw my bag onto the bed, then started in on what I always did when it was just the two of us: I told Mom everything. It was kind of like a reality-TV confessional; I just vented and said whatever was on my mind. In a way, it did feel like having a conversation, even though I never got a response. Usually she just sat there, staring out the window and not even looking at me. Occasionally she'd contribute something off topic, like "Why, this pancake isn't very good at all" as she took a bite out of a catalog.

It was okay. I didn't expect much.

But today, when I was right in the middle of telling her about how the new girl in school wanted to join our babysitting club, I looked at her, and she was sitting straight up, almost leaning forward in her chair, her eyes wide and clear, totally focused on me.

"Mom," I said, not able to help myself, "what do you know about babysitting?" Just then, Dad walked into the room behind me, in the middle of a conversation with one of the staff, and by the time I turned back to Mom, I'd lost her again, and she was back to just staring out the window.

• • •

The sun was beginning to set as Dad and I were pulling out of the parking lot, and the sky was the colors of candy corn. Dad was tired, and I could tell he was worried by the way he drummed his fingers on the steering wheel and quoted *The Big Lebowski* when the Eagles came on the radio. He was trying to be lighthearted and pretend nothing was wrong. When my phone rang with an unknown number, I didn't answer—I rarely answered even when I did know the number.

I honestly probably would have continued to ignore it if Dad hadn't been sitting right there, looking at me as we sat at a stoplight, just waiting to make some sort of Dad-ish comment like "Why do ya even have a phone if you're never going to answer it?" So I hit accept and said hello.

"He took a poop!" a voice screamed into my ear.

I was about to hang up on this soon-to-be-obscene caller when she continued, breathlessly, "Esme, it's Cassandra! He pooped. What do I do?"

"Brandon?" I asked.

"Yes, of course! This holy terror that I'm babysitting. Who else would I be talking about?"

"I don't get it," I said. Brandon Harrison was only two and a half years old, but he was already about the best-behaved kid I'd ever babysat for, as long as you steered clear of anything itsy-bitsy. "You mean in his pants?"

"No, in the thing that looks like a smaller toilet that sits next to the big toilet. Like, what is that anyway? A planter?"

"Oh my God, Cassandra," I said, realizing what was

going on. "He's supposed to do that. It's part of potty train-ing. Surely you've seen one of those before!"

"No . . . ," she started, then changed her mind. "I'm mean, yes, of course. But it's been a while. I don't remember. So I just leave it there?"

Was she serious? "No, you dump it into the toilet and then wash it out."

"That's disgusting."

"Cassandra, where is Brandon?"

"He's right here," she said. Then she lowered her voice and said, "Esme, I think he wants me to help him wipe his butt." Her voice was crackling with fear.

Something was dawning on me. Something that I'd been suspecting but hadn't wanted to admit to myself.

"Cassandra," I said, "have you ever babysat before?"

A beat of silence. Two beats. "Yes," she said. And then she hung up.

Dad and I stopped for Mexican, but I felt too queasy for queso. I sent Cassandra several texts and eventually tried calling her back, but she never answered. This was one of those times when I really cursed myself for not being able to drive, because if I could have, I would have come up with some excuse and driven straight to the Harrisons', to make sure their house was still standing and their kid was still alive. I kept checking my phone, wishing I knew what time they were supposed to get home.

I hadn't told Janis about Cassandra's panicked phone call, but she had the burner phone, so if the Harrisons called to complain about our new sitter's total ineptitude and obvious lack of childcare experience, Janis would be the first to know. Would she ever forgive me?

The babysitters club was really important to me, and now I was terrified that Cassandra Heaven was going to make me lose it. Why in the hell had she wanted to babysit in the first place if she knew nothing about kids?

I must have fallen asleep shortly after midnight, because that was the last time I looked at my phone, and the next thing I knew, I was awake and the sun was streaming through my windows.

I grabbed my phone to see if I'd somehow slept through Janis's angry texts, but there was nothing. Usually I was as conscious as a corpse at this hour on a school day, but I was too wired to go back to sleep, so I lay in bed staring at the ceiling and tried to make a mental list of what I knew about Cassandra Heaven.

Good hair.

. . .

And that was as far as I got. Nothing to suggest competence, responsibility, or knowledge of the Heimlich maneuver. What on earth had possessed me to hand over one of our prized babysitting clients to a girl I knew literally nothing about?

Finally, at an appropriately late hour, I dragged myself out of bed and got dressed for school. I'd been so distracted the night before that I hadn't planned my outfit. So shirt and pants were just going to have to do. I called it "Sorry I'm late, I didn't want to come."

When I saw her at lunch, Janis could sense that something was wrong, but I think she chalked it up to the gray mood I was always in after a visit to Mom. When she asked me if I'd heard anything from Cassandra, I just shook my head and pretended to shrug it off. "No news is good news, right?" I said, then forced a laugh and immediately tried to change the subject.

"So, your house or mine?" I asked. Since it was Friday, I assumed Janis and I would do what we always did when neither of us had a babysitting job lined up: see how many episodes of *The Office* we could watch in one night. Our current record was twenty-one.

"I've got to pack tonight," she said. "This is that weekend we're going to Chicago for my mom's thing."

"Oh yeah," I said. Janis had told me about her travel plans weeks ago but hadn't mentioned them since, and I hadn't asked why she hadn't mentioned them because I knew. Janis's mom was speaking at a conference the following Monday, and they were going early so Janis could low-key check out the campus at Northwestern, one of her backup schools. "That's cool. That'll be fun."

Fortunately, the bell rang, cutting off our chances to have a conversation about how I would amuse myself for forty-eight hours in Janis's absence. I'd have a lot of real conversations with my dog and a lot of pretend conversations with Michael Scott.

I spent most of my school day looking for Cassandra, but it felt about as useless as trying to get followers on Twitter. I didn't know where her locker was. I didn't know what classes she had, and her phone went straight to voicemail. I might as well have just written a message in lipstick on a bathroom mirror and hoped that she had to pee.

For the first time ever, I was actually looking forward to gym, hoping I could finally corner Cassandra there. Then, of course, she skipped it again. Was it me she was avoiding, or the forty-five minutes of aggressive badminton? Thankfully, racquet sports were not Stacey Wasser's forte, and class had barely started when she got sent to the principal for telling the teacher to shove a birdie up . . . well, it wasn't somewhere nice.

I saw Janis briefly, and she graciously tried to hide her excitement and even went so far as to say she wished I was coming with her, then an uneventful Friday rolled into an equally uneventful weekend. It at least gave me time to plan my next two months of outfits.

I never heard from Cassandra, and for the first time ever, I was actually grateful when Monday rolled around. School might be awful, but at least it was a distraction.

Of course, I didn't see Cassandra until after school, when I was walking to my locker and happened to glance out the door. There she was, standing in the middle of the sidewalk, looking right at me. I turned and made a beeline for the doors, pushed through them, and headed straight for her. Her face transformed into a smile when she saw me coming, which pissed me off. By the time we were standing face to face, I was so mad that I was foaming like an overfrothed cappuccino.

"You lied!" I hissed. "You've never babysat before!" If Cassandra had been worried about me finding her out and being mad about it, nothing on her face showed it, and the smile stayed firmly in place.

"Okay, so I panicked," she said. "I shouldn't have called you, but I didn't know what else to do, and I didn't want the kid to, like, die or anything." Then she crossed her arms and leaned back like she'd just dropped her verse in a rap battle.

I sucked in a breath. "I don't want a kid to, like, die or anything either, Cassandra," I said as calmly as I could manage, even though I hadn't been this pissed since a ten-year-old babysitting charge had dumped a half gallon of milk into my book bag. (Ten-year-olds should know better.)

"I thought I could fake it, but it was way harder than I thought it was going to be," she said, flipping her hair over her shoulder, casually.

"You said you liked kids!" I was trying hard to keep my voice from rising. "You said you had tons of experience!"

"I know," she said. "I do like kids, and I've always wanted to babysit. But, first time for everything, right?" Cassandra raised her hands in a don't-blame-me gesture that was completely inappropriate, since this was unquestionably her fault.

I actually smacked my forehead in disbelief. "It doesn't make any sense! Why on earth would you lie about baby-sitting? Why do you want to be a babysitter? Just get a job at the froyo place like everyone else our age!"

"Listen, Esme. I do want to be a part of the babysitting club. I've always wanted to babysit—and," she said, "I wanted an excuse to talk to you."

Maybe I should have been flattered, but I wasn't buying it. Anyone who wanted to use me to social climb wasn't going to get far off the ground. "No one wants to talk to me that bad, Cassandra," I said.

The smile on her face faded, and she looked somber. "I do, Esme. Trust me. I'm sorry that I went about it the wrong way, but maybe we could go somewhere and talk now?"

"No," I said, brushing past her and heading down the sidewalk. "I don't even know you, and you already risked my professional reputation and put a kid in danger."

"The kid is fine," she said.

I spun around so that I was facing her again. "Brandon! His name is Brandon. And he is fine, but no thanks to you!"

"Okay, fine. Brandon is fine! We had a great time, and he only cried for, like, ten minutes, when I made him go to bed."

"He usually doesn't cry at all!"

"Okay, my bad." She pumped her hands like she was try-ing to calm me down. "Just listen for a minute."

"I'm going home." I was suddenly filled with the urge to put as much distance between us as possible.

She grabbed my sleeve. "Come on. We'll give you a ride home."

"I don't need a ride," I growled, then turned and started walking away again.

"I saw what happened in gym," she called. Her words stopped me in my tracks, but only for a second. I forced myself to keep walking. I wanted to pretend what she had just said was no big deal, because, really, she could have been talking about anything.

She caught up with me so that we were shoulder to shoulder, and I kept looking straight ahead. "Yeah," I said. "So, what does that have to do with anything? I suck at dodgeball, just like every other non-sadist on the planet."

Out of the corner of my eye, I could see that she was smiling, like she was finding our whole exchange funny. "How do you know I'm talking about dodgeball?" she said.

Crap. I felt like I'd just copped to something, even though I didn't really know what. I paused, then said, "I don't know what you're talking about."

"Yes, you do," she answered. "You threw a ball without touching it."

My hands were shaking like cold Chihuahuas as I folded my arms across my chest. Cassandra had just confirmed what I'd been thinking. What'd I'd been fearing. I shook my head, my mouth feeling like it was full of stale cotton candy, and repeated myself. "I don't know what you're talking about."

"You do," she repeated. "You just haven't admitted it to yourself."

I'd stopped walking, and now when Cassandra took another step toward me, I took a step back. I forced myself to smile and laugh. "So I make one good play in dodgeball and you think . . . I'm . . . there's something . . ."

She shook her head. The sun was behind her now, glinting off her hair and illuminating her flyaways like an autumnal aura. "There's driver's ed too," she said. "One of the guys who was in the car swears you didn't touch anything and suddenly you were mowing down a tree."

"They also said I was the one who farted," I said, "so don't trust them for a minute."

A smile flickered across her face, but I could tell she was serious. Dead serious. "I pay attention to this kind of stuff, and I know it when I see it."

She was still walking toward me, and I was still walking backward.

"Know *what* when you see it?" I asked.

"Magic," she said with a smile. She held her hand out, and a tiny flame sprang from the center of her palm, hovering there like a hummingbird.

Maybe I tripped, or maybe my legs gave out, because that was the last thing I remembered before my head hit the sidewalk and I blacked out.

CHAPTER 6

I woke up lying in the back seat of a van—or, more precisely, in the back of a van where a seat should have been—not knowing where I was going, not knowing who I was with. Which could only mean one thing . . .

I'd been kidnapped! I panicked, and bolted upright, smashing my forehead into something hard. I fell back down to the floor, seeing stars.

"Holy crap, she headbutted me!" As my vision came into focus, I saw Cassandra Heaven sitting next to me, and I realized that the concrete block I'd just smashed into was actually her nose. I could tell by the tiny bit of blood trickling out of a nostril and the fact that she was now looking at me like she wanted to headbutt me back.

I wasn't sorry.

I pushed myself up onto my elbows, and the front and back of my head were throbbing.

I could tell by the motion of the van that we'd just turned a corner. "Where the hell am I?" I asked, feeling equal parts confused, angry, and like I wanted to take a nap.

"We're taking you home," Cassandra said, wincing as she pinched the bridge of her nose and gave it a tiny wiggle.

"Who is *we*?" I asked. "And how do you know where I live?"

"Well, *our* home. We didn't know what else to do, and we couldn't just leave you lying on the sidewalk."

"Lying on the sidewalk where?" I was trying to piece together how I'd ended up there, lying in the back of a van, but I was missing major chunks of information. She didn't totally answer me either, and I still didn't know who was driving. Kidnapping remained a possibility.

"In front of the school. Where you tripped and hit your head."

I groaned again, only this time the pain was colored with embarrassment. So in one week of school, I had wrecked a car people thought I farted in and blacked out on the front lawn. This was awesome.

Then I realized she hadn't actually answered my question.

"Who's driving?" I asked hesitantly.

"My brother."

Cassandra was dabbing at her nose with the sleeve of her flannel. "Don't worry," she said. "I don't think it's broken."

"I wasn't worried," I answered. I sat up so that I was no longer lying on the floor, and I put one hand on the side of the van to steady myself against the rocking. As soon as I felt like I wasn't going to fall over, I looked up toward the front of the car and locked eyes with someone in the rearview mirror.

"Hey," a voice said. "Sorry we had to meet like this, but man, you scared us."

We stopped at an intersection, and the driver turned around and smiled at me. I blinked several times, taking in the entirety of his face. This was the most gorgeous guy I had ever seen IRL.

Then I leaned over and threw up on the floor.

I'd puked right as we were turning into their driveway, and before I knew it, they were on either side of me, pulling me out of the back of the van and then basically dragging me up onto their porch and into their house like I was a dead body. I was still too woozy from the fall and nauseous with humiliation to protest much, though.

I could swear that there was something in the water in Spring River that turned teenage guys into potatoes—lumpy-looking, with a mashed personality to match. It was immediately clear that Cassandra's brother had not grown up drinking out of the Spring River taps. Rather, it looked like celestial beings had spoon-fed him ambrosia and he'd received a pheromone IV. He was hot. He had a face that made you want to read poetry and get a stick-n-poke of his initials in a place no one else could see.

He was tall and thin, but not skinny in a bobblehead sort of way. Wiry. That was the word for it—like he didn't hit the gym but spent a lot of time working on motorcycles or moving concrete blocks. He had the same black hair and tawny skin as Cassandra, and wore the same kind of beat-up clothes. Dusty boots, a faded black T-shirt that stretched over his chest and arms, and jeans that dissolved into a dirty fray at the hem. Looking at him, I had the kind of thoughts that had previously only been inspired by guys on album sleeves or in the nineties movies Janis and I watched every weekend. I didn't know guys like him actually existed.

I had time to think about all this, because Cassandra and her brother were dragging me into their house and talking about me like I wasn't there.

"If she barfed, she might have a concussion," Cassandra was saying, "so we should keep her awake."

"Well, she doesn't look sleepy to me," her brother said as they dumped me onto a couch. Her brother disappeared through a doorway, and Cassandra stood there looking at me for a second before she reached out like she was going to touch me. I swatted her hand away and growled like an injured dog. The male model returned and passed me a zip-lock bag of ice cubes wrapped in a dish towel.

I thanked him and held the bundle against the rapidly growing bump on my head. "I don't have a concussion," I said. "I just have a nervous stomach. Other than that, I'm fine." At least, as fine as I could be.

He was staring at me with concern in his gorgeous eyes. "Do you know where you are?" he asked.

"Of course not," I said. I pulled my ice pack away and

touched the back of my skull gently, then winced—it felt soft and squishy. "Because you haven't told me."

"How many fingers am I holding up?" he asked, holding his hand in front of my face.

"Four," I said, and his forehead creased with concern. "And one thumb." The crease relaxed.

I looked around. The couch I was sitting on was ripped, the stuffing spilling out of the cushions. The curtains were stained brown and yellow to match the faded carpet. Now that I was no longer worried that I'd been snatched by a human trafficker, I was starting to find all this ridiculous.

"Listen, I'm fine. I just have no freaking clue what is going on here. You guys basically kidnapped me and brought me to this dump. What do you want?"

He grinned in a tight way that was more of a grimace. "Maybe we should start over," he said. "I'm Dionysus, but everyone calls me Dion. And this is my house."

Before I could stutter out an apology, the Greek god offered me his hand, and I took it. He was smiling at me with these perfect teeth and these eyes like melted chocolate, and the feeling of his fingers wrapped around mine stopped all words from forming in my mouth and made me forget I should probably be trying to escape.

It also made me self-conscious. When was the last time I'd shaken someone's hand? Was I doing it right? How hard do you grip? How fast do you pump up and down? How long do you hold on? I worried that my hand felt as slimy and limp as an uncooked chicken breast. I was wearing a white collarless shirt, not from Fred Segal, with suspenders and a short plaid skirt, and I hoped he hadn't been able to see the holes in the crotch of my tights when I was sprawled in the back of his van.

"I'm excited to meet you," he said, and if I hadn't already been knocked unconscious once, I probably would have fainted right there. What on earth could Cassandra have told him that would make him excited to meet me?

All she knew about me was that I babysat, and unless this guy was a single teenage dad, I doubted that was what he was talking about. My eyes flickered back to Cassandra, who hadn't taken her gaze off me the whole time I'd been sitting there.

"So," she asked, sitting down beside me, "how long have you known you were telekinetic?"

That was the word for it, the one that had been locked away in a corner of my brain. The one that I'd never planned to think, much less say out loud.

I still couldn't seem to form words. I sat there, trying to process what Cassandra had just said, and she pressed on. She held out her hand, fingers splayed, and a flame appeared at the tip of her index finger, just like a candle. Then it moved to her middle finger, ring finger, and pinky, then back again.

"Cass, don't burn the couch," Dion said, as blithely as if he were telling her not to get ice cream on his shirt.

She rolled her eyes and pressed her hand flat against the cushion, right by my thigh. The smell of burned polyester threaded through the air, and I watched, stunned, as a scorch mark spread between her fingers. I felt torn. One half of me wanted to get up and run out the door. The other half wanted to ask her to do it again.

"Esme's right," she said. "This place is a dump. Setting it on fire would be an improvement."

I glanced at Dion, whose face hardened for a second. "Well, it's the only place you've got," he said. "So if I were you, I would resist turning it to a pile of ash."

Cassandra rolled her eyes at him again and turned to me. "I can create fire out of nothing," she said. "I'm a pyrokinetic. Pretty cool, huh?"

I looked down at the burned handprint she'd left behind on the couch. It looked like someone was trapped inside the cushion and was trying to push their way out. It was creepy. Cassandra and her brother were creepy. This whole thing was creepy. So why wasn't I more creeped out? Instead of being overwhelmed, I felt almost relieved.

I sat there for a second, all my unacknowledged thoughts from the past couple of days coalescing into words. It felt like I'd been sitting in the dark and now the lights were slowly coming on.

"That thing in gym, with the ball," I said, "and in driver's ed, with the car—it's not like I meant to do it, you know? It just happened. Stuff has been happening because of me, but I don't think I control it." From the other end of the couch,

Dion wasn't taking his eyes off me, and it made me too self-conscious to look up. I traced Cassandra's handprint with a finger.

"Yeah. It took me a couple of weeks of things going up in flames around me before I realized I was doing it," Cassandra said. She kept talking, telling me about piles of leaves that started smoking, and a pickup that caught fire after it almost ran over her foot, and as she talked, her words peeled back the layers on the last several weeks of my life.

"You can control your"—I wasn't sure what to call it—"*powers* now?" I asked.

Cassandra nodded.

"So it only happens when you want it to?"

She nodded again.

"When did it start?" I asked her.

"I turned seventeen in June," she said, "and it was pretty much right after that."

I nodded slowly. "It was the same for me," I said. I told them about rushing to get ready for school and dropping a perfume bottle in the bathroom and somehow managing to catch it before it hit the tile floor, because it seemed to just hang there for a second. Also about the very realistic dream, which I now knew probably wasn't a dream at all, that my globe lamp was floating in the middle of my room in the middle of the night.

I looked over at Dion and knew that my hormones were raging, because even though this was the weirdest afternoon of my entire life, I couldn't help but notice the way the muscles in his forearm undulated as he took a sip from a bottle of red Gatorade.

"What can *you* do?" I asked him.

"You're looking at it," he said, and flashed me a smile that faded just as quickly as it had appeared. In my book, looking that hot did count as a superpower, but I didn't think that was what he was talking about.

"Dion doesn't have powers," Cassandra said. "We've tried, but he can't do anything." Dion gave her a look, and she corrected herself. "I mean, nothing extraordinary. Dion can do plenty of normal stuff, like change a tire or make spaghetti. . . ."

I wondered if maybe it was a touchy subject for them, but Dion just looked at me and shrugged.

"So, if you're pyrokinetic, and I'm telekinetic . . ." My mind was trying really hard to string this stuff together and make it all fit, but it felt like trying to squeeze into a too-small skirt. It just wasn't going to work. "Well . . . I mean . . ." I gave up and fell backward into the couch cushions. "Why?"

Cassandra snapped her gum. "Beats me. I was hoping you knew."

CHAPTER 7

As I sat, staring at Cassandra, Dion got up and poured me a glass of lukewarm Coke. "Sorry there's no ice," he said. "It's, uh, all being used." I took the soda with my free hand, still holding the bag of ice to the back of my head with the other. It was melting, and the cold drips ran down my neck.

"Wait," I said. "Let's start over. You guys just moved here? With your parents?"

"Yes and no," Cassandra said. "It's complicated." And it was. I had a hard time following as she explained that their parents had died in a car wreck when they were young, and after bouncing around to a few different relatives, they'd ended up in foster care and didn't have much contact with family.

"Dion and I grew up knowing nothing about who we were or where we came from. It's like people thought 'they're dead' was all we needed to know about our parents," she said, untying her Converse and then kicking them off so that they landed across the room with a thud. "Then, all of a sudden, Dion turned eighteen, and we found out that our mom had deeded him this house. Which is super strange, because he was barely four when she died. But oh well. We figured we'd take it, you know? I got the state to let Dion be my legal guardian, and here we are."

"How'd you do that?" I asked, thinking it was pretty odd that Dion was her guardian, since they were basically the same age.

"I threw the biggest fit the state of Kansas has ever seen," she said. Something about the set of her shoulders and the grin on her face told me that she probably wasn't exaggerating.

She paused dramatically, and I realized she was waiting for me to urge her on.

"So, you moved to Spring River . . . ?"

She nodded. "And once we got here, guess what we found in the house?"

"Um . . . squirrels?"

She sighed. "No. A note."

"Okay."

"Guess who wrote it?"

"I don't know. A neighbor?" I wished she'd just tell me what she wanted to tell me instead of trying to make me guess everything.

"No," she said. "It was tucked into a book, and it was from my mom!" She jumped up from the couch and headed down the hallway to what I assumed was her room. Dion and I sat in silence, and I could hear the fizzing of my drink. The hall was lined with black plastic trash bags, and Dion must have seen me looking at them.

"We're cleaning it up," he explained. "No one's lived here since our parents died, apparently, so it was full of junk, dust, and actually, a couple of squirrels. . . ." He was smiling slightly at me, in a way that made my ears get hot, and I wondered if he could hear my heart flopping around in my chest.

"Sorry I called it a dump earlier," I said.

"It's okay." He shrugged. "It *is* a dump."

"But it's *your* dump," I said, then realized that had sounded like I was making fun of him. "I mean, you own a house, and you're only . . ."

"Eighteen," he finished for me, and I still couldn't believe it. I went to school with guys who were eighteen, and none of them, not a one, looked anything like Dion.

Cassandra came back into the room and thrust a ziplock baggie at me. There was a note in it, sealed up like it was evidence from a crime scene. The paper was yellowed, with an illustration of roses in the corner, and a few lone words were written in a feminine script. "Dear Cassandra, Find the babysitters. Love, Mom."

I was taking a sip of Coke and choked, sending soda squirting right out my nose. How many fluids could possibly come out of me in one afternoon? I wiped my chin with the back of my hand and took the note from Cassandra, still in the plastic bag. I stared at it, as if I might be able to read between its meager lines. This was clearly why Cassandra had wanted to join the babysitters club, but I couldn't believe that her mom's note was just about finding a way to make a couple of bucks. I looked back up at Cassandra. "What does this mean?"

Cassandra rolled her eyes. "I think it means to find the babysitters," she said. "So that's what I did. Now we have to figure out what to do next."

We. Without asking me, Cassandra had just assumed that we were in this together.

What did I want? I wasn't sure. I had to admit that part of me felt good. It was like this thing that I hadn't even admitted to myself was now out in the open. I, Esme Pearl, high school junior with a mediocre GPA, one friend, no driver's license, chin acne, and zero college prospects, had special powers. Supernatural powers.

It was terrifying.

I took a sip of my soda and swallowed carefully this time to make sure nothing came out of my nose again. Cassandra had gotten up and was standing a few feet away from me, in the middle of the living room, but Dion hadn't moved, or said anything. His eyes flicked back and forth between me and Cassandra like he was watching a tennis match. Me, his sister. Me, his sister. Every time they landed on me, I flushed. "What if I don't want to do anything next?" I asked finally.

"That's an option," Cassandra said. "If you want to go through life with uncontrollable powers that just go off whenever you fart or something."

Oh God. Did she think I was the one who'd farted in the driver's ed car? Did Dion?

"That's not what I want. I mean . . . it wasn't me," I said, and now I really was blushing. But Cassandra wasn't paying attention. She had jumped up and grabbed a dying plant from the windowsill and set it in the middle of the floor.

"Try," she said. She stared at me intently, and if I hadn't known she could start fires with her hands, I would have guessed that she could start them with her eyes. It was clear that she was waiting for me to do something with the plant.

I held my hands up in protest. "I can't," I said. "I mean, I don't even know where to start. . . ."

"Come on," Cassandra said. "It weighs nothing. It won't be hard to move. And once you figure it out, it's easy." She pivoted so that she was facing the plant, and one of the dry vines burst into flames. Dion was next to it in an instant, stomping out the fire and sending Cassandra a scorching look of his own.

"Just look at it, and use your mind to tell it what to do," Cassandra directed. Dion stood back a few feet away from her, and was looking at me curiously. "You're going to have to learn how to control it eventually."

"You don't think it'll just go away?" That was what I had been secretly secretly hoping ever since I'd secretly started to get an idea of what was happening.

"God, I hope not!" Cassandra said, genuine fear in her voice at the thought of that happening. "Come on," she urged. "We're all friends here."

Were we? I wondered, but I looked at the plant anyway. The ice in my ice pack had all melted, and now I was just holding a bag of water to my head. The throbbing had subsided, and my stomach had settled from a roil to a slow roll.

What the hell.

I tried to make my mind blank, just like in those meditation tapes Dad was always listening to, and I looked at the plant. Okay, I thought. *Move*, you stupid thing, *move*.

Just like that, it started to rise. First a wobbly inch off the ground, then two, three, until finally it hovered a foot and a half in the air.

Dion sucked in his breath, and my concentration broke, sending the plant falling back down. It landed on its side and bounced, tumbling out of the plastic pot and spilling white-flecked soil out onto the carpet.

I stood up, and Cassandra was beside me immediately, throwing her arms around me in a hug, and then we were literally jumping for joy. I had never felt so good in my entire life.

I spent the next hour practicing. The poor plant got beat to crap, but by the time I was done, I could hold it in the air for a full minute without even a wobble.

Finally, it was getting late and I figured I should leave, as I still had homework to pretend to do. Dion insisted on giving me a ride home, and as he walked me out, he kept a hand on my elbow to steady me. I felt totally fine now, but I wasn't going to tell him that. On the way to their house, I'd been too out of it to really notice anything about Dion's car, but now that we were walking down the driveway, I got my first good look.

The car was a minivan, the kind driven by people who wear Snoopy pajama pants in public and drink diet Sprite instead of water. It was light blue. Mostly. One front side panel was a burnt umber, and the sliding door was fire-engine red. The back fender was smashed, and there was silver duct tape and black plastic around one of the back windows. But what really made the car a wreck was the bumper stickers: one said "Coexist" in religious symbols, and one said "Mean People Suck." I decided I was going to give him the benefit of the doubt and assume they'd come with the car, because it was impossible that someone with such exquisite cheekbones could have such crappy taste.

"I inherited the car too," Dion said, as though he could read my thoughts. "A guy I used to work with gave me most of it. I just had to add the door myself."

I nodded, as if this were a totally familiar way to get a car.

Cassandra was coming with us, and while most people would have offered me—"the guest"—shotgun, I wasn't surprised, even though I'd only spent a few hours with her, when she climbed in and left me to sit on the floor in the back. I tried to do so as gracefully as possible, then finally gave up and sat leaning against the passenger side with my legs sprawled in front of me.

From my place on the floor I could see how clean it was.

The carpet had been vacuumed. There wasn't a speck of dirt anywhere, and the spot where I'd emptied my guts earlier had already been shampooed. He must have snuck back outside to do it while Cassandra and I were practicing.

"There's a blanket back there if you're cold," Dion said, and I shivered. Not from a chill but from, well, him. When we pulled up at the first intersection, he rolled down the window and waved his arm out, and that's when I realized the car didn't have turn signals. I gave Dion directions to my house, and the ride took less than ten minutes. We were all quiet, and I wondered if they were as exhausted as I was. I felt almost unconscious, like I could curl up and sleep in a folding chair. When we got to my house, Dion put the van in park, then got out and walked around to open the sliding side door.

"Sorry, Es," he said. "It's broken and doesn't open from the inside." Cassandra was absorbed in changing the radio station, but Dion gave me a hug and brushed his hands across the bump on the back of my head. "I really hope that's not a concussion," he said, the wrinkle reappearing in his forehead.

I'd known him for less than an afternoon, and he was already abbreviating my name like I was someone he had on speed dial. I wanted not to like it, but I did. It wasn't broishly overfamiliar. It was just comfortable, like someone ordering you fries you hadn't asked for, just because they knew that, as a human being, there was a 98.9 percent chance you liked fries.

"It's not a concussion," I said, not totally convinced that

it was the truth, but not wanting him to worry his pretty little head about it.

"Don't be a stranger," he said, and all I could do was smile dumbly and nod until he turned away.

I was walking up the sidewalk when Cassandra yelled my name out the window. "Keep practicing!" she said. "You got this."

I watched them drive away, and at the corner, the van sputtered and died, then started up again and drove off with a squeal. I marveled at my afternoon. It was the weirdest few hours of my life, no doubt, and had left me with more questions than answers. Was the note really all that had led Cassandra to me? That hardly seemed likely, but she hadn't said what else her mom had left her, and I hadn't asked. In fact, I'd hardly asked anything at all. Aside from what she'd said about her parents, we'd skipped almost all the basic getting-to-know-you kind of stuff, which made this the second time I'd hung out with Cassandra and failed to learn anything about her.

A wave of panic washed over me. Letting her into the babysitting club without a background check had come around to bite me in the ass, so maybe this was going to turn out the same. What if I'd messed up by revealing so much of myself to people I barely knew anything about?

I sighed. If I *had* messed up, it was too late to do anything about it now.

I let myself into the house and was greeted by a tail-wagging, drool-dangling, very-excited-to-see-me Pig. Pig only cared about two things: her family, and food, and not necessarily in that order. I knew her well enough to know that such an enthusiastic welcome meant that she probably hadn't had dinner yet.

I went straight to the kitchen, and as I dumped kibble into her bowl, a laugh track exploded in the den. I peeked in to see that the TV was still on, but Dad was asleep on the couch, his head thrown back and his mouth open like a gasping fish. I put the food down for Pig and went to the den. When I shook Dad by the shoulder, he jerked awake like he'd been shocked.

"What time is it?" he said, pushing himself up into a sitting position.

"Almost eight."

"Is it?" He took off his glasses and rubbed them on his T-shirt, a nervous tic that meant his glasses were almost always gross and greasy, as his T-shirts were never clean. "Make any moolah?"

This was one of Dad's favorite questions, and it took me a second to realize that this meant he thought I'd been baby-sitting.

"Thirty-five dollars," I lied, because it seemed easier than explaining that I'd just been hanging out with two people he'd never heard of before. Dad had only ever known me to hang out with Janis, because, prior to today, I'd only ever hung out with Janis.

Dad sighed and held his glasses up to the light. "You're going to need it. The school sent me the driver's ed bill today.

Their insurance will cover most of it, but you're still responsible for the tree."

I stared at him, feeling like the bump on the back of my head had a heartbeat of its own. I'd managed to completely forget about the wreck, even though now I knew, without a doubt, what had happened in that driver's seat.

"Oh," I said, and swallowed.

Dad smiled. "It's not actually that bad," he said, "and it's nothing that hasn't happened at that school before." His brow crinkled. "Is your head okay?"

I nodded, realizing that I was still standing there with my hand on my skull. I quickly dropped it to my side.

Dad continued. "Going over the financials got me thinking about your future, Esme. I think we should sit down and do a real frank evaluation of your options." He looked at me like he was waiting for me to say something, but I wasn't going to humor him by turning this into anything more than a one-sided conversation.

"I was talking to Jed the other day, and his son just started at SRCC and really likes it. . . ." I turned away from him and started up the stairs. I stopped outside my room, as I realized that Dad had actually gotten up off the couch to follow me and was standing at the bottom of the staircase. "I'm just thinking we need to be realistic," he said.

"I know," I said, trying to keep from sounding too annoyed. "Can we talk about this later, though? I'm tired, and I have homework." I went into my room and shut the door without waiting for him to answer. The afternoon had made me feel like I was floating along with that dead plant, and now Dad was yanking me right back to earth. We'd had this conversation a dozen times before, and the thing was, I knew Dad was right. We didn't have the money for me to go someplace like Pratt or FIT, and even if we did, I probably wouldn't get in.

All the babysitting money I was saving would barely buy a bus ticket to Cleveland. My grades were just okay, and my only extracurricular was thrifting. A huge part of Janis's and my friendship was based on the fact that we both wanted to GTFO of Spring River, but just because we wanted out didn't mean that we would make it out. Janis's parents were professors. She got a 3.9 in her sleep, and went to coding camp every July. When Janis was thirteen, she actually built an app that mimicked Cher Horowitz's closet. Would Janis still text me every night when I was studying communications at Spring River Community College and she was in Paris channeling Phoebe Philo at Celine, or at Central Saint Martins in London?

I waited a few seconds, until I heard Dad's footsteps retreat. Then I opened the door a little bit. "Come on, girl," I said, and Pig came trotting in and made herself a nest out of some clothes on the floor. I shut the door behind her, and she settled, giving a sigh of contentment, then started snoring with her eyes still open. I flopped down onto my bed, careful not to bump my head again, as it was still throbbing. I sighed and looked over at the door as I heard Dad come back up the stairs. There was no way he would come in without knocking, but I stared at the lock anyway. What the hell? I thought. It was worth a try. I focused, and the lock gave a little shiver, then clicked into place.

In spite of myself, I smiled a bit. If I tried really hard, maybe I could even learn to like this.

CHAPTER 8

Dad considered rising with the sun to be a sign of integrity and good character.

I disagreed.

Who knew how long he'd been up by the time we met in the kitchen. He was working on a crossword, which he did diligently every single morning and still sucked at. He did them in pencil, and usually ended up erasing so much that he rubbed a hole into the paper.

"You're going to be late," he said without looking up.

I poured myself a cup of coffee. "No, I'm not," I said, giving the barely warm coffee a loud slurp. "I've timed it perfectly so that I'll get there at 7:57."

"That's almost late," he said, licking the eraser and then grinding it into the paper.

"I like living on the edge," I said. I felt bad about the night before. Dad wasn't deliberately out to squash my dreams; he was just being practical. I was determined to be extra nice to him today, so I leaned over to give him a kiss on the top of his head. As I did, the front page of the local section caught my eye. I swatted his elbow so that he'd move it and I could slide that section of the paper out.

In Spring River, the local section was usually good only for a laugh and as proof of how pathetic our town was, like coverage of a planned protest against the new roundabout going in at the intersection next to the park. ("'This ain't Europe!' said Fred Gregorson when asked why he was in opposition to the city's new roundabout." Janis had actually cut that one out and taped it to her bathroom mirror. It was motivation, she said, to never forget why she wanted to leave.) Or the local section might provide a serious review of the latest chain restaurant opening. ("When dining at Olive Garden, the breadsticks are a must.")

But today there was an article I wanted to read. A demo date had finally been set for the Triple Lakes mall, which had been pretty much abandoned for the past several years. It was scheduled to be knocked down on December 31.

"Why would they blow up the mall on New Year's Eve?" I asked, and Dad scanned the article.

"Probably something to do with taxes," he said, and I kept reading. Until then, the mall's last gasp of life would be as the Mall of Terror, a haunted house where "prices aren't the only things that get slashed." The article was illustrated with a picture of the mall, which was now totally decrepit and creepy enough without any decorations, and the Mall of Terror poster, which was illustrated with a blood-soaked shopping bag full of eyeballs and severed limbs.

I couldn't help but feel somewhat nostalgic for the days when I could still buy stuff at the mall, and the food court wasn't just for zombies snacking on rancid brains. That mall was where Dad had taken me back-to-school shopping before I'd discovered thrift stores, and it was where I used to go to spend my babysitting money on cupcake-scented glitter body lotion and multipacks of earrings that turned my skin green, back in the original babysitters club days.

Dad clearing his throat snapped me out of my memories and back to the kitchen. "Esme," he said. "Clock's ticking. You better move it, unless you want to take the bus."

"I know, I know," I said, draining the last of my coffee. "I'm practically ready."

My look today was "Y2K VMAs," a nod to the pre–Rachel Zoe glory days before celebs started using stylists," and was entirely plastic from head to toe—vinyl, polyester, rayon, oh my! But in spite of what I knew was a really good outfit, I felt nervous and on edge. As I walked down the hall to my first class, I scanned every passing face to see if it was Cassandra's. The only thing I could compare this to was the feeling I'd had sophomore year after I'd kissed Jordan McFadden, my longtime crush, at the mini-golf course and wondered if things would be any different between us at school. (News flash: they weren't.)

What would I say to Cassandra if I saw her? What would she say to me? In the same minute, I'd go back and forth between hoping she'd want to talk about it more, and hoping she'd pretend that we'd never talked about it at all.

Even though I still wasn't even sure what "it" was.

Finally, in the middle of US History, I couldn't take it anymore. We were watching *Braveheart*. Again. In *US* History. The teachers typically didn't start in with the movies until at least December, but the rumor was that Mr. Hedgeman was going through a divorce. This would certainly account for the motorcycle he now rode to work every day, the black leather jacket he wore, and the fact that he'd walk into class, slap a DVD into the player like he was about to blow our minds, and then promptly fall asleep at his own desk.

In the midst of a scene of good ol' anti-Semitic, misogynistic, long-haired Mel Gibson running up a hill in a skirt and yelling (which was basically the whole movie), I got up and walked to Mr. Hedgeman's desk. I didn't want to startle him, so I used a low, calm voice to ask for a bathroom pass. When that didn't work, I tapped him on the shoulder. First with just one finger, then with my fist. He sat bolt upright, blinking like he wasn't sure where he was. Which was entirely possible. "Can I get a bathroom pass?" I asked.

"Of course, of course," he said. "I was just resting my eyes. Gotta recover from all the screen time of grading essays."

"I bet," I said, smiling as widely as I could. "You teachers work really hard."

"So, what can I do for you?" he asked.

"Um, bathroom pass?" I said again. He nodded, and fumbled around on his desk. When he couldn't find the passes, he settled for scrawling his name on a Post-it, which would at least hold up in a detention court of law. He was asleep again before I'd even left the room, which meant I could spend the rest of the period wandering the halls and dip back in right before the bell to pick up my backpack.

I was digging through my locker, looking for a granola bar that I was 99 percent sure was in there somewhere, when a "Hey" from behind me made me jump. I spun around, and Cassandra was right there.

"Nice outfit," she said, and I nodded. I pushed my hair out of my face, my heart beating so fast that I thought it might burst out of my cropped turtleneck. "You seem nervous." I nodded again, not sure what to say to that. She spun halfway around so that she was leaning up against the locker next to mine, and she was smacking her gum. "You know, I was thinking about you last night," she continued. "And how yours really is the superior power. Think of everything you could do with it. You could take whatever you wanted, from wherever. You could even kill someone and never get caught."

I swallowed. "I doubt it. Even if I wanted to kill someone, which I don't, I can barely control it."

"Did you practice any more last night?"

"A little," I admitted.

"I practice all the time," she said, and a few lockers down, a wadded-up napkin on the floor began to smolder, then caught fire. I went over and stamped it out.

"Careful," she said, a wry smile on her face. "Your shoes might melt."

"Cassandra," I said finally. "I don't understand what's going on here. At all."

"I don't either," she said simply, "so we'd better figure it out. What are you doing tonight?"

We agreed to meet up at five-thirty, and since Cassandra had some stuff she had to do after school and I didn't, I killed time in the library, actually doing my homework in advance. I worked there until five, then gave myself thirty minutes to get downtown to meet her. She still didn't know much about Spring River, so I'd picked where to meet and had chosen the Park Perk, a dingy downtown coffee shop that Janis hated because it always smelled like ham and pickles, even though neither were on the menu. I didn't want to run into her and have to explain why we were having a "club meeting" without her.

The days were getting shorter now, and the sky already had a hazy sunset glow when I opened the door to the Perk and ham smell hit me in the face. Cassandra had gotten there before me and was already sitting in a booth in the back with a large mug. I ordered an iced coffee at the counter and set it on the table as I slid in across from her. I looked at her mug, the contents of which were dusted with a sprinkle of chocolate. "Mocha?" I asked.

"Hot chocolate. I don't like coffee." My mouth dropped

open. Who was this person? This dislike of the elixir of life might cancel out everything else that we had in common.

"You're joking, right?" I asked.

"Why would I joke about coffee?" She had a point. I mean, I didn't joke about coffee either. She sat back in the booth, ripped open a Sweet'N Low packet, and dumped the contents onto the table, then drew designs in it with her finger.

"So, everyone says your mom is . . ."

"Crazy," I finished for her, and she raised an eyebrow. "It's kind of apt. She doesn't have a diagnosis. They've ruled out bipolar, schizophrenia. . . . Sometimes it's like psychosis, sometimes PTSD. Every time she gets a new doctor, they spend a couple of weeks determined to figure it out, but they all eventually give up. Drugs don't help either, no matter what they try." I faked a smile. "So, medical mystery, I guess."

"What happened?" she asked.

I ripped open my own packet—Sugar in the Raw—and gave her the abbreviated version.

"It's like something in her brain broke," I said, "and now there are oceans between her and the rest of the world."

"Do you ever wonder what caused it?" Cassandra asked.

"Sure," I said. "When I was younger, I filled notebooks with theories."

"But now?"

It made me feel like a horrible person, but I told Cassandra the truth. "It hurts too much," I said, "so I try not to think about it."

I waited for the kind of reaction I normally got when

I told people about Mom, awkward fumbling for the right words, looks of pity, and the eventual hints at questions about whether we knew if it was genetic.

When all she said was "Dude, that sucks," I was actually relieved.

Over the course of my story I'd drained my drink down to the ice, but Cassandra had barely touched her hot chocolate, with the whipped cream melting into an oily skim on top.

"Okay," I said. "Now your turn."

"I told you," she said, running her finger along the rim of the mug. "We don't know much. I was three when our parents died in a car accident; Dion was four. We ended up in foster care because I guess there wasn't any family that could take care of us, or who wanted to take care of us."

"Why do you say that?"

"I don't know, really," she said. "I was pretty young. But kids pick up on things, you know?"

I nodded, because as a babysitter, I definitely did know this.

"I think my mom's family was scared of her," Cassandra continued. "As weird as it sounds, I think they were scared of us too, even though we were just kids. Like, I distinctly remember waking up one night to my aunt sprinkling me with holy water."

"You weren't eating a lot of pea soup, were you?" I asked.

"Ew, gross. Why?" she asked. "I hate peas."

"Never mind." I said. If she hadn't seen *The Exorcist*, now wasn't the time for me to stop and explain.

"What about your dad's family?"

"Who knows?" she said. "Even if they were out there somewhere, no one showed up to take us in."

Cassandra leaned forward, her hair falling around her face like a privacy curtain for our conversation, and she lowered her voice to a whisper. "So, the note wasn't all I found."

I nodded, wondering if she was going to try to make me guess everything again. Instead, she didn't say anything and reached into a tote, and pulled out another ziplock bag, then slid it across the table toward me. Inside was a black spiral notebook. It was battered and creased so that veins of white showed on the cover.

"Take it out and open it," she said.

"Should I wear gloves?" I asked, and I was only half joking. The notebook was well-used but clean, and the way Cassandra kept it sealed in plastic told me that it was very, very important to her.

"Just don't spill on it," she said.

I nodded and unzipped the bag, and pulled the notebook out. I flipped the cover open, and the pages were as soft as fabric. The handwriting was neat and precise, like it had been carefully copied from somewhere else. Cassandra didn't take her eyes off me as I flipped through it. Each page had a different word written at the top, in a language that was not one I spoke, i.e., English or any Spanish that was covered freshman or sophomore year.

Underneath each word was a list. Some of the things were stuff I'd never heard of, like mugwort and tourmaline sand. Some were normal grocery-store gets, like pumpkin pie spice or frozen gyoza. And then others, like the hair from a Barbie doll or a used pink razor, seemed like the kinds of things a stalker would keep in a special box.

I looked up at Cassandra, baffled. "What is all this?"

She shook her head. "I don't know. I thought it was maybe a scavenger hunt, or even just a grocery list, but none of it really makes sense. And that's not all. There's also this." In her other hand, she was holding yet another ziplock—she had more baggies than a drug dealer. In it, I could see the back of a printed photo.

Slowly I reached out and took it from her, then turned the photo around. It was two women and two babies. One woman and one baby I'd never seen before. This first woman was hands down one of the most gorgeous creatures I had ever seen outside of the pages of a magazine, with long, curly dark hair that swooped haphazardly over her forehead, like she'd just run her fingers through it to get it out of her face, deep brown eyes with mile-long lashes, and pillowy lips that were accented with perfect dark-maroon lipstick.

I'd seen those eyes before, and that hair that wouldn't stay put. It was clearly Cassandra and Dion's mom, and from the diamond studs that glittered on the model baby's ears and the fact that it was wearing a dress, I could guess the baby was Cassandra, even though I couldn't imagine her wearing anything sparkly now.

The other woman and baby I did recognize.

In fact, I knew them well.

The woman was my mom, and the baby was me.

My hands were shaking, half with shock, half with anger. "Where did you get this?" I spat the words at Cassandra.

"It was in the notebook."

"And you didn't bother to show me when I went to your house?"

"I didn't want to blow my load right away."

"Nice, Cassandra," I said, my voice rising. "Very classy. I'm leaving." I stood up to go at the same time that her coffee mug arced into the air and crashed to the floor, where it cracked into a dozen pieces.

"Oh crap," Cassandra said loudly, looking around. "I'm so clumsy." She turned to me, and in a lower voice said, "Esme, sit down, and don't get mad or you might send the table flying out the door. We're in this together. We need each other."

"Maybe that's true," I said, "but that doesn't give you the right to manipulate me." I could feel tears seeping into my eyes. "If you knew something about my mom, Cassandra, you should have told me right away."

Her face softened. "I'm sorry. I really am. I keep messing up." I sat down, because she looked like she meant it. "But you can't deny that we're connected," she continued. "And there has to be a reason behind all of this. Something that's bigger than you and me put together."

"That may be true," I said, "but we have no idea what that is."

"Well, then we have to find out. And I say we start with this book."

She tapped it, and with that, every candle in the coffee shop flickered to life.

Cassandra wouldn't let me borrow the notebook or take pictures, because she was worried about spies in my iPhone. But she did agree to let me make copies, so we walked three doors down from the Perk to a copy shop, and I made copies of every page, Cassandra standing under the fluorescent lights with her back to me, scanning the place like she was my bodyguard. Or, to be more precise, the book's bodyguard. When I was done, I handed it back to her, and she carefully sealed it up in plastic and tucked it back into her tote.

Her phone was dead, so she used mine to text Dion for a ride, though, much to her chagrin, he didn't respond. And to my chagrin too, since I was already wondering when I would see him next. I had big plans for when that happened—like to not pass out or puke or anything.

"What does Dion think about the book?" I asked.

"Nothing," she said. "I haven't told him."

"Why not?" That surprised me. It wasn't like she was hiding her powers from him.

"It doesn't have anything to do with him," she said.

"You found it in his house," I pointed out.

A cloud crossed her face. "I guess," she said, "but I want to figure out what all this stuff is first. And then I'll see if it has anything to do with Dion."

With no ride on the horizon, Cassandra and I took the

bus together, and as soon as she got off at her stop, I pulled out my phone to see the text she'd sent, but she'd deleted it, not even leaving his number. When it came to cell phone etiquette, I didn't know if this was polite or rude.

I got off at my stop and pulled my jacket around me as I walked to the house. Dad wasn't home, and when I let myself in, I went straight to my room, Pig at my heels, without detouring through the kitchen to see what we didn't have for dinner. I dropped my backpack and sat down on my bed to pry off my shoes. In my mind, I kept seeing all the candles in the Park Perk igniting as Cassandra just sat there and smiled. She wore her power well, like it was something that was owed to her.

When I'd started to figure out what was going on with me, I'd felt the opposite. Like it was a curse instead of a gift. I'd never felt powerful in my entire life. I mean, I was forever paying with large bills because I was too scared to hold up the line while I dug for exact change. I lived in fear that a stranger would ask me what time it was. But I could do things that other people couldn't. Not that I wanted to, but if I had, I could even have smashed the hell out of everything Stacey Wasser made in pottery class, and really made her pay for touching my turtle.

With my chunky Mary Janes finally off, I lay back on the bed and flexed my toes at the ceiling, then flipped over so I was looking at my closet. I focused, and Pig howled as a black crushed-velvet minidress and an oversized black hat flew through the air above her. I knew just how she felt. I didn't bark, but I did feel my cheeks stretch into a smile. As the clothes arranged themselves into an outfit on my chair, I texted Janis.

> **lydia deetz goes to the beach. small dress, big hat.**
> **U?**
>> rich black bitch
> **lol**
> **u watching the nina simone documentary again?**
>> u know it. C u tomorrow with my headwrap on.

CHAPTER 9

Thank God for online dating, because it meant Sharon needed a babysitter at least once a week. I was nervous about what had happened last time, but my savings account needed me to get over it, and I headed to their house just after six the next day. Kaitlyn answered the door when I knocked. I could tell it was her, because although I could hear lots of clicking from the other side, and see the knob turn a little bit, the door remained closed. It made me uneasy, and something dark welled up in me—a toddler who couldn't work a door-knob could not have opened the window—but I pushed that aside and I let myself in, to be greeted by a two-year-old in footie pajamas, wearing a unicorn horn and a rainbow tail, sticking her tongue out at me.

I returned the gesture and stuck my tongue out at her. "Does Mommy know you're opening the door?" I asked, as it didn't seem like a habit she should be getting into. Her answer was to throw her hands into the air and run around me in circles, screaming at the top of her lungs. When she stopped, she wrapped those chubster arms around me to give my knees a hug. That was when I realized she was also covered in a fine layer of glitter, because my tights sparkled as soon as she pulled away.

"I thought I was just babysitting a kid tonight," I said. "I didn't know that there was a magical beast here!" Kaitlyn neighed, and I followed her as she galloped off down the hallway. In the kitchen, Sharon scooped her up and deposited her back at the table, in front of a plate of peas and mini pizza bagels. Sharon was wearing a shimmering silver camisole and a pair of sweatpants.

"Oh, Esme," she said. "I love that hat. It's so chic. Is it Michael Kors?"

I smiled and shook my head. "Salvation Army," I said, but Sharon was already heading back down the hallway.

She yelled to me through the open door to her room. "Doll, can you please make Kaitlyn eat her dinner? I have to finish getting ready."

"No problem," I called back. Kaitlyn was already back out of her booster seat, galloping laps around the table.

Part of being a good babysitter was doing what you had to do to get the kid to do what it needed to do, so I cut up some bites of pizza bagel and put them and some peas into my hand. Then I held out my flat palm and said, "Does the unicorn want some magic rainbow nuggets to make it fly real high and real fast?" The unicorn nodded, then trotted over to eat out of my hand, sliming it in the process. Thank God for hand sanitizer.

I was used to Sharon being about as scattered as birdseed, but tonight she seemed extra flustered. By my count, she changed outfits five times, all the while complaining, in detail, about some stomach issues she'd been having all day ("I thought I should just glue my ass to the toilet seat, 'cause I wasn't ever coming out of that bathroom," she said at one point), and telling me about the fish massacre Kaitlyn had staged earlier that afternoon by squirting dish soap into the aquarium. I complimented her on her combo of black cigarette pants and kitten heels, and asked what they'd done with the dead fish.

"Oh, they're still in the aquarium," she called over her shoulder as she rooted through the closet looking for a rhinestone clutch. "I was hoping you could take care of it for us?"

Internally I groaned. Externally I said, "Not a problem at all."

As soon as Sharon's car pulled out of the driveway, after she'd finally settled on a pink silk blouse and a gray wiggle skirt, Kaitlyn and I got right down to dead-fish-disposal business. Kaitlyn watched quietly and patiently as I scooped them out with a slotted spoon and laid each goldfish on a paper towel, their blobby bodies shimmering like chunks of orange Jell-O.

When I'd gotten all three out, we carried them into the bathroom. I made sure to keep my voice somber as I gave the eulogy, as I didn't want Kaitlyn to think that a fish funeral was a fun new game. "You were good fish," I said, "smart fish, beautiful fish, talented fish. Master swimmers, so good at eating little fishy flakes and just being very fish-like. We will miss you, oh noble and true fish friends." I dropped the first one in with a splash. Flush. Then the next one. Flush, and final flush.

All in a day's work.

"Isn't it sad," I said to Kaitlyn, "that now you don't have any pets?" She nodded, and her expression transformed. Suddenly she looked like she was going to cry. Seeing the look in her eyes, I realized I'd laid it on a little thick. To cheer her up, we went to the living room so that she could jump off the couch. She landed maybe eight inches from where she'd taken off, but I screamed and clapped like a gymnast's momager.

"Oh my goodness," I cried. "You're like an Olympian! Triple gold medals, for the longest jump, the highest jump, and the most beautiful jump!" She grinned like she really had just won a prize, and when she took a bow, I could see all the glitter stuck to her scalp.

She went to bed without a fuss, and as soon as she was asleep, I made myself a cup of hot chocolate and sat down outside her door. I didn't move until I heard Sharon's car in the driveway. I wasn't taking chances anymore.

I wouldn't say I practiced on Thursday. That sounds like setting an allotted time for something and doing it over and over until you get it right. But I did use my powers here and there. I fed Pig without getting off the couch. I got more toilet paper without getting off the . . . well, that's obvious. I repiled some junk in my room without getting off the bed. I was entering a new period of power, and peak laziness, and I had to admit that it was kind of cool.

It was crisp and sunny on Friday, so Janis and I sat outside at lunch, next to the pond that had once been home to several koi but that now housed just one sad turtle that might have actually been dead. (It's hard to tell with turtles.) The senior class had TP'd the school, an early Halloween prank, and dreadlocks of toilet paper twirled from the trees. It was pretty, in a weird sort of way.

Janis's look today was "be all you can be Barbie," which translated to a camo-print minidress, a military overshirt with a name patch that said "Raul," and unlaced hot-pink Doc Martens that required deft steps to avoid tripping. The front of her hair was twisted into tight rows, with curlicues of baby hairs on her forehead and the back natural and puffed. She had finished her look with gold door-knocker earrings that said "Patrice."

Janis loved things with someone else's name on them. Maybe that was because she hated her own name, which was Janis Jackson. It was one of my favorite things in the world when someone met Janis for the first time and snickered, "Janis Jackson?" and she snarled back, "It's a family name!" She already had the forms filled out to change it the minute she turned eighteen.

My own look was "feminist rodeo queen," as I was wearing my "The Future Is Female" T-shirt under a fringed denim shirt, with high-waisted jeans and turquoise suede cowboy boots that were seven dollars on the super-deep-discount rack at Dad's favorite western-wear store.

Our lunch today came from the snack machine, not the caf line, so I was eating Cool Ranch Doritos and drinking a Red Bull, and Janis had a ginger ale and Sour Patch Kids. It was Friday, and since neither one of us had a job lined up, the night yawned before us, wide open.

Janis picked out a green kid and popped it into her mouth.

"So, what do you want to do tonight?" I asked. When Janis had been in Chicago, we'd texted nonstop, but she played down her trip from last weekend, at least to me. Her stories still looked like a "cut here" line. I was happy for Janis, that she was out there exploring her options for the future, but I was still happy to have her back. We had a routine, and I liked it.

"Yeah, I was going to talk to you about that," she said. "I know that you really want to hang out in your room and watch *Bring It On* while we eat pizza and scroll to the ends of the internet, but Bernie Goodman is having a party, and I think we should go."

"*Bring It On* is a really good movie," I said. "You always like the cheer routines."

Janis sighed. "I'm not saying I don't."

I shoved a chip into my mouth, chewed, and swallowed, the ranch coating thick on the roof of my mouth. "A party?" As of late, my social anxiety had taken a back seat to the discovery of my telekinesis, but at the mention of a party, it clamored to get back behind the wheel. Nothing sounded less appealing to me than going to a party.

"Yep. A gathering of like-minded people talking to each other, listening to music, drinking, maybe even—God forbid!—having fun."

"At Bernie Goodman's?" I was stalling.

"Yes, Bernie Goodman, a junior at Spring River High School whose parents are away for the weekend because his sister got caught trying to buy Adderall from her RA. Bernie's about five feet eleven inches tall, with brown hair, cheek acne—"

"I know who he is," I interrupted her. "I'm just surprised you want to go. It seems like Bernie Goodman's parties are probably lame."

"Esme, it's not like I think it's going to be Studio 54. I just think we could go, because it's not like we have anything else to do."

I saw more than enough of my classmates, well, in class, and all I really wanted to do that night was hang out with my pillow, Pig, and a bottle of nail polish, but that was how Janis and I had spent the previous three weekends before she went to Chicago. It was clear she wanted to go.

I ignored the signs telling me not to feed him, and threw my last chip to the turtle. "Okay," I said, "I'll go. But I can't promise that I'll like it."

"I'll pick you up at six-thirty," she said. "And no one said you had to like it."

It was 6:32 when my phone dinged.

Outside

Janis was waiting at the curb.

Unlike me, Janis had gotten her learner's permit as soon as she'd turned fourteen and her full license the day she'd turned sixteen. She drove a Honda Accord, which had been a nice car when she'd inherited it from her mom six months before. Now it was littered with soda bottles, coffee cups, abandoned school assignments, and a hot-pink smear on the upholstery from when an uncapped lipstick had spent a week skittering around the back seat. Next to my bedroom, I was more at home in Janis's car than anyplace else in the world.

I opened the passenger door, threw a magazine and a pair of socks into the back seat, and climbed in. My nose wrinkled as it took in a not-good, not-totally-bad odor— chocolate, with undertones of aquarium.

"What's that smell?"

Janis shrugged as she simultaneously cranked the music and the wheel. "I left the window down last week when it rained," she said. "I think there's mildew growing in the passenger seat." I looked down between my legs. I was sitting in the passenger seat. No wonder things felt squelchy.

Janis's outfit tonight was "lead singer of Jewel Tonez," a fictional nineties all-girl R&B trio. She wore purple eyeshadow that matched her halter top, a pair of teal hip-huggers with a hidden zipper in the back, and a cropped satin magenta baseball jacket.

I had put extra effort into my outfit tonight in an attempt to camouflage the fact that I really didn't want to go, and my look was "Edie Sedgwick loves LeBron." I had on thick black tights, black flats, and a minidress made from a Lakers jersey. I'd slicked my hair behind my ears to show off sparkly purple-and-gold waterfall earrings, rimmed my eyes with about a half inch of kohl, and topped it off with a black fake fur coat to keep me from freezing.

"Nice," Janis said as I climbed in. "Most people don't know that Edie was actually from California."

"That's because most people don't care," I said.

"Most people are stupid." Janis stepped on the gas and pulled away with a squeal.

Bernie Goodman only lived about ten minutes from me, in the next neighborhood over, and I'd barely picked out the song I wanted to hear, Siouxsie and the Banshees' "Halloween," when we turned onto his street. We pulled up behind a long line of cars, and Janis nosed her way into a spot by knocking some trash cans out of the way. I popped open my door and could hear music coming from the house several buildings away. The gutter by my feet was littered with beer bottles, even though it was still early, and for every car that pulled away, two seemed to pull up.

Bernie Goodman's house was a split-level painted bright orange and gray. Like all red-blooded suburban families, the Goodmans had gone all out on the seasonal decorations, and said decorations were now being thoroughly pillaged. A headless dummy slumped on the porch swing, and a few feet away, a guy in a werewolf mask lay sprawled across the walkway. Nearby, two seniors kicked a plastic jack-o'-lantern back and forth like a soccer ball, and as we walked up, a freshman I recognized from gym class pushed past us to dry heave into the mums.

It was as grim a social scene as I'd ever encountered, and I missed everything I'd left behind at home. I wondered what my nail polish collection was doing right now.

The inside of the house was in the process of being defiled by teenagers. The carpet was beige, the drapes were floral, and there were footprints and purple stains trailing across the cream-colored couch. All flat surfaces were covered with half-empty bottles, cans, and every mixer imaginable. Bob Marley blasted from the speakers, signaling that this was still considered the pre-party. The official party would start when a shrieking group of girls stormed the stereo, demanding some of-the-moment incoherent pop song that would give them an excuse to dance like baby strippers and be the center of attention. The lights were on, fully illuminating everyone's bloated cheeks and smeared makeup, and I could see shiny trails of spit stringing between the lips of a couple drunkenly making out in Bernie's dad's maroon La-Z-Boy.

Who named their kid "Bernie," anyway?

A crowd had gathered around a Solo-cup-covered dining room table to watch a girl and two guys try to throw a tiny plastic ball into them. Upon catching sight of it, Janis practically squealed, "Beer pong! I love beer pong."

That was one of the last things I would have expected to come out of the mouth of an intersectional feminist. It was also something I had never heard her mention before. I grabbed her sleeve. "Janis! That's for frat bros. How do you even know about beer pong?"

"One of Dad's students taught it to me when I was little," she said. "He'd come over and babysit, and we'd play juice pong in the backyard. Come on. It's fun."

She tried to pull me along with her, but when I resisted, she let go of my wrist and pushed her way up to the table. Before I could even blink someone had handed her a Ping-Pong ball and she'd sunk it, with a splash, right into one of the beer-filled cups. Suddenly the other people were yelling, and clamoring for Janis to be on their team. Someone handed her a cup of beer, and she took it.

A guy I'd never seen before, with a red face and hair so blond it was almost white, reached across the table to give her a high five. Steven Marshall, who slept next to me in history, reached out to touch her hair, and when she whipped around and poured her beer down the front of his shirt, the crowd fell silent.

Only for a second. Then they cheered again, even more loudly. Janis was the queen of beer pong.

Watching her, I felt like she was on a ship sailing out to sea and I didn't know how to swim. Sometimes I felt like this about Janis. Like if we lived someplace else, where she had more options, we probably wouldn't be friends. Janis was cool. She had normal parents and could have fit in if she'd wanted to, and I was just lucky that she didn't.

She lined up to take another shot, and I could tell the second the ball left her hand that it wasn't even going to be close. I held up my palm and made a little kinetic adjustment, so that the ball switched directions midair and landed, with a splash, right in the middle of a cup. The crowd cheered. Janis beamed, and I turned to go outside.

I didn't have to wander far before I saw Cassandra sitting in the corner, talking to Craig Lugweather, and I sincerely hoped she knew better than to let him anywhere near her "pearly gates." She caught my eye, and I was relieved when all she did was smile and wave, instead of coming over. I didn't want Janis wondering when Cassandra and I had gotten so cozy.

I'd never kept a secret from Janis before. It wasn't like I couldn't tell her. It was more like I didn't know what I'd tell her—"Hey, bestie, just FYI, I can move things with my mind." Yeah, right.

I felt like my brain was starting to look like one of those string conspiracy walls that you always see on crime shows when the detectives finally discover the shooter's storage unit. All day, it had been jumping around, but instead of things beginning to make sense, they were just becoming more tangled and complicated.

Cassandra and I had powers.

Our mothers knew each other. Were probably even friends.

This has something to do with babysitting. Maybe?

From across the room, Janis caught my eye, and the look on her face told me I must have been scowling. I flashed her a smile and a thumbs-up, then motioned that I was going outside. I'd planned to just sit down on the porch for a while, but I kept walking, my feet carrying me down the path to the sidewalk, then down the street. Before I knew it, I'd passed Janis's car and was more than a block away. In a little bit, about the time when she'd notice I was gone, I'd text her and say I'd gone home because I wasn't feeling well. She knew enough about my stomach's habits to take me at my word.

It was still early enough that I could catch the city bus home. Thanks to my car-less lifestyle, the city's bus maps and schedules were etched into my brain. One might even have said that I was a connoisseur of the bus, if one used words like "connoisseur" for a thing that had no air-conditioning or heat and often smelled like pee and Fritos.

I was putting my earphones in when a familiar minivan pulled up beside me.

Dion.

It took him a minute to roll down the window, because it appeared to be stuck, and by the time he got it fully down, I was standing right there. Up close, I could hear that the car was making a low, rhythmic rattle.

"You going to this party?" he asked.

I shook my head. "Just leaving, actually."

"That's a bummer," he said. "I was just going to meet my sister, because why stop going to high school parties just because you graduated, right?" He shrugged and held up his hands in a look of mock cluelessness, and I couldn't help but laugh.

"Exactly. Don't let a little diploma come between you and your love of bad music and people who can't hold their liquor."

Dion smiled. "So, why are you leaving?"

"Bad music and people who can't hold their liquor?"

"Get in," he said. "If I can't convince you to stay, at least I can give you a ride home."

You could convince me to stay, I thought, but I kept my mouth shut as I opened the door and got in.

I tried to ignore the beauty sitting beside me, and we drove in silence for a while until I finally broke it.

"I feel bad about you missing the party," I said.

"Don't. I didn't really want to go. I just didn't have any other options, and now I do." He turned to look at me, drumming his fingers on the wheel. "Honestly, I'm kind of jealous of Cass, that she's making friends."

I wanted to scream "I'll be your friend, Dion!" but I bit my tongue. *Keep it casual, Esme,* I told myself. *And play it as cool as you possibly can.*

"So, what have you been up to?" I asked instead, and he responded with a sigh and a shrug.

"Looking for jobs," he said, "which is basically just like letting people use your self-confidence as a punching bag."

"What kind of jobs?" I asked, thinking that I couldn't imagine anyone who looked like him ever feeling less than perfectly confident.

"Right now, just construction."

"That's cool," I said, and meant it. "You know how to build stuff." He smiled as he cranked the wheel in a way that clearly took some effort. No power steering, apparently.

"Well, I'm learning. When I was little, I wanted to be an architect. I would draw buildings all day in my notebook."

"I did that," I said, surprisingly myself that I had just said something without totally overexamining it in my head first.

"You drew buildings?"

"No, I drew outfits. I wanted to be a fashion designer. Still do, actually." This was something that I'd only ever talked about with Janis, not even with Dad, but talking about it with Dion felt okay. Somehow, I just knew that he'd understand. "I mean, only if this whole babysitting thing dies out."

He gave a little laugh. We stopped at a light, and he turned and looked me up and down. I knew that he was examining my clothes, not me, but still. I couldn't meet his eyes, so I stared straight ahead with my hands folded in my lap like a nun.

"I can see that," he said. "You always look good. Or at least, you have the two times I've seen you." I looked down at my feet and flexed my toes, grateful for the night camouflage that was helping me keep my cool.

"Thanks," I said. "It's my way of making the days less boring." I looked up at him, feeling like I owed him a compliment in return. Where did I start? The dark hair that wouldn't stay off his forehead no matter how many times he ran his fingers through it? The eyes that contained galaxies? The stubble on his chin, bisected by a thin scar that ran up into his bottom lip, this sole imperfection only serving to make a perfect face more perfect?

Instead, I settled on his tattoo. It was on the inside of his left forearm, the part where the skin is usually smooth and pale. I'd noticed it the first time we'd met, but had been too overwhelmed by other stuff to give it a good look. Now, as we idled under a streetlamp waiting for the light to change, I could see it as plain as day, right below the rolled-up sleeve of his flannel shirt. It was big, and went almost from his wrist to his elbow. It was a cactus. Sitting on the cactus was an eagle with a snake in its mouth, and the eagle was wearing a flower crown, like it was on its way to Coachella.

As soon as I mentioned it, though, Dion clamped a hand over it and groaned. "I hate it," he said. "I got it when I was sixteen, and I designed it myself."

"What does it mean?" I asked. "And you don't have to answer if you're the kind of person who hates getting asked what their tattoos mean."

"It's the eagle from the Mexican flag, wearing a crown of laurels. It's supposed to represent my mom. She was

Mexican but loved Greek myths—people even called her Circe. Hence my name and Cassandra's name and this." He gestured at the hippie-child eagle. "But it doesn't look victorious. It looks, I dunno, kinda dumb."

"It's not the worst tattoo. I mean, you could have Mickey Mouse making the 'suck it' sign or something."

He laughed. "You're right. Everything could always be worse." The glowing green light of a Starbucks had come into view, and Dion glanced up at it. "I could really use a coffee," he said. "You?"

I nodded, thrilled that a ride home was turning into something that could, in some cultures, be considered hanging out. "Always."

"Do you like living in Spring River?" I asked as he nosed the minivan into the drive-thru lane.

"I like having a house," he said. "I'm learning how to fix it up. I can use things I learn on the job at home, and use things I learn at home on the job. I'm hoping I can sell it. Maybe make some money and have something for once."

We had inched up to the menu, and the crackling speaker announced that it was our time to order. Dion got a Grande black coffee, and I got an iced Venti with milk but no sugar.

"What do you mean?" I asked once the speaker had gone silent. "'Have something'?"

"It's tough growing up like Cass and I did. Just being bounced around all the time, always staying in someone else's house, some other kid's room, never being the first person to wear your clothes."

Huh. I'd always loved vintage clothing because it meant I *wasn't* the first person to wear something, and that my clothes had stories, but maybe I'd feel differently if I'd never owned anything new.

"When we had to move, which was often, they'd pack up our stuff in trash bags," he went on. "Like it was a way to remind us of who we were or something. I'm sick of being at the bottom. I want to make something of myself, make people pay attention." We pulled forward to the window. "Sorry," he said, running his hand through his hair again in a way that made me wilt. "I know that sounds stupid."

"No, not at all. I get it."

I tried to stop him, but Dion had pulled out his wallet and insisted on paying for my coffee. He faked a shiver when he handed it over to me.

"Iced in October?"

I stabbed the lid with a straw and took a sip. "Iced all year round."

I directed Dion to my house, and the rest of the drive went by way too fast. "So, what are you up to for the rest of the weekend?" he asked as he pulled up and shifted the van into park.

"I'll probably just go visit my mom and hang with Janis, my best friend." I didn't add that Janis was also my only friend. "And if a job comes up, I'll babysit."

"Ah, yes," he said, "the mythical babysitting. You know, the way Cassandra talks about babysitting, you'd think it was saving the world."

"She kind of sucked at it," I said.

Dion smiled. "I'm not surprised. I can't imagine my sister with kids, but she seems pretty determined, ever since she found that stupid note."

Now I felt bad for having outed her as a sucky babysitter, especially if it was so important to her. "You think the note is stupid?" I asked.

He shook his head. "I don't really mean that. I mean, I think it's just a note about, like, making friends or something, but Cassandra treats it like it's our mother's dictum from beyond the grave."

Somewhere, a few houses down, a dog howled, and Dion looked out the window.

"But isn't that what it is?" I asked.

"Yeah, I guess, but . . . Can I say something, Es?" he asked.

My heart thumped at the promise of something important. "Of course."

He took a sip of his coffee and looked over at me. "I don't mean to downplay Cass's powers, or yours. It's crazy, that's for sure. I just know my sister, and after a lifetime of dealing with her BS, I . . ." He trailed off, like he was considering what he was going to say next. "It's just that she's dramatic, and causes a lot of problems without even noticing how they affect other people. Like, with babysitting. It's obviously really important to you, and Cass didn't think twice before she jumped in there. So just be careful, okay?"

Of course he hadn't wanted to tell me anything that had

to do with me. I nodded, half relieved, half disappointed. "Like, don't get burned?" I said.

He smiled. "Exactly. Take everything she says with a grain of salt. Or start carrying a fire extinguisher."

I thanked Dion for the ride, climbed out of the van, and walked up to the house. Just like last time, he waited until I had the door open before he waved and drove away. Part of me wanted to be elated and proud of myself. I'd just spent several minutes with my crush and had managed not to say or do anything dumb. But instead I couldn't stop thinking about what he'd said. Why was Dion trying to warn me away from his own sister? Why would he care? I hardly knew him. But then, I guess I hardly knew Cassandra either.

CHAPTER 10

I slept late on Saturday morning, per usual, and woke up around ten-thirty to Dad knocking on my door and a muffled "Esme, you got a package." Those words were sweet, sweet music to my ears, and I was up and out of bed in no time, practically pushing Dad out of the way to get to the kitchen.

A padded envelope addressed to me lay on the table, and I ripped it open. A fluorescent orange mesh vest fell out, and I yelped out loud when I saw it. Dad had caught up with me. "Construction-worker chic?" he asked.

"It's not for me. It's for Pig!" She started to wag her tail when she heard her name, and ambled over to lick my knees. I bent down and wrangled her into the vest. "Hmm," I said, taking a step back to admire her. "It's a little small, girl, but it's not your fault you're so busty."

"Certified therapy dog?" Dad said, reading the side of

the vest. "What's she going to do, listen to all your problems?"

"No. This means she can go visit Mom now."

"Oh," Dad said, his voice softening. "I didn't know you were doing that. What a good idea."

It was hard for Dad to talk about Mom. I'd realized that when I was about six, and so had stopped asking about her shortly after that. There was so much about her that I didn't know—like, what music had made her dance? When she went to a restaurant, would she try something new, or always order her favorite? Had she cried at movies? The list went on and on.

But I knew that she loved animals almost as much as she loved kids. One of my only memories of her was of her catching a spider in the kitchen and carefully carrying it outside. "It has eight legs, Esme," she'd said. "And we don't want to hurt a single one."

When I'd read about how easy it was to get your pet certified as a therapy dog, I instantly thought of Pig. If people couldn't get through to Mom, maybe a dog could. I'd actually applied for the certification months before, but Pig's application kept getting rejected because they said they didn't certify farm animals. Finally I resubmitted, saying her name was Susan, and she was approved the same day.

"Come on, girl," I said, tugging the vest back off her. "A big day like this calls for a bath."

●   ●   ●

Pig knew she was going someplace special. Even though it was chilly out, Dad rolled the window down for her, and she sat in the back seat with her head hanging out the window like she was a beauty queen in a parade. Having Pig along made the whole situation seem less grim, and for the first time in years, I was actually looking forward to our visit.

Dad parked, and she jumped out of the car the second I opened the back door. She held her head high as I led her across the parking lot on her leash. Pit bulls may have a gnarly reputation, but Pig was a love dumpling, and she straight-up pranced as soon as we were inside the door.

Everyone oohed and aahed over her, and she certainly acted like a therapy dog. She discreetly passed anyone who seemed scared or nervous around her, but stopped to give kisses to anyone who even smiled in her direction. When she stopped at Harold, an older man who'd been there as long as Mom, I sucked in my breath. Harold was afraid of everything, and who knew how he'd react to a big dog, but when Pig started to lick his hand, he moved it so that she could get a better angle.

Dad squeezed my shoulder. "Good job, Esme," he said. "It looks like you've found her true calling."

"Come on, girl," I said, happily steering her down the hall to the whole reason she was there in the first place. He went into Mom's room first, and I was starting to follow, when Pig's leash jerked me to a halt.

"Come on," I said, and gave the leash a tug. "Move." I turned around, and she was planted on the ground, her legs stiff and a ridge of fur standing up along her back. It was a sight I'd only ever seen once before, when a family of raccoons had traipsed across the backyard and Pig had felt the need to defend her territory. I yanked the leash again, but she didn't budge.

From inside the room, I could hear Dad talking to Mom. "Theresa, we brought you a special visitor." I walked around behind Pig and tried to give her a shove, but she'd become a fire hydrant. She wasn't going anywhere.

Dad appeared in the doorway, a confused look on his face. He was holding Mom's hand, and as soon as Pig saw her, she started to emit a low, guttural growl.

"Esme, what's wrong with her?"

"I don't know! You saw her. She was fine just a minute ago." I grabbed Pig by the collar and tried to pull her into the room, her nails scraping on the tile floor. I looked up at Mom, just as a single tear rolled down her cheek. Then Pig pulled away from me and took off, barking as she tore down the hall.

I caught up to her in the waiting room. She was huddled under a chair, shivering. I got down on my knees and tried to coax her out. "Come on, girl," I said, grabbing her collar and trying to pull her. "There's nothing to be afraid of. Mom is going to love you. I've told her all about you."

"Esme, you'd better take her out to the car," Dad said behind me, slightly out of breath from running to catch up with us. I nodded and got up. Pig came willingly when she saw that I was headed to the car and wasn't trying to get her to go back to Mom's room. I opened the car door for her so she could climb into the back seat, then cracked the windows. Before I turned to head back in, I gave her a pat on the head. "You're such a good girl, Piggy. What happened?" Her eyes met mine, and I swear I could see terror in there.

Everyone looked at me as I walked back to Mom's room. Inside, things were proceeding as they normally did. Dad trying to maintain a cheerful attitude while Mom stared off into space. Except this time, there was one big difference: Mom was crying. Tears rolled freely down her cheeks, and it made me feel horrible.

"This is my fault," I said.

"No, it's not," Dad said, putting a hand on my shoulder. "You just never know about these kinds of things. But I think maybe this was enough of a visit for today, and we should go." I went over and gave Mom a kiss, which got no response, then followed Dad numbly back out of the room.

We didn't talk much on the drive, and when we got home, Pig headed straight to my room and didn't come out for the rest of the day, not even for her dinner.

Saturday had been a true bummer, and I woke up on Sunday determined to salvage the weekend. Janis and I belonged to the Church of CDT. It was our Sunday morning ritual, and what we looked forward to all week: coffee, donuts, thrifting. Janis and I did not go vintage shopping. We went thrifting. Vintage shopping was just shopping. Thrifting was a treasure hunt. A race that required focus, strategy and lots of hand sanitizer. The risks were great—no one expected that piece of chicken hidden in the sleeve of that rabbit-fur coat, or cat poop in a box of scarves—but the rewards were priceless: a bootleg Madonna concert tee where her name was spelled "Madomna," an adult-sized Brownie uniform, red velvet bell-bottoms, Betsey Johnson, Marc Jacobs, once even Miu Miu (who knew how that skirt made its way there, but Janis was still bitter that I saw it first).

We had a strategy, and we did the same thing every time. We walked up and down each aisle. Janis took one side, and I took the other, each of us with an eye out for anything that either one of us might like. We looked first for colors, patterns, and textures that caught our eye. If there was a burst of blue mohair or the glint of silver sequins, it would be pulled out for closer inspection. If there was a section of all black, whoever had that section looked at each item individually, because there could be some truly avant pieces hiding in there, like my turtleneck shoulder-pad dress with one sleeve and an asymmetrical hem. I hadn't worn it yet, because I was saving it for prom.

Anything that looked remotely cool got thrown into our shopping cart, and after we'd made the rounds, we would hold each find up for inspection. If we had to, we'd try things on over our clothes—that was why leggings and a tank top were ideal thrifting wear. And the final rule of thrifting: when in doubt, just freaking buy it! You didn't want to spend all summer thinking about that parrot muumuu you let slip through your fingers because you didn't want to spend the seventy-five cents. True story. I finally had to tell Janis that if you loved something, you had to let it go, and she's been looking for it to come back to her ever since.

Today the thrift store was extra packed with people looking for Halloween costumes, like dudes who planned to just wear a dress because they thought nothing could be funnier than a man dressed as a woman (and also because they secretly wanted to wear dresses every day). Such a crowd normally warranted extra strategizing, but today I couldn't concentrate, and Janis could tell. "Earth to Esme," she said, holding up a zippered A-line dress with a Scandinavian pattern that could pass for Marimekko. "You just passed this up. Are you okay?"

I reached out and touched the fabric. It was even better up close—no rips or stains, and it was priced at a mere four dollars. "Sorry," I said. "I'm a little distracted."

"Seems like a lot distracted to me," she said. "And you've been like this for a while. What's going on?"

Where did I start? With Cassandra? Pig? Mom? Dion? I hadn't even told Janis that I'd met Cassandra's brother, much less that I couldn't stop thinking about him. Or maybe the fact that I could move things with my mind and was kinda, sorta scared of myself now?

Instead I just shrugged and told her I was tired.

Normally, Janis and I could hang for weeks on end and never get tired of each other, but when she dropped me off, I felt relieved and ready for some alone time. In my room, I sat down on my bed and stared at the photo of Mom baby-sitting. It was my favorite, and I kept it in a frame on my bedside table, next to my collection of half-finished lip balms and half-read paperbacks. I had so many questions, and I knew that if I could only talk to her, I'd probably get some answers. Now no matter what I learned, I just ended up with more questions.

I decided to do what I always did when I was depressed: watch horror movies and try to scare the sadness out of myself. Not because it was October either. Like iced coffee, horror movies are in season all year round. I'd take a scream queen over a manic pixie dream girl any day. I had even made an entire queue of horror movies where the baby-sitter gets killed, and then a second—and much better—list where the babysitter fights back. That was the kind of movie I needed right then—maybe *Halloween* so that I could cheer on Laurie Strode, who was about the most badass babysitter to ever read a bedtime story and go blow for blow with a psycho killer.

But of course my laptop was dead.

I dug through my backpack and groaned when I realized my charger was MIA. I hadn't used it all weekend, which meant that it was probably still in my locker at school. I stuck my hand into the back pocket to double check, but all that was in there was a stack of papers. I pulled them out—the photocopies of Cassandra's notebook. By now they were kind of wrinkled, and I stared at the top one as I tried to smooth them out on my bed. Cassandra's mother, or whoever had written them, had had beautiful handwriting. The letters were perfectly slanted and delicate and all connected together in textbook cursive. The top of the page said "Fytó," and the list underneath read "green jelly beans, a round river rock, rainwater, garden gnome."

The second page said "Kryo," and underneath that "Popsicle sticks, peppermint candy, Vicks VapoRub, feverfew."

I flipped back and forth between the two, sure that there was something I was missing. Something obvious.

The items seemed random at first, but the more I thought about them, the less accurate that seemed. All the items under "Fytó" were kind of about nature. The jellybeans weren't, of course, but they were green. And for "Kryo," I didn't know what feverfew was, but the rest of the stuff evoked a chill, like an open window in the winter.

What was more, I realized that they were all like the things Mom had gotten caught shoplifting—small, seemingly insignificant, yet clearly chosen with a purpose. There was a lot I couldn't remember, but that was burned into my brain. She hadn't just grabbed anything. Everything she'd pocketed had been very deliberate, the kind of stuff she still stockpiled in drawers in her room at the hospital. The pages in the notebook were like shopping lists, but like what you would need if you were going to make something specific. Like a recipe, almost. A recipe for magic—a *spell*.

CHAPTER 11

With each ring, I grew more impatient for Cassandra to answer. When she finally did, I didn't even bother to say hello. "In your mom's notebook, were there any pages other than those lists?"

"There was one," she said, "In the front. It just said 'kinesis.'"

That was when it really clicked. "Cass," I said, "they're spells. Put the word 'kinesis' after the word at the top of the list, and you get a new power. Like my telekinesis and your pyrokinesis, but for other stuff."

Cassandra was silent, and when she finally spoke, all she did was whisper an obscene word. "You'd better come over," she said, "and fast." Then she hung up on me.

• • •

Waiting for the bus felt like it lasted decades. I had an Uber account linked to one of Dad's credit cards, but he'd been very adamant that it was for emergencies only, and I imagined trying to explain a Sunday afternoon ride to him. "You see, Dad, I wanted to see if I could cast a spell . . ." Uh, no.

The bus finally came, and when I got to Cassandra's house, I tried to tell myself that I wasn't disappointed when I saw that Dion's transportation heap wasn't in the driveway. The front door of the house was open, and through the screen, I could see that the living room looked like it had been ransacked. It would have been enough to send someone running away and screaming about a burglary, but I knew better.

I knocked, first softly, then more loudly, and when no one answered, I let myself in and called for Cassandra. In the living room, I got a better look at the damage. The couch was charred and sitting in a puddle that had several feathers floating in it. In the corner, a light flickered on and off, and I noticed with a start that it wasn't even plugged in.

There were also weird, small things strewn everywhere: a plastic aquarium castle, chocolate gold coins, Mardi Gras beads, paper party hats, a kazoo, condoms, lefty scissors. It was like the guts of the world's most eclectic piñata had exploded across the living room.

"Hey."

I spun around to see Cassandra standing in the doorway, her face streaked with dirt and her hair looking like she'd just crawled out of a grave. Then some squawking thing buzzed the top of my head and made me jump three feet in the air.

"What the hell was that?" I asked, swatting at my scalp.

"Ugh, a stupid bird," Cassandra said, chasing it into the living room. "Shoo! Go! Shoo!" She picked up a magazine and swung it wildly through the air at the open door, but the bird had other ideas, and flew in the opposite direction down the hall, straight into a bedroom that, from the pair of work boots that I could see right inside the door, I assumed was Dion's. "My Poulikinesis was strong enough to get it in here, but then it wore off," she said, "and now I can't get the bird back out. I tried to lure it out with cornflakes, but I think that's a really smart bird."

It had looked like a plain old pigeon to me, but that explained all the yellow crumbs crunching under my feet.

"Poulikinesis?" I asked.

"Power to manipulate birds: one packet airplane peanuts, lungwort, cotton balls, and a feather."

"What's lungwort?"

"I don't know. I didn't have it, so I used basil, and I think maybe that's why it didn't work?" With an angry squawk, the bird came tearing down the hallway, and Cassandra and I both flattened ourselves against the wall to get out of the way.

She walked into the dining room, stepping over an overgrown plant that had been turned on its side, potting soil and long green tendrils spilling out everywhere, and ate a green jelly bean off a pile on the table.

"Plant manipulation?" I asked, and as she nodded, I realized that the lush green giant nearly blocking the doorway was the same philodendron that had been nothing but a few dry stalks when I'd lifted it into the air just a few nights before.

I picked the book up off the table and read aloud from the open page. "Kréaskinesis—"

"The power to manipulate meat," Cassandra interrupted, before I read the list of steak sauce, Saran Wrap, mesquite chips, and soybeans. She waved a hand behind her, and through the kitchen door, I could see a large red hunk of raw meat sitting on the counter. "I tried to make myself a hamburger," she said, "but it didn't really work." It looked nothing like a hamburger, but it was dripping blood down onto the cabinets below.

"Let me guess," I said. "You didn't have mesquite chips, so you substituted . . ."

"Charcoal," she said. I nodded, shivering at how the kitchen looked like a murder scene ripe for a blood-splatter expert. It was not sanitary.

"You did all this in an hour?" I asked, but she ignored me and took the book back, flipping through several pages. When she found the page she wanted, she looked up at the mess in the kitchen. "Katharikinesis," she said. "Dish soap, a sponge, paper towels, and disinfectant spray. Dang it, that's cleaning power, but it also sounds just like actual cleaning." She carefully stepped over the blood pooling on the kitchen floor, and pulled the requisite items out from under the sink, then walked back and held them out to me. I shook my head. She'd made this mess, and she could clean it up.

"Oh, come on, Esme," she said. "I don't want you to actually scrub. I want you to try the spell." She arranged the four items in a line in front of my feet, then took my arm and pulled it out in front of me, flexing my hand up at the wrist like I did when I told Pig to stay. "Now say it. Kath-ari-kinesis."

I repeated it, just like she'd said, and watched as the blood drips vanished from the floor, up the cabinet doors, and along the countertop, as if an invisible paper towel had just wiped them away. The charcoal briquettes zoomed back into the bag, and the dripping chunk of dead cow evaporated into thin air.

Cassandra yelped and clapped her hands. "Yay. So that's one that you can do!"

She was thrilled, and I was shaking. "What the hell did I just do?"

She held up the book. "Katharikinesis," she repeated. "The power to manipulate cleanliness. I can't believe you got one on the first try! I tried about fifteen different ones before I finally found a spell I could do."

"And what was that?"

She got a weird look on her face. "Malliakinesis." She said it so softly that I had to ask her to repeat it. "Malliakinesis," she said again, her palms running reflexively over her hair. "The power to manipulate hair. I tried to give myself beachy waves. All I got was frizz, but that was at least a start."

• • •

It didn't take long for me to see how the house had gotten so wrecked. Cassandra and I ripped through the book, trying everything we could with what we had, and making a list of what we'd need to find and buy to try the rest. For some of the powers, we got absolutely nothing. Others, we got a tiny flicker, and for a few, they actually worked like we assumed they were supposed to. We finally got the bird to fly back out the front door, but I think that had more to do with being in the right place at the right time than it did with magic.

It was stupid that it had taken us so long to figure it out. It wasn't some made-up language, just rough Greek translations, which wasn't surprising at all since it had come from Cassandra's mother. I wondered briefly if maybe Dion would have guessed it sooner, then quickly put that thought out of my mind.

I tried ypnokinesis—chamomile, a radio tuned between stations, an ankle sock, and lavender oil—which didn't succeed in actually making Cassandra fall asleep, but it did make her start yawning. Weirdly, we both seemed to be particularly adept at tyrikinesis, the power to manipulate cheese. I turned a block of Muenster into Colby Jack, and then Cassandra grated it with a wiggle of her fingers. "Hmm," she said as the last nub was shredded. "A hit at Taco Tuesdays, no doubt, but not exactly the stuff that Marvel makes movies about."

I knew exactly what she meant. The initial excitement at seeing that I could do all of this weird stuff was wearing off, and now I just felt confused. Fortunately, it seemed like the ingredients and objects were needed the first time we used a spell, but once the power was activated, we could use it at will just by saying the word. I stood looking at the pile of cheese in front of me, pinched off a little bit, and put it into my mouth.

It tasted like fiesta blend, all right. I chewed and swallowed, then looked back at Cassandra. "What are we?" I asked. Her mouth was too full to answer.

When I got home, Dad was sitting on one end of the couch, and Pig was sitting on the other. She came trundling to meet me when I opened the door, her tail wagging like a whip.

"That dog doesn't understand who pays the bills around here," Dad called out. "So she loves you more."

I knelt down so that I was eye level with her, and scrunched up her face. "That's supposed to be a secret, Piggy," I said in a mock whisper.

"I made dinner," Dad said. "It's in the kitchen."

I went to go investigate, and Pig followed, close at my heels.

By "made" he meant "ordered," and by "dinner" he meant "pizza." Which was fine with me. I pulled a plate from the cabinet and helped myself to a couple of pieces.

"I'm going to eat in my room and catch up on homework," I yelled from the kitchen, because that seemed like a good excuse and I needed some time to decompress before I launched into a round of Dad small talk.

"You don't want to watch football with me?" he called back.

"I do," I said, pausing in the doorway. "But you know my rules about watching football, and last time I checked, hell had not yet frozen over."

Pig followed me into my room. I realized how ravenous I was as soon as I took a bite of the cold pizza. Spellcasting really worked up an appetite. I took another bite, and looked around my room as I chewed. I could use my newfound powers to pick all the stuff up off the floor and sweep the dust bunnies from the corners, but that would alert Dad instantly to the fact that something was up. He'd probably haul me right back into therapy, saying, "My daughter hasn't been acting like herself lately. I'm afraid an alternate, cleaner personality has taken over." So the mess would remain the same. Besides, I'd never been more exhausted in my entire life. Magic was even harder than babysitting, though maybe not as messy.

I finished my pizza and set the dirty plate on top of a stack of magazines on my desk. I gathered my remaining strength and willed it to be halftime, because I figured tonight was as good a time as any to ask Dad about Mom. Surely she was the missing link between me and Cassandra and whatever it was we were. Cheese witches? Kinetic wonders? Babysitting banshees?

I steeled myself to push through any impending awkwardness, because Mom was a topic that made Dad so uncomfortable, he would start scratching at his hands and neck.

Dad and I were both good at living with unanswered questions, and we just worked around them like they were houseguests who were never leaving because they had no place else to go.

Back in the living room, the TV screen was filled with large men in even larger suits, talking about tonight's game as if the fate of the world depended on it. I plopped myself down onto the couch and tucked my feet under me.

"Shoes," Dad said, so I straightened my legs and kicked my slip-ons onto the floor, then pretzeled them again. I wanted to be comfortable so that Dad felt comfortable.

"Hey, so can I ask you something?" I was trying to sound casual, and this seemed as good a way as any to start the conversation.

"Sure, kiddo," he answered, only half looking away from the television.

"It's about Mom," I said, and I could feel him stiffen. I could see his Adam's apple bob as he swallowed. He took a few seconds to answer.

"Of course." His voice sounded tighter than it had just a moment before.

I decided it was best to go with the truth, albeit a very shallow version of the truth. "Who were her friends, and what was she into?" I asked. I pulled at a string on my leggings, and then tried to smooth it back out. "There's a new girl at school, and it turns out that her mom was friends with Mom. She even has pictures of them together. And I don't know, it just got me thinking. I don't really know much about what Mom was like before she was . . ." I paused. "Like she is now."

Dad took a sip of his Coors Light. I could tell the can was almost empty by the way he had to tip it almost all the way upside down to get some to pour into his mouth.

"What's the new girl's name?" he asked.

"Cassandra Heaven." I was careful to keep my voice neutral and not sound too excited.

"That's quite the name, but it doesn't ring a bell. Your mom had a lot of friends," he said finally. "Her phone rang all the time. She even had her own line when we still had a landline." He paused and gave a little laugh. "She said it would save me the trouble of answering her calls when she wasn't here. She was like that, you know, always thinking of little things to make someone else's life easier."

I nodded. This did sound very nice. And also very suspicious.

"What were her friends like?" I asked.

"I didn't know a lot of them all that well. She had this women's group that she would meet with all the time, and they would do stuff. Some would come from out of town for meetings."

Ah, yes. I was definitely getting somewhere.

"What would they do?" I pressed.

His brow wrinkled up. "Like, organizing and stuff. Non-profits. Your mom was big into feminism, so I let her have her space. Tried not to pry too much. Wanted to make sure she was her own person, you know?" He trailed off, and stared at his empty beer can like it held all the secrets of the universe.

"Were any of her friends babysitters?"

He scrunched up his nose. "That's a weird question."

"Well, were they?"

"I think so? I'm not sure, but she was always running out to take care of someone's kid."

That was good enough for me. "Thanks, Dad," I said. "I'm going to bed." I got up, but he called me back as I was about to head up the stairs.

I walked back to the couch, and Dad shut his eyes, pinching the bridge of his nose. "Kiddo, I'm sorry we don't talk about your mom much," he said. "Everything that happened with her was very stressful. You were just a little kid, and I was scared. I guess I blocked a lot of it out. I'm ashamed to admit there's a lot I don't remember." He paused, and swallowed. "Your mom was an amazing woman, and I'm sorry you didn't get to know her as she used to be. So whatever you want to know, ask. I'll try to tell you."

I nodded. "Thanks, Dad. I will." I gave his shoulder a squeeze, then got out of there before he could see that I was about to cry.

Back in my room, I pressed my palms to my eyes and took a deep breath. This was not a day for crying. Anyway, I'd spent most of my life crying about Mom, and I was pretty freaking over it by now. Crying was worthless. It accomplished nothing.

There was a grunt outside my door, and I opened it to let Pig in. She settled down by my bed, and as we looked into each other's eyes, she made a noise like the air slowly escaping from a balloon. I raised an eyebrow at her. It was truly mind-blowing to me that a living creature could be so unaware of its own farts. I went over and cracked the window.

No matter how tired I was, I knew I was still too wired to sleep, so I lay down on the bed and shuffled through the spells again. One of the few that we hadn't attempted at Cassandra's was for milókinesis, the power to induce speech. Pig made another squeaking noise, and I looked at her as I tried to breathe in and out through my mouth.

I mean, why not? I had to try new things, and the ingredients for this spell were stuff I knew we had—a lemon, a cough drop, cherry ChapStick, and a blue obsidian crystal, which was left over from my rock collecting phase in middle school. I gathered them all up, then got down on the floor and sat across from Pig. Which was her invitation to come over and lick me, but I held out a hand and told her to stay as I placed the items in an arc on the floor between us. Keeping my hand extended, I looked back at her, let my mind go as blank as it did in calculus, then recited the name of the spell.

Pig's long pink tongue came out and licked her nose, and her big brown eyes stared at me. Then she said, "Hello."

If I hadn't been sitting on the floor, I would have fallen out of my seat.

It wasn't cute. It wasn't funny.

It was weird. And not the good kind of weird. Pig was an experienced lurker, but now she watched me more intensely than she ever had before.

"What's for dinner?" she asked.

"Dog food," I said.

"The brown stuff?"

"Yeah, the brown stuff." Wow. This conversation was riveting.

"Ooooh, goodie. I love that stuff. I saw a squirrel today."

"Oh yeah?" I said, not mentioning that I'd seen probably two dozen squirrels just since lunch. I didn't want to one-up her.

"The squirrel ran fast. Fast, fast. But I would have caught it if I was outside." I hadn't expected Pig to be Simone de Beauvoir or anything, but I had expected a little more than squirrel talk. I tried to think of what else she would want to talk about.

"Piggy, do you want to go on a walk later?"

"Oh my goooooooshhh, a waaaaalk. We're gonna go on a waaaaaalk? You're kidding? A walk! We're gonna go on a walk. I'm the luckiest girl, I'm the luckiest girl in the whole wide world." She paused to chew on an itch. "I'm the hungriest girl. What's for dinner?"

"You had dinner. It was dog food."

"Yum. I looooooove dog food." Pig's voice wasn't male or female. It was low and scratchy, like she'd been smoking two packs a day for thirty years. I guess eating rocks and sticks wasn't the best for the vocal cords.

She looked around my room, her nostrils twitching. "You have any dirty underwear around here?" she asked. "I love dirty underwear, and I haven't eaten any in months."

"You ate a pair just last week," I corrected her.

She cocked her head to one side as if she was thinking hard. She made the hissing noise again, and my eyes started to water with the fumes.

"Pig," I said, trying not to breathe. "You have to do something about that."

"About what?"

"About the gas."

"I don't know what you're talking about." She lay down on the floor with a huff, and I found myself worried that I'd offended my farty dog. I reached over and scratched her ears. Pig was nothing if not sweetness and light—pure love—and I suddenly felt tears pricking my eyes.

"Piggy, would Mom have been able to tell us what's going on?"

She gave me a long look, then raised an ear like she was listening for a rabbit a hundred yards off. I know it was nuts to think my dog could tell me the truth, but after that day in the hospital, I would bet my babysitting money that Pig knew something about Mom that the rest of us didn't.

"What's for dinner?" she asked.

I sighed. "I told you. Dog food."

"Have I had that before?"

I sighed. Pit bulls were known as the nanny dog, but now that I'd had extra insight into the inner workings of her dog brain, I shuddered to think what would happen if Pig were ever left in charge of a bunch of kids: "Uncooked hot dogs for dinner. Then everyone drinks out of that old bucket under the porch!"

I held out my hand and stopped the spell the way I'd seen Cassandra do earlier. I didn't relax until Pig looked at me and barked. Then I took her on a quick walk around the block and fed her dinner number two. She ate it like it was the most gourmet meal she'd ever had in her short little life.

CHAPTER 12

My eyes popped open at five a.m., a full hour before my alarm was set to go off and a full two hours before I usually got out of bed. It was that kind of awake where I knew I wasn't going back to sleep, so I did the unthinkable: I got up early. Before I knew it, I was dressed, as "Wino forever," in a leather jacket, a Tom Waits shirt I made myself, and mom jeans. I took a look in the mirror, scribbled a note for Dad, then left the house, quietly locking the door behind me.

When I stepped off the city bus at school, it was barely six a.m. There were a few lights on inside the building and a few cars scattered in the parking lot, but everything looked pretty quiet. I knew that some teams of overachievers, like the swimmers and the cheerleaders, were insane enough to squeeze in a practice before school, so the building would be open, if mostly empty.

I walked down the hall as if my feet were moving of their

own accord, straight to the school office. I tried the door, just in case, but it didn't budge. I looked up and down the hallway to make sure no one was watching, and then I held my hand out and concentrated until I heard the lock slide out of place. When I tried the door again, it opened and I ducked inside and locked it behind me.

The school office was filled with posters meant to inspire you and posters meant to scare you—there was a permeable line between the two—and it had always reminded me of a cross between a waiting room for infectious disease treatment and the visitors' holding pen at a juvenile detention facility. There were several smaller offices off the main one, and I walked straight to the one I wanted—the one for Mr. Loompah, the unfortunately named guidance counselor in charge of schedules. It was barely bigger than a broom closet, and when students sat down across from him to try to plead their way out of Algebra II, their knees touched the front of his desk.

Mr. Loompah had made it easy for me. He hadn't locked his door or turned off his computer, so when I sat down in his chair, after taking my backpack off and setting it on the floor, I was greeted by a slideshow of snapshots of all the little Loompahs. It looked like there were a lot. I moved the mouse, and the slideshow vanished, revealing a wallpaper of an obese wiener dog. I had half hoped that there would be a folder on his desktop that just said "student schedules," but I knew that even Mr. Loompah wouldn't have it set up to be that easy, so I sat and thought about where to start. Janis would have known immediately how to get onto the school servers, but I could just imagine how that phone call would go if I called her now. Janis sitting up in bed in her pajamas, her hair still wrapped, screeching into the phone, "You broke into the counselor's office before sunrise to do what? Have you lost your freaking mind?" I was on my own with this one.

At the bottom of the screen was an Internet Explorer icon, and I clicked on it. After what seemed like ages, and an actual, physical whirring sound coming out of the computer, the browser opened to the school's home page, which was still advertising the date for the previous year's graduation. What if cyberkinesis only worked on servers that had been built within the last ten years? This one seemed like it probably dated back to the eighties. But I'd come this far, so I had to try.

I reached into my backpack and pulled out the spell ingredients I'd brought with me: a receipt from RadioShack (thank you, Dad, for never throwing receipts away), a pack of Tic Tac Freshmints, a quartz crystal, and a number two lead pencil. I lined them up in front of the monitor, then held out my hand. I was going to either do what I came to do or crash the entire school district's system. Here goes nothing, I thought.

Almost immediately lines of type began to fill the screen, and page after page of student information appeared. Finally, though I almost couldn't believe it, the program stopped . . . at my name. Underneath my name was my entire school record, every class I'd taken and every grade I'd gotten since entering high school. I tabbed down to my freshman year and highlighted where it said "Band." In its place, I typed "Physical Education," and in the field for grade, I gave myself a C minus. I wanted this to be realistic.

Then I scrolled back to junior year, deleted gym, and replaced it with a study period. Then I deleted driver's ed and thought for a second. What else could I do to kill a class period with minimal effort? I finally settled on photography, which was taught by the wrestling coach, and Ansel Adams he was not. All I'd have to do to get an A would be to take some arty shots of the water fountain and lots of photos of my feet.

I hit save, gathered up all my spell objects and carefully put them back into my bag, and then got the hell out of there. Not just out of the office but off campus entirely. The last thing I wanted to do today was look suspicious, so I had to roll up to school at 7:55, at the earliest, just like I always did.

Today Janis was "Bauhaus janitor," wearing acid-washed-denim coveralls with a Mondrian head wrap, one red and one blue sock, and Swedish clogs.

"Were you not just Lydia Deetz, like, two days ago?" Janis asked, picking up on my scheme immediately.

"Whatever, you Lisa Bonet freak," I said as we went through the lunch line. "It's Wino forever because there is never enough Winona."

Janis grabbed a bottle of water and shook her head, then launched into a griping session about her upcoming evening. She was scheduled to babysit for Andrew Reynolds, who was a holy terror if there ever was one.

"Last time, he pulled out one of my extensions and threw it over the fence!" she said. "The neighbor's dog buried it!"

I sighed, then took a bowl of something that looked okay and put it on my tray. "You can handle Andrew, Janis. You've done it before."

"You know that's gravy, right?" Janis asked. "And you don't have anything to put it on."

"Oh," I said, putting the bowl back. "I thought it was veggie curry. Would it kill this school to serve food that was green for once? Or even just white? I'm sick of brown."

"I'm sick of babysitting," Janis said, paying for her corn dog. "I just want to clock in and clock out, and not have to worry about whether or not a kid's going to get hurt. Or ruin my hair. I mean, aren't you sick of it?"

I thought for a second. "No," I said honestly. "Not at all. I like it. I like kids, because they're funny, and they have a cool way of seeing the world. They're innocent and imaginative. They're not all beaten down like adults. Besides, babysitting's an important job. I mean, somebody's got to watch the kids."

"Yeah," Janis said as I followed her to our regular table, "but that somebody doesn't have to be me."

• • •

After lunch, I headed to the library to spend my newly acquired study period catching up on all the chemistry memorization I'd been avoiding for the past six weeks. It really was more boring than trying to explain Snapchat to my dad for the seventy-fifth time. I found an empty table in the reference section, which was the quietest part, since the only reference section anyone ever seemed to use for writing reports was Wikipedia.

I had my books and papers spread out in front of me when I heard a strange sound coming my way. It was a *swish-swish* sound, and it was drawing closer and closer. I looked up, and tried to keep my eyebrows from knitting into a frown. I should have recognized that nylon-on-nylon whisper anywhere.

"Hey, Brian," I said to the large man suddenly towering over me. "Whoops, I mean Coach Davis. What's up?" I swallowed. It was just my luck to run into Coach Davis on the same day that I'd abracadabra'd myself out of gym, but I told myself I had no real reason to be scared. There were three thousand kids in the school—Brian didn't get an email every time one of them dropped gym.

When I first got to high school, I lived in fear that Brian would try to be all buddy-buddy with me there, but he seemed to get that I wasn't the kind of student who would want to flaunt football-coach privileges. He kept a pretty good distance. We'd smile and nod when we passed each other in the hallways, but until I had gym I rarely saw him outside of that. It was weird now to be seeing him in the library, of all places. . . .

And then I realized.

He didn't just *happen* to be in the library.

He was there for me.

I rearranged my expression to look as innocent as a kitten. Brian smiled down at me, and from this angle, he had a bit of a double chin, and I could see gray whiskers dotting his mustache. He looked, actually, a bit more haggard than he had the last time I'd seen him.

"Hi, Esme," he said, smiling a smile that looked more like a grimace. "I saw that you dropped gym class from your schedule."

Crap. Was this really happening? Didn't he have anything better to do?

But I just nodded and tried to keep that I've-done-nothing-wrong look in my eyes, while wondering if he had also noticed that my records now looked like I'd suffered through gym freshman year with everyone else. "I needed an extra study period," I said as lightly as I could. "I have to start thinking about college."

He looked like he was about to say something, but after a few seconds of silence, I added, "I'm going to make up for it in summer school." I was talking out of my butt basically, since I had no idea if gym was even offered in the summer.

He nodded again. "If you were having problems with PE, I wish you had come and spoken with me before you made any big decisions. We could have worked out an independent study."

Why did he care so much about me taking PE? It wasn't like a few times around the track was going to flip some switch in my brain and turn me into an athlete. Plus, it made me shudder to think what he meant by "independent study." Doing tai chi in the corner by myself? Or some other form of social suicide, like golf?

"It's okay. Really," I said. "And I'm looking forward to it. In the summer, I won't have any other classes, so I can really focus on my, uh, physical development and uh, playing sports . . . and I won't have to worry about showering after. I can just walk around all sweaty, and no one will notice." Brian almost always acknowledged my jokes, at least with an eye roll, but now his face stayed serious. He looked like he was about ready to walk away, but then he paused.

"How is the babysitting going, by the way?" he asked.

I surprised myself by answering honestly. "Ah, it's okay. I think Janis wants to quit the club, and there's a new girl who wants to join, but I think she's a pretty crap babysitter, so . . ." I caught myself before I went any further. Why was I being so honest? I was so used to trotting out the rote answers that adults wanted to hear, but Brian had totally caught me off guard. Since when did he care about my babysitting?

I gave him a quizzical look. "Why do you ask?"

He toyed with the plastic whistle that hung on a cord around his neck. "Just interested, that's all," he said. "Babysitting's a big job. A young woman, in charge of so many lives . . ."

"Well, when you put it that way . . ." I smiled at him, forgetting that Brian didn't have a sarcasm meter. "I know," I said, switching back to serious, "but I'm up for it."

Teachers were usually so bad at camouflaging their feelings that you could read them from across the street, but Brian was different. I couldn't tell what he was thinking at all. "I know you are," he said, "You're very capable."

"Okay," I said, wondering where this conversation was going, but then he just turned and walked away, leaving me completely confused.

Had Brian and I just had the thing I'd been trying so hard to avoid, a heart-to-heart? It was baffling. He didn't even seem that mad about gym.

Photography was as much a joke as I had expected it to be. Half the class just used their phones to complete their assignments, since Mr. Briggs couldn't tell the difference between overexposure and a filter. In Earth Sciences, we were still on geology, so the whole room smelled like baking soda and vinegar since that week's lesson was volcanoes. When the final bell rang, I was more ready than usual for the day to be over. I was speed walking toward the bus after school when I heard someone yelling my name. A *guy* yelling my name. I turned, and saw his car first. It was hard to miss the car, even in a sea of clunkers like the Spring River High parking lot. But then

I saw Dion, leaning against it, his arms crossed over his chest, one hand up waving at me. I had to resist the urge to do the movie thing—exaggeratedly looking over my shoulders, then pointing at myself and mouthing "Me?" Of course he was talking to me. I was the only Esme at school, probably the only Esme in town. Still, it seemed unreal that my name could come out of the mouth of someone who looked like that.

I walked toward him, trying to instill each step with nonchalance. I wanted to say something like "What's up" or "Hey, what are you doing here?" But what came out was "Hey, what are you doing up?"

He smiled. "Just can't sleep that late anymore," he said, and I could feel myself blushing.

"Are you looking for Cassandra?" I asked.

He shook his head slowly, and smiled. "I was looking for you. Where you headed?" I tried to keep my eyebrows from skyrocketing up my forehead in shock. It was really nice of Dion to give me a ride home on Friday, but I'd assumed that was it. A ride home. But now he was here, *looking* for me? I must have fallen through a hole in the universe, and this was the Twilight Zone, an alternate dimension where I was someone a hot guy sought out.

"Home," I said finally. "I was just on my way to catch the bus." Behind me, the bus ground into gear and pulled away. I corrected myself. "I was gonna walk."

"Come on. Let's go do something fun," he said. "It's a

beautiful day, and I just got a job, so I need to do something to celebrate."

I smiled, hoping it hid my confusion. Was I really the only person he knew, aside from his sister? That was the only possible explanation for it—for why he was here, asking me to hang out. He must not have had any other options. I glanced around behind me. Where was Cassandra, anyway? I had a million questions, but I also had a hot guy who was standing in front of me, waiting.

"You know," I said, walking over to open the passenger door, "this is Spring River, so finding something 'fun' to do is asking a lot. I could take you on a tour of strip mall parking lots that have been home to abandoned-car fires, or would you rather visit chain restaurants known for food-poisoning outbreaks? I hear the Chili's on West Street has a pretty good molten-chocolate-E.-coli cake." I climbed in and heaved the door shut behind me, then fumbled for my seat belt.

"Been there," he said. "Still recovering."

"Congrats on the job," I said. "What is it?"

"Working for a contractor," he replied. "It's nothing special. Just working on a new housing development out west, building McMansions out of cardboard. But I'm going to learn a lot about drywall, which will be cool because I haven't done much of that before."

"Oh, that's awesome!" I said, probably a little too enthusiastically. I sounded like I was a huge drywall fan. I didn't know what drywall was.

Dion mashed the van into drive, and with a squeal pulled away from the curb. "Okay, so where are we going?"

I looked out the window at the clouds racing through the sky like in a regatta, and had a breath of inspiration. I shifted in my seat so that I was almost facing him. "I have an idea. I'm going to take you to the one place in Spring River that might actually be considered beautiful. Do you want to know what it is?"

He shook his head. "Nope. Surprise me."

I nodded, and hoped he couldn't hear my heart caterwauling around in my chest.

If you started at the center of Spring River and drove in any direction, in fifteen minutes you'd be out of town, flying down roads that didn't have curbs—nothing but fields, the occasional tree or the even more occasional cow on either side. I talk a lot of crap on Kansas, but backwards politics and the lack of good shopping options aside, it's pretty okay sometimes. Like now. The sky is huge and close, as if you could touch it if you just found the right tree to climb, and the landscape is as subtle as no-makeup makeup. There are no mountains intimidating you into appreciating them, and there's no ocean throwing itself on the rocks to demand your attention. The plains are just like, we're here and we're chill.

Dion drove with the windows down, and the rush of air made the droopy ceiling liner flap like a one-winged bird trying to take off. I had to yell to tell him where to turn, but when we were just driving straight, I settled back in the seat and put my hand out the window so that my fingers could ride the waves. It was a little chilly, but I liked it, and just pulled my jacket tighter around me.

We were getting close, and I made Dion slow down so I could read the street signs. It'd been years since I'd been there, so when I finally saw the one I was looking for, I told him to stop. I could see that he was confused about why I was having him stop in what seemed like the middle of a field, but I could also see a smile playing on the edge of his lips. He was intrigued. I'd done good.

"We have to walk a little bit," I said, trying and failing to open my door.

"Hold on a sec," Dion said, jumping out and running around. "It works, but it might be stuck." I stumbled a bit when my feet hit the dirt, and without thinking, I grabbed on to his arm to steady myself. I pulled away just as quickly, as the ripple of muscle under his flannel threatened to make me woozy.

Big, round hay bales dotted the fields like gumdrops, and the late-afternoon sun made their pale beige seem gilded. I started across the field toward a row of trees, picking out each step carefully since the ground was uneven and kind of wet. From behind me, I heard Dion say " 'Nature's first green is gold, her hardest hue to hold,' " and I spun around. The words practically knocked the breath out of me.

"What did you just say?" I asked.

He looked almost sheepish. "It's a Robert Frost poem,"

he said. "'Nothing Gold Can Stay.' I always think of it when the light looks like this."

"I know. Me too. It's—it's one of my favorites," I stammered. It was almost like he'd read my mind. Was this what people were referring to when they talked about "having a moment"?

"I'm not all literary or anything," he said. "I just know it because of—"

"The Outsiders," I finished for him.

He smiled. "Yeah, but you probably read the book. My dumb ass just watched the movie."

"I've read the book, and I watched the movie about three hundred times," I said. "I know every line by heart. I used to want to be Cherry Valance."

"I used to have a crush on Cherry Valance," Dion said. Swoon. He was looking into my eyes, but I quickly turned away. What was going on here? Was he flirting with me? I had no idea what being flirted with felt like, but maybe this was it? If I'd been cooler, if I'd been Cherry Valance, I would have flirted back, acted coy and playful. Maybe taken his hand and made him close his eyes, something to play this up and make it seem adventurous and romantic.

Instead I just crashed through the bushes, caught my jeans on a twig, sneezed, almost fell down, and said, "Well, this is it."

At first he didn't say anything, and I panicked. What if I'd misjudged, and this wasn't his kind of thing at all? Then his eyes widened, and his mouth fell open a little bit. "What . . ."

He slowly turned back and forth so that he could take it all in. "This is incredible. What is this place?"

I couldn't help but grin. "No one knows," I said. "It's been here forever. It's kind of like the only magical thing in Spring River, since no one's ever claimed it and it keeps growing." It was a DIY sculpture garden of a couple of acres, with concrete statues placed every few yards. There were elephants, tigers, and giraffes. Greek gods, mermaids, and centaurs. Biblical figures, Shakespearean characters, and angels. They weren't organized in any particular way, with a winged fairy next to a pickup truck next to a snake-haired medusa. Some were brand-new and still a smooth, pale gray. Others were decades old, their faces weather-beaten and falling away, and though there were a million theories about who had built the sculpture garden and why (my favorite was that it was an old man whose wife had died young, and he added a sculpture every year on her birthday), none had ever been confirmed. It was a mystery of the best kind.

We split up to wander, and I watched Dion smile as he ran his hands over a devil's broken horns. "How'd you find this place?"

"My mom loved it," I said. "You know, she's in a facility now." Dion was nodding like he knew what I was talking about, which didn't surprise me at all. "But we'd come here for family picnics, and Dad and I came a few times by ourselves. I was, like, four years old, and some of the sculptures scared me."

"Like this one?" he asked, pointing to the devil.

I shook my head. "More like that one," I said, pointing to one of Adam offering Eve an apple. We didn't talk much as we wandered through, and I noticed that Dion took out his phone to snap pictures of a couple of the statues. Finally we met at a cement bench in the middle of the garden. The sun was starting to set, and the shadows were growing longer. A slight breeze left a trail of goose bumps along the back of my neck, and I involuntarily shivered.

"Do you want my flannel?" Dion asked.

If I'd been a hot girl, I would have scoffed at this rote method of seduction. But since I was just his little sister's friend, I only shook my head. "No, because then you'll be cold," I said.

He laughed, and then the unthinkable happened. He put his arm around me and pulled me into him. I tried not to hyperventilate at his heat or his smell, and tried to seem relaxed, even though I felt like I was being electrocuted. Was I supposed to do anything? Was I supposed to say anything? I opted for nothing, as that seemed like the safest option. We sat in silence, watching the sunset, and I really, really hoped that Dion wouldn't know I was freaking out. He spoke first.

"I don't have that many memories of either of my parents," he said. "But I remember Cass's second birthday. Mom made her this banana cake that she just smashed everywhere. Then my parents and I joined in. All four of us were eating cake by the handful."

I nodded against his shoulder. "It definitely tastes better that way," I said. "What was your dad like?"

"He was cool, I know that," he said. "He had a motorcycle, and he was in a band for a while. If I remember right, Mom was kind of all over the place, but Dad really held it down. It sucks to not have gotten to know him, you know?"

"I feel the same way about my mom," I said. "My dad and I have nothing in common—I mean, everything he wears is moisture wicking. So I have to think I'm more like my mom, but I might never know for sure."

"When I was younger," Dion said, "I spent a lot of time daydreaming about how my life would have been different if my parents were still alive, my dad especially. Their car caught fire when it wrecked, and burned up so bad that it was hard to identify the bodies. So I'd tell myself that maybe it wasn't really our parents in that car, and that someday I'd walk out of school and Dad would be waiting for me."

I felt like I knew exactly what he was talking about, how hope could lodge in your chest and then harden until it felt like a thing that was weighing you down instead of buoying you up. "I used to think stuff like that about my mom," I said, "like maybe she was just pretending, or playing a joke."

"But you grew out of it, didn't you?" he said, and I nodded. "Cass didn't," he continued. "She still thinks our parents might be out there somewhere, and she can't accept that they're gone. It's all part of her thinking there's something special about her."

Almost against my will, my body stiffened and pulled away from him at those words, because, well, what a weird thing for him to say. "There *is* something special about her, Dion," I said. "I mean, she can set things on fire. That's going to mess with her head a little bit. It's hard to feel like you're just . . ."

He put his other arm around me and pulled me into a hug. "I'm sorry," he said. "That's not what I mean. I didn't mean to sound like such an asshole. There's something special about both of you. You especially. You've got all this crazy stuff going on around you, but you're still really . . ."

I sucked in my breath as anticipation ballooned in my chest. I was freaking out inside, wondering what he was going to say. I was really *what*?

"Nice," he said.

I exhaled. Balloon deflated.

Nice—it's the chicken Caesar wrap of compliments. Acceptable, but never very exciting.

"Thanks."

"Come on," he said, standing up. "We should get going."

"Righty-o," I said, and didn't even worry that it sounded stupid.

CHAPTER 13

Dion dropped me off at home, and I went in and sat down on a chair in the kitchen, and stayed in the dark for several minutes. I felt stupid, yet relieved that I'd kept my stupidity to myself. I didn't have much experience with guys, but I did have enough to know that guys like Dion were not into girls like me. He was so hot, you could probably use his driver's license photo to make s'mores. And me? On my good days, when I woke up early and had no zits and my hair was co-operating and I managed to blend my under-eye concealer just right so that I didn't look like a ghost or a panda and I'd stopped myself from eating a sixth piece of pizza the night before, I could pass for cute.

Cute and smoldering were not in the same orbit.

Besides, Dion was an adult. Sure, he was basically only a year older than me, but he owned a house. And a car. He could leave to go buy Flamin' Hot Cheetos at two in the morning, no questions asked, and no one was garnishing his babysitting wages to pay for a driver's ed disaster. There was a snow cone's chance in hell that anything would ever happen between us. So why had I spent all afternoon waiting for him to kiss me? Shouldn't I have known better?

I heard Dad's car turn into the driveway, and moments later the slap of the screen door announced his entrance into the house. He flicked on the kitchen light, and jumped when he saw me sitting there. "Geez, Esme, why are you sitting in the dark?"

"I was trying to decide what to eat for dinner," I said.

I could tell by the flush in his cheeks that he'd been at the bar. He had a Styrofoam take-out container in his hand, and he dropped it onto the table in front of me. I opened it up—chicken fingers and fries. Brown and brown.

"So, I met up with Brian for a beer," he said as I picked through the browns, looking for the least soggy fry.

"Oh yeah? How's he doing?" I didn't want to let on that I had any reason to fear Dad spending time with the school's athletic director.

"He's good. He thinks we've got a good chance at going top three in the state this year. Our offensive line is full of juniors too, which bodes pretty darn well for us next year." Sometimes I had a hard time understanding how Dad and I were related. Like when he used the term "us" to talk about the high school football team. "You know, you'd probably know that if you ever went to a game," he continued.

"You know me and football, Dad. We don't mix." I took a bite of chicken.

"Yeah, but Brian's a good friend, and he's really been there for our family. Even if you're not into it, it'd be nice for you to show some support."

I was starting to get an inkling of where this was going. Then Dad turned around and set his plastic cup of water down on the counter, a little harder than he needed to.

"He also tells me you dropped gym."

I groaned and rolled my eyes. Every time I thought that maybe it wasn't totally a bummer that my dad was friends with a teacher at my school, something like this happened. It felt like being spied on. "I didn't drop it. I'm going to take it later. It just didn't work with my schedule this year."

"Esme, you can't just go through life avoiding everything you don't like."

"Dad, it's not that. It's . . . complicated." Like, in an I-outed-myself-as-telekinetic-in-dodgeball kind of way.

"If you were having problems with the other students, you could have talked to Brian about it. I don't like seeing my daughter run from bullies." *Crap.* How the heck did Brian even know that Stacey Wasser was the reason I'd dropped gym? I hadn't even told Janis.

"I'm not being bullied." I stood up and slid the chicken fingers back toward him. "Like I said, gym just didn't work with my schedule this year."

I left Dad standing in the kitchen and headed to my

room. My phone started to ring, and for a second, before I could stop it, my heart leapt with the hope that it was Dion.

Instead the screen said it was Janis. I answered with a groan, knowing that she'd ask what was wrong and give me a chance to vent about Dad and his weird obsession with gym and all things Coach Davis.

"Esme?" She was whispering, and her voice was small and shaky. I froze instantly, every hair on my arms standing on end.

"Janis? Are you okay?"

"There's someone in the house."

Instantly my mouth went dry and my heart started to race. "What do you mean?"

"I'm babysitting, and there's something in the house." Her whisper was urgent and came out with a scared hiss.

"Oh my God, Janis. Where are you?"

"I'm with Andrew. We're hiding in the closet. I locked the bedroom door."

I didn't tell her she was imagining things. I didn't tell her to hang up and call the cops. "Stay there," I said instead. "I'm on my way."

Then I turned around and ran right out the front door.

I was already at the end of the block when Dad realized what had happened, and I heard him screaming from the porch. He'd probably never seen me run so fast in my life. He'd probably never seen me run.

But I kept going, even when I heard a bark behind me.

Great. Now I was being chased by a dog.

I glanced over my shoulder, and it was Pig, ears flapping in the wind as she raced through the dark to catch up with me. I didn't have time to turn around and take her home, so I just called out to her to keep up.

Andrew's house was less than a mile away, and as my combat boots slapped the sidewalk, my lungs hurt so bad that it felt like I was inhaling pure gasoline and sandpaper. I didn't dare stop, though. I ran through an intersection and dialed Cassandra.

"Janis is babysitting, and something's happening," I gasped as I nearly collided with a Subaru. "We need to save her!" I flipped the driver the finger as he laid on the horn. I yelled the address into the phone.

"I'll meet you there," she said, and hung up without asking any questions.

When I turned onto Andrew's street, every muscle in my body was on fire, but I didn't stop running until I was on the front porch. I went to pound on the door, and it swung open as soon as my fist hit it. I stepped inside and surveyed the hallway to see what sort of heavy object I could swing through the air if I needed to take somebody out. A brass umbrella stand would have to do. I grabbed it with one hand, and with the other told Pig to sit and stay. I felt better knowing that she was guarding the front door.

The house was quiet, and all I could hear was the sound of my own breathing. The living room and kitchen were both empty, and I made my way slowly up the stairs. The door to Andrew's room was open, and in the glow of his night-light,

I could see that the window was wide open. It gave me the creeps, and I used my powers to slam it shut and lock the night outside. Then peeked in the closet. Empty.

The bathroom was empty too; the only room left was his dad's at the end of the hall. The door was shut, and it was locked. I assumed this was where Janis was hiding, but I still didn't dare to call out to her. If there was someone else in there, my best bet was to surprise them. I put my hand on the knob and concentrated on unlocking it, until it turned under my fingers.

I scanned the room and noted that the bedside lamp had a thick metal base, so I could grab that if I needed it, and set the umbrella stand down right by the door. I crept in slowly, then dropped to my knees to peer under the bed. Nothing. So I tiptoed over to the closet.

"Janis? It's me," I whispered, and the closet flew open. Janis came tumbling out and sat Andrew down before throwing her arms around me. It was obvious that she and Andrew had both been crying, and a freaked-out-looking dog was at their heels.

At that moment, someone burst through the door behind us.

Janis screamed. I held out my hand, and the lamp, the bedside table, the pillows, the duvet, and a pair of dress shoes all rose into the air above our heads, then began to launch themselves at the intruder like missiles.

Fortunately, she had good reflexes.

The next few seconds were chaos and barking as first

Janis and then Andrew took in what had just happened, and Pig came running down the hall to check on the noise.

Andrew started crying, and Janis looked panicked as she backed away, her head swiveling rapidly back and forth between Cassandra and me.

"What the f . . . ? Esme, wh-what was that?" she sputtered. "Did you see . . . ? How . . ."

I decided to deal with the scared-out-of-his-mind three-year-old first, and picked him up.

"I'm sorry you had a nightmare," I said softly, stroking his head and trying to smooth some of his hair back into place. "That must have been so scary. Everything's okay now." I carried him over to a corner of the room, and stood so that I could see everything. Cassandra grabbed Janis and pulled her over to us.

"Stay with them," she whispered, then turned and crept out the door.

Janis was shaking and had tears streaming down her face. Still holding Andrew, I grabbed Janis's hand and squeezed. "It's okay," I said. "Cassandra will—"

I was interrupted by a loud crash and a scream from the other side of the house. Janis gasped, and Andrew cried harder. My nerves blinked like Christmas lights as I waited for what would come next, but it was pure silence, and each passing second of quiet made me even more convinced that something horrible had happened out there.

Wordlessly I sat Andrew down and motioned for him and Janis to stay put, then crept out to the hallway and down the stairs. Cassandra was standing in the foyer, her hand on the knob of the open front door. The coatrack was lying on its side on the floor.

"You okay?" I asked.

She nodded, then pushed her hair out of her face and motioned at the coatrack. "It attacked me," she said, "but I think I won."

CHAPTER 14

In the kitchen, I sat Andrew down on the counter and poured out some cheddar bunnies, then put a sippy cup of milk in the microwave to warm it up a bit.

"Hey, buddy," Cassandra said, approaching him. "High five. You're so brave! That nightmare is never coming back!" She held out her hand. Andrew considered it for a few seconds, and I breathed out in relief when he raised his palm and slapped Cassandra's, a smile playing at the corner of his mouth. I took the milk out of the microwave, made sure it wasn't too hot, snapped a lid on it, and then handed it to him.

Cassandra seemed to have recovered, and I could see that with a little more experience, she could actually be a pretty good babysitter. She was entertaining Andrew by tossing cheddar bunnies into the air and deliberately missing them with her mouth so that they bounced off her forehead and cheeks. Pig was having a field day gobbling up any that hit the floor, and wasn't letting Andrew's dog get a single one. Andrew was laughing now, but Janis still hung in the doorway, a look of horror on her face.

"Come on, Janis," I said softly. "Let's go talk." I motioned for her to follow me into the living room, and when she didn't move, I reached out and put a hand on her arm. She shook it off immediately, and when she looked at me, I could see she was mad. Like, rappers-beefing-on-Twitter levels of pissed.

"You did that, Esme. I know you did. You made all that stuff float. And you know what's going on here." Her bare arms were covered in goose bumps, and she rubbed her hands briskly over them.

"Here, let me get you a blanket," I said, ignoring her accusation.

"I don't want a blanket," she snapped. "I want you to tell me what just happened."

"Janis," I said, "it's a long story, and one that I don't even really understand."

"You're not denying it. You made all that stuff float up into the air. You threw it at Cassandra without even touching it."

I nodded slowly.

"Why didn't I call the cops? Or Andrew's dad? It just seemed natural to call you. Something told me to do it, even though you're just a babysitter like me. Why did I think of you, Esme? Do you have something to do with what was in this house?"

My best friend was looking at me like she was scared of me, and I didn't know how to make it better. Cassandra appeared in the doorway before I could think of what to say to Janis. "He's asleep," she said. "I had to use ypnos on him, but he shouldn't remember much when he wakes up."

"Ypnos?" Janis asked, raising an eyebrow.

"It's like a spell to make someone fall asleep," I said. "It's totally safe." Mentally I added "we hope" to the end of that sentence.

"Spell?" She inched even farther away from me.

Cassandra didn't seem to notice, and came over and sat down right next to her.

"Janis, tell us exactly what happened tonight," she said.

"It was just past bedtime," Janis said, her voice hesitant. "And I got this feeling like I should go and check on him, which I never do—not after he goes to sleep."

Cassandra nodded.

"His door was open an inch or so, and I was pretty sure that I'd closed it on my way out, so I went into the room, and I was standing there looking at him. Then out of the corner of my eye, I saw something move down the hallway."

"Did you get a good look at it?"

Janis nodded.

"What did it look like?"

"Voldemort."

Cassandra blinked. "Voldemort?"

Janis nodded, deadly serious.

"Voldemort broke into this house and tried to kidnap

Andrew?" Cassandra asked, and I could detect a note of incredulity in her voice.

Janis could too, and it pissed her off. "No," she said. "Someone dressed like Voldemort broke into this house and tried to kidnap Andrew. They were wearing a costume." She huffed. "It'd be easy to get. There's a Halloween store on practically every corner right now."

"That's so impractical. Why would a kidnapper dress like Voldemort?" Cassandra asked.

"Are you serious?" Janis said, looking at her like she had a subzero IQ. "It's perfect. Think about it—if a kid tells their parents that Voldemort broke into their room, the parents are going to laugh it off. They'll think it's just a case of overactive imagination."

"Oh my God," I said, feeling like I'd been shocked as it came together. "David Bowie!"

Janis glared at me like I was trying to change the subject.

"No! I know what you're talking about," I said. "I was babysitting for Kaitlyn, and she said a not-nice man came into her room. The way she described him, he looked just like the Goblin King. I didn't believe her."

Janis pointed a finger at me. "See! Exactly! I wouldn't have believed Andrew if I hadn't seen it myself."

"Why didn't you tell anybody?" Janis asked me, and I knew she meant "Why didn't you tell me?"

I looked down and picked a piece of lint off my knee. "I don't know," I said. "I thought it made me look bad. Like I was a babysitter who didn't know how to deal with a little nightmare." They were both staring at me. "And," I continued, figuring I might as well lay it all out there, "I was scared. Like, really scared."

Janis nodded. "It freaked me out. I didn't look back. I just picked him up, then went and hid in his dad's closet. That was when I called Esme." She looked over at me.

"Should we call someone now?" I offered.

"Like who?" Cassandra asked.

"Like the cops, or Andrew's dad?"

"No way," Cassandra said, shaking her head. "They wouldn't believe us, and we don't have any evidence. They'd ask too many questions, and I don't want to be questioned by a bunch of old men."

I looked back at Janis, and to my surprise, she was nodding in agreement with Cassandra. "I don't want to drag this out," she said. "All I really want to do is go home."

The thing was, Janis couldn't go home, at least not until Andrew's dad returned, so we settled on the next best thing. We didn't want Janis to get in trouble for having friends over, but she understandably didn't want to be left by herself, so Cassandra and I crossed the street to watch the house until Andrew's dad got back. Pig sat between us on high alert. I had a feeling that, after tonight, Janis really *was* going to kick babysitting to the curb. The cookie-cake job might have required an apron, but at least there was no worry that someone was going to come in and try to kidnap the cookies.

We sat there for a little over an hour before Mr. Reynolds pulled up and went inside. When Janis came out of the house and started to walk to her car, I stood to meet her.

"Esme," Cassandra said, standing up next to me, "before you go, there's one thing I wanted to ask you. You're not falling for my brother, are you? I know you guys text and hang out."

The question caught me off guard, because in the excitement of the night, I'd somehow completely forgotten about Dion.

"I don't know," I answered truthfully. Janis's car beeped as she unlocked it.

"I don't care," Cassandra said. "Honestly. You wouldn't be the first of my friends to like my brother. Just be careful. I love him more than anyone else, but he can be a real jerk."

My mouth fell open in shock when I heard this. But before I could ask her to clarify, she was already crossing the street.

Janis gave us rides home, her mouth set in a grim line and her hands at ten and two as she drove four miles below the speed limit. No one talked except Cassandra, who gave Janis succinct directions about where to turn. When she got out of the car, I moved into the front seat. Janis started driving toward my house, and I figured now was as good a time as any to address the mastodon in the car.

"Janis—" I started, and she exploded.

"What the actual hell, Esme?" She took one hand off the wheel and pressed it to her forehead. "This was the scariest night of my life. There was something in that house, and it wanted to hurt me, or hurt Andrew, and then you show up and you can move things with your mind? And your new BFF Cassandra Heaven knows all about it, but I don't?"

"I'm sorry. I was going to tell you," I said. Though, as soon as I said it, I realized it was a lie. Before Cassandra, I hadn't even thought about telling Janis, or anyone else, about what I could do.

"How long have you known about this?"

I sighed. "I guess I started to suspect that something weird was going on a while ago. But know for certain? Like, maybe a week? A little more? It's all brand-new to me too."

"Why does Cassandra know? Is that why you wanted her in the babysitting club so bad?"

"Janis, it's not that at all. She didn't even know until after she'd joined the babysitting club. She's not even a good baby-sitter!" Normally this was the kind of news that would have piqued Janis's interest, but she didn't bite. "I didn't tell her," I continued. "She figured it out. Before I did, even. The stuff that happened in driver's ed, it was because of these weird powers. I didn't tell you, but it was why I dropped gym too. Stuff happened. With balls. Bad ball stuff." I was babbling, so I tried to get to the point. "I couldn't control them, and Cassandra helped me. She gets it because she has powers, too."

"She's a Carrie?" Janis asked.

"No, she's more of a Drew Barrymore than a Sissy Spacek."

"What the hell are you talking about?"

"Sorry," I said. "I mean, she's only a pyrokinetic."

"Ha," Janis said. "Only."

"Well, Carrie was both, because she—"

"I've seen the movie," Janis snapped.

"Are you mad?" I asked.

We were at a stoplight, and when the light turned green, Janis just sat there, the car idling at the intersection. "What would I be mad about? It's just really . . ."

"Weird?" I finished.

She nodded.

"Are you freaked out?" I asked.

"Honestly, yeah." The light turned red, and she finally went. "I mean, I know you better than I know anybody else, but the stuff you just did, I thought that only existed in books and movies."

I nodded, even though I didn't want to end up covered in pig blood, and didn't want Janis to think that I was like Carrie.

"Tonight, whatever was in that house," she said, "you're connected to it, aren't you?"

I hadn't wanted to think about that, but as soon as she said it, I was pretty sure Janis was right.

"Esme," she said as she finally pulled up to my house, "what is going on with you?"

"I don't know yet," I said, "but I have a feeling I'm about to find out."

I had so much to think about. What Janis had said, and who she had seen. What the hell was I, and what did it mean? It sounded like a bad country song (as if there were any other kind), but when I crawled into bed, all I could think about was Dion. Especially what Cassandra had said about him, and what he'd said about her. Every time I saw them together, they acted like the chummiest of chums. Every time I saw them apart, it didn't seem like they liked each other all that much.

I knew I wasn't her first friend to fall for him. Anyone who was around Dion for any amount of time would probably fall for him. But she'd called him a jerk. "A real jerk" had been her exact words, and that was a not a phrase I would have associated with Dion. Nor was it something I would have expected to come out of Cassandra's mouth when talking about him. I wasn't quite sure what to make of her warning. I mean, it wasn't like I hung out with Dion 24/7, but I'd never seen anything even remotely dickish from him.

When he had talked to me about Cassandra, he'd just seemed tired, and maybe a little sad even. I always got a protective vibe from him, even though Cassandra didn't exactly seem like someone who needed protection. But what did I know? I was an only child, so I didn't expect to understand what went on between siblings, especially when they'd been through so much together.

I texted Janis, hoping to close the night with some semblance of normality.

> 2morrow's look?

I had to wait several minutes for a reply.

> Thankful to be alive.

I could tell from the period that she was still mad.

I woke up the next morning to another text from Janis.

> the McAllisters want someone to babysit on Halloween. last minute, but can u take it?

I stared at the text for a minute, not knowing how to respond. Janis and I always hung out on Halloween, even if that just meant sitting on her couch in costume and watching scary movies. We always coordinated our costumes too. We were Cher and Dionne once, which was awesome, if a little obvious, and last year, we were the twins from *The Shining*. We should have won the costume contest at school, except the judges were a bunch of football players, and they gave first place to a couple of girls who'd dressed as . . . *Baby One More Time* Britney. The patriarchy is nothing if not predictable.

But now, if Janis was asking me if I wanted to babysit on Halloween, that meant . . .

> **U don't want to hang out?**
>> yeah, no offense, but after last night, i want
>> to avoid everything spooky for a while
> **that's cool, I get it. u don't want the job?**
>> I think i want to avoid babysitting too

I didn't know what words would properly express how sorry I was. About everything, and not just what had happened the night before. Finally I just said I'd take the job and told her I'd see her at school.

I wasn't surprised that Janis didn't want to babysit anymore. People evolved. They moved on. You weren't going to like the same stuff at seventeen that you did at twelve. But maybe, just maybe, we could have eked it out until the end of high school if a creep in a costume hadn't tried to kidnap her babysitting charge. And if Janis hadn't seen me chuck a bedroom set through the air using nothing but my mind.

When I saw her before first period, I couldn't help but notice how subdued her outfit was. Forest-green skinny jeans and an oversized silver sweater, with leopard-print motorcycle boots, a black leather backpack, and bags under her eyes.

"Here," she said, holding something out to me. "You should have this."

I looked down. It was the burner phone. "But, Janis," I said, not taking it from her, "you've always been in charge of the phone. You know I'm crap at managing the schedule."

"I know," she said, not denying it. "But like I said, I think I'm done with babysitting. I'm not up for it anymore."

"Janis . . . ," I started, something inside me deflating. "You're a really good babysitter. Kids love you."

"Yeah, but I don't want to be the one left holding the blankie when someone gets hurt."

"What are you going to do instead?"

She shrugged, her gold hoop earrings shimmering with the movement. "I'll go back to making smoothies or something. It wasn't that bad. I just have to keep my opinions to myself."

"But . . ." I had a million protests inside me. We'd had the babysitting club for so long that I couldn't imagine *not* having it. "It won't always be this way," I said. "We're going to figure out who was trying to kidnap the kids, and everything will go back to normal."

"Esme, you can move things with your mind and you're talking about hunting down a kidnapper," she said. "Nothing is ever going back to normal."

Ugh. I wanted to protest more, but deep down, I knew she was right.

• • •

I was used to Cassandra appearing at school whenever she felt like it and not according to the school's schedule, but today I saw her between every period. She was usually waiting for me at my locker, for no apparent reason, snapping her gum and looking up and down the hallway like she was on a stakeout. She never had a backpack, and didn't carry textbooks, paper, or even a pen.

"What class do you have now?" I asked, envious of her light workload as I walked to my next class, laden down with books and my heavy laptop.

"Chemistry."

"You have chem?" I balked. "Where's all your stuff?" That class was notorious for tons of homework and painful, hunchback-inducing textbooks.

Cassandra smiled, and something twinkled in her eye. "I'm trying out gnosi." She said that like I was supposed to know what it meant.

"Gnosikinesis. Knowledge manipulation," she said at my blank stare. "It makes it so I know something front to back after seeing or hearing it once. It works. I already got a hundred on the last pop quiz."

We had turned to take a shortcut behind the annexes, and before I could pepper Cassandra with more questions, we saw them and I lost my train of thought.

Five of them. All with their arms folded across their chests, and just standing there like they were waiting for someone. Standing there like they were waiting for . . . us.

CHAPTER 15

The word "cheerleader" conjured up a certain image. High ponytails. Shiny nails. Cheeriness.

Not here, though. Our cheerleaders were straight-up thugs.

They'd taken the mantra "cheerleading is a sport" to the extreme, and had biceps to rival the baseball team. They'd been state champions three years in a row, and had the bro-bravado to match. They cut class, were rude to teachers, and were rumored to have slashed the tires of a rival squad's bus. But true to our school's whack priorities, all of that was forgiven every time they were clapping their hands and doing backflips on ESPN 24 or whatever channel it was that aired that kind of stuff.

So when I saw Stephani Riggs, a junior who seriously spelled her name with no *e*, leaning against a wall, smacking her lip gloss and looking Cassandra up and down, it made me stop in my tracks. Cassandra either didn't notice or was new enough to still be naive about the squad's reputation, because she kept walking.

"Hey, new girl," Stephani called, pushing herself off the wall, with Shannon Clinton, her bulldog second-in-command, right behind her. Stephani's ponytail looked like it had been dipped into a deep fryer, and Shannon's eyebrows looked drawn on with Sharpie.

"Cass," I said quietly, trying to get her attention, but I failed.

"New girl! She's talking to you," Shannon growled, which finally made Cassandra stop.

"Wait, you're talking to me?" Cassandra said, seeming genuinely confused.

"Of course I'm talking to you," Stephani snapped. "How many other new girls are there?"

"I have no idea," Cassandra said. "See, since I'm new, I wouldn't know if someone else was also new. Right?"

It was a very practical point, and one that was completely lost on Stephani, Shannon, and their three minions, Sheryl, Shauna, and Tonya, the lone *T* in the squad's top squad.

"I hear you were chatting up my man last weekend," Stephani said. She started to walk toward us, and the other four followed her like they were a five-headed, athleisure-clad Hydra. I tried to appear calm as I glanced around us, looking for other students—or, better, a teacher or faculty member—who might prevent this from turning into the confrontation I was 99 percent sure it was about to turn into. I also frantically sent Cassandra mental messages not to say anything that would make SSSST any more pissed off than they already were.

She didn't get them.

"Your man?" Cassandra said, doing the unthinkable and actually taking a step toward Stephani. "I don't even know who your 'man' is."

Oh God, did she really just make air quotes at the cheerleaders?

"You know who he is," Stephani hissed.

"No, I don't," Cassandra said, smiling like she knew a secret. "I'm new here, remember? I've seen a bunch of little boys sniffing around campus, but men? I don't think so."

I did not like where this was heading. I did not like it at all.

"Craig Lugweather!" Stephani practically yelled, at which point Cassandra did the worst thing she could possibly do and burst out laughing. Now I was panicking. Cassandra was either completely oblivious or knew and did not care at all that she was about to get jumped. I didn't know what to do. I wasn't about to run off and leave my friend when it was five-on-one, but realistically, what was I going to do if it was five-on-two? I was a hider, not a fighter.

"Your 'man' is Craig Lugweather?" Oh God, not the air quotes again. "The one with the bacne and the premature beer gut?"

To Stephani these weren't insults. Just more proof that Cassandra's eyes, and maybe even her hands, had been roaming where they shouldn't have been.

"You little slut!" she squealed. "How do you know he

has bacne?" Shannon put an arm out in attempt to hold Stephani back that was totally just for show.

"Because it creeps out of his shirt, up his neck, and down his arms," Cassandra said. "He sits in front of me in English and scratches his pustules until they bleed. Your 'man' is disgusting." She smiled again. "Which is why I did not give him my number when he asked for it last weekend."

At that, Shannon's arm went up, releasing Stephani to fly at Cassandra in a rage. It happened so fast that I was frozen in place. With two hands, Stephani shoved Cassandra in the chest and sent her flying backward. Cassandra stumbled but didn't fall, and went straight back at Stephani. Cassandra grabbed Stephani's hair with one hand, held her head down, and started hitting with the other—slaps and punches connecting with Stephani's face, neck, and shoulders.

Stephani had a hold of Cassandra's sweatshirt and was swinging at her face. I winced when her closed fist hit Cassandra in the chin and they both fell to the ground, where they rolled on top of each other.

"Stop it!" I screamed, running to them. I grabbed Stephani's shoulders to try to break them up. Out of the corner of my eye, I could see Shannon run in too, and I had a momentary rush of solidarity with her, as there was no way I was going to be able to break this up myself.

Then she kicked Cassandra in the chest.

"What the hell are you doing?" I screamed at her. Then the next thing I knew, Shauna was in my face, and I felt like I was being scalped as her ham-hands grabbed at my hair.

Oh, hell no. I managed to get a palm up and pointed in her direction, and with a blast, I lifted her whole body three feet off the ground. She let go of my hair, and I threw her into the side of the annex.

Holy moly. I guess this is that "power of adrenaline" people are always talking about. Sheryl and Tonya started screaming like banshees, and I turned to see that Shannon's pants were on fire, flames licking up past her knees. She didn't know whether to keep trying to kick Cassandra in the face or stop, drop, and roll.

So much for passive resistance. Cassandra and I had escalated this from routine fight to full-on catastrophe in about thirty seconds.

Stephani was now on top of Cassandra, one knee digging into Cassandra's arm and pinning it to the ground. There was no going back now, so I pointed my palm at Stephani and gave her split ends a good hard pull. She squealed, not knowing why her head was suddenly being yanked back, but she pushed forward with her attack. I did the only thing I could think to do.

When we'd gotten a pit bull, Dad had read up on how to break up a dogfight, just in case Pig had turned out to be anything other than the bucket of soft-serve that she was. Kicking and hitting a fighting dog will just make it angry and it will bite down harder. What you have to do is disorient it, and the quickest way to do this is by grabbing its back legs and lifting it into the air so that it's suddenly dangling upside down.

Stephani wasn't a dog, but she sure as hell was a bitch, so I raised both hands in her direction, then used my powers to grab her ankles right above her Nikes and hoist her up until she was dangling like she was doing a handstand. She was the heaviest thing I'd ever lifted, and keeping her dangling in the air felt like doing crunches with my brain. Cassandra made a tiny flame appear in her hand and then smashed it onto Stephani's forearm. Banshee screams echoed off the school walls.

Then someone yelled "What in the world are you doing?" from behind me. Startled, I dropped Stephani Riggs into a crumpled heap on the ground.

I knew that voice well. Too well.

I spun around to see Brian storming toward us. I had never seen anyone in a tracksuit look so angry. In fact, he seemed so pissed that I wondered what he'd seen—the fire, or Stephani hanging upside down like she'd been strung up on an invisible clothesline?

If he'd noticed anything unusual, surely he'd have been less mad and more confused. Or scared, even.

Sheryl ran up to him with tears streaming down her face. "Coach Davis, did you see that? They're evil! One of them made Shauna fly, and the other tried to set Shannon on fire!"

"Shut up," Brian said, and sidestepped her like she was nothing more than a yapping Yorkie. Sheryl's mouth hung open in disbelief, as she was clearly not used to being told to shut up, especially not by a teacher.

He stalked over to me, grabbed my arm in a grip that

was tighter than necessary, and dragged me along until we were both standing over Cassandra. Stephani was still on the ground too, looking dazed, but Cassandra's eyes were clear and fiery.

"Get up," he snarled at them, and they both hastily struggled to their feet. He whipped me around so that I was standing next to Cassandra, our shoulders practically touching. Then he turned to the cheerleaders.

"The five of you are coming with me, *now*," he said. Then he turned back to us. "And you two are staying right here until I come back. Do not move." Behind him, Stephani smirked, sure that there was no way the head of the athletic department would get her into trouble. Fighting earned a suspension. A suspension earned an absence from the cheerleading squad, and no faculty member would risk that, since everyone knew that no one could double-backflip like Stephani Riggs.

Brian was starting to usher the girls away, when he suddenly turned around and walked back to Cassandra and me. "Do not try to get out of this by running off," he said, his voice low enough that the cheerleaders couldn't hear it. "Remember, Esme, I know where you live. And, Cassandra, I can find you too."

I nodded and tried to swallow, but my mouth was so dry that my tongue just stuck to the roof of my mouth. My body was still shaking as my breath slowed, and I turned to look at Cassandra. For someone who had just gotten jumped by five girls in Lululemon, Cassandra seemed pretty unfazed. She was still breathing hard as she ran her fingers through her hair and adjusted her clothes. Aside from a small rip in her jeans, she didn't look any worse for the wear.

I, on the other hand, was shaking, reeling from what had just happened. When Cassandra started to walk away, I grabbed her and dug my nails into her arm.

"Where do you think you're going?"

"I don't know. Home? I'm certainly not just going to sit here and wait for that guy to come back and punish us. That was really creepy, what he just said."

I tightened my grip on her arm. "That guy is my dad's best friend. I'm not going anywhere, and since this is all your fault, you're not either."

She pried my fingers off one by one. "It's not my fault. It's that girl's fault. I don't even know who she is, and she started this whole thing."

"Stephani's an idiot. She can't even spell her own name. You could have walked away, but you played right into her." I had a vision of the consequences that were going to be waiting for me, especially since I already seemed to be on treacherous ground with Dad after driver's ed. "I'm going to be grounded for a month, or worse."

Cassandra rolled her eyes. "Where I'm from, walking away isn't really an option," she said. "Neither is running away, because that just leads to a lifetime of being picked on in gym class."

Anger flared in my chest, and my cheeks burned. "Excuse me?" I almost spit. "Run away? I saved your butt back there, and the only way you can think to thank me is to call me a coward?"

"I didn't call you a coward." She exhaled a stream of air and the hair around her face fluttered. "I'm just saying that you still think of yourself as someone who needs to run from other people, when other people should be running from us." She leaned in closer to me so that her face was only a few inches from mine. "We're the scary ones. Did you hear that girl screaming? She's terrified of us. Because we're power-ful, and we're still discovering everything that we can do. We could rule this school if we wanted to. We could rule this town. But I'm thinking bigger than that, even if you aren't."

"What the hell are you talking about?" I snapped. "You think this is some sort of magical pyramid scheme you can use to get the best seats at Outback Steakhouse? I don't think—" I stopped midsentence when Brian reappeared, looking no less angry than he had moments before. I was waiting for him to lead us straight to the principal's office, or at least his own office, which was hidden away off the gym at the back of the guys' locker room. Instead he motioned for us to follow him and walked away from the building, into the teachers' parking lot, and finally to his car. Brian's car was a black, two-door Ford Explorer. I'd ridden in it, years before, but I was very familiar with it because of his frequent visits with my dad. He opened the passenger door, popped the seat forward, and motioned for Cassandra to get into the back seat.

"No way," she said. "I'm not leaving campus with a male teacher when I don't even know where we're going." I knew Brian, and I trusted him as much as I trusted any adult, but I also had to admit that this was a little unusual.

To my surprise, though, he didn't offer any explanation. He just stood there and crossed his arms. "Get into the back seat," he said, his voice low and threatening, "or I will make you." For a second, Cassandra seemed unsure of what to do, and I thought she might actually turn and run. She shifted back and forth on her feet; finally, with a sigh that made it clear she was just humoring him, she climbed in. Then he shoved the passenger seat back into place, and when I got in, he slammed the door with equal force.

"Someone woke up with their Under Armour in a bunch," Cassandra mumbled as he walked around the car to the driver's side, but I didn't respond. I just stared straight ahead. I was growing more scared by the second, and not just of a grounding from Dad. Brian hadn't asked if I was okay. So far, he hadn't asked us anything. He just seemed mad. Beyond mad. Furious.

Brian drove in silence, and as he made turn after turn, I realized we were going to his house, and at this thought, I started inching my hand toward the door handle. If he slowed down at an intersection, I could always jump out. Sure, I'd be leaving Cassandra, but she'd be okay. Right?

"Don't even think about it, Esme," Brian said, as if he were reading my mind, and I moved my hand back to my lap. I knew where Brian lived because I'd gone with Dad before to drop something off or pick something up, whatever it was that adults did on Saturday mornings. But I'd never been *inside*. Brian always met us on the porch. My mind started to spiral. What if he was a serial killer, and the whole inside of the house was lined with plastic? It was still the middle of the school day. Had he even told anyone he was leaving and taking two students with him? Maybe someone had seen us and the police were already on the way?

I felt my stomach rising into my throat, and then Cassandra's words came back to me. Why was I scared? I could yank the wheel right now and send this car straight into a tree. Brian should have been scared of me. From the back seat, I could hear Cassandra going to town on her gum. It was oddly comforting. Whatever Brian had in store for us, we could handle it.

CHAPTER 16

Brian still didn't say anything as he parked in his driveway, got out, and walked to the front door. He unlocked it and stood there, which I guess was our cue to get out and follow him.

"Is he going to murder us in there?" Cassandra asked. "Or worse?"

"Don't worry," I whispered back. "That tracksuit is definitely flammable."

As soon as we stepped through the front door, Brian shut and locked it behind us, and my jaw dropped in shock. From what I knew about Brian—football coach, never married, middle-aged man—I would have expected his house to be mostly television sets and microwaves.

Instead I wanted to double-tap his living room. It was the coziest place I'd been in a long time—overstuffed couch dotted with indigo-dyed throws and sheepskins, succulents in smooth terra-cotta pots circling the fireplace, a diffuser in the corner that made the whole place smell like Tahitian vanilla and jasmine.

"Okay," Cassandra said, flopping onto the couch and sinking into the pillows. "It's cool if you're kidnapping us, so long as we're staying here." She picked a candle up off a side table and sniffed it.

"We're not," he said. "Get up."

We followed him through the kitchen, which was sunny and filled with viney green plants and bowls of bright citrus, through to the bedroom, where a queen-sized bed held more pillows than Pinterest. At the back of the bedroom, he opened the closet and shoved all the clothes to one side. I was so distracted by the fact that he had about twenty nylon tracksuits—and that they were all on hangers—that it took me a second to realize that he'd taken off his necklace and I could finally get a glimpse of the charm. It looked like a sacred geometry version of Prince's symbol, and holding it flat, Brian pressed it against the wall. The area all around it started to glow purple, there was a beep, and then a door slid open. Brian put the necklace back on, and I started to back away. Cassandra had been right, and I had been wrong. There was something off about Brian. Way off.

"I like your cozy vibes and all, but I am not going into your dismemberment chamber," Cassandra said, reaching into her pocket and pulling out her phone. "In fact, I'm calling the school right now and telling them that a teacher forced me to leave campus with him and to go to his *house*."

Brian sighed. "I'm going to force you to do a lot of things." Then, with a shove, he pushed us both through the door and followed us inside.

Instead of panicking, Cassandra and I raised our hands at the same time, Cassandra to throw flames, me to grab the first thing I could to whack Brian right in the back of the head.

Except nothing happened.

"Stop it," Brian said, sounding annoyed, as if we'd done nothing more threatening than blow him a raspberry. "And sit down. Your kinesis won't work in here."

I froze. What was going on? I would have been less surprised if he *had* tried to murder us. How did he know about the kinesis? I felt stunned, so I did the only thing I could think to do, which was exactly what he'd told me to. I sat down. Cassandra wavered, then followed suit.

I looked around as I tried to catch my breath. This room was entirely different from the rest of the house—there was nothing cozy about it. It was sharp and modern, with a large metal desk on one side and a sleek flat-screen on the other. The walls were a deep purple, and lined with glass display cases. When it registered what was in them, I struggled to swallow the lump rising in my throat. They were full of ropes, handcuffs, muzzles, shackles, things that looked like

Taser guns. On the other wall hung several framed photos of teenage girls, some of whom were bloody, bruised, and barely standing.

So, he *was* going to kill us. He was just going to take his time. I started to think of all the things I was going to miss when I was dead: Dad, Janis, Pig, my closet, even stupid school. I liked being alive, and I didn't want it to end.

"Relax," Brian said. "You're not going to get murdered or dismembered. But you *are* in trouble." He walked around and sat down behind the desk.

"What you did today was very, very dangerous. You revealed yourself in a highly public, and highly unnecessary, way. And over what? A boy you don't even like?" He closed his eyes and massaged his temples with his fingertips. "Fortunately, I was able to take care of it, and the cheerleaders will not remember anything other than crossing paths with you by the annexes." He gave us a hard stare, waiting for his words to sink in. "But that will be the last unnecessary use of any of your kinetic powers. Do you understand me?"

I was completely lost, but I still nodded. "Esme, it's bad enough that you manipulated the entire school server to get out of the classes you don't like. And, Cassandra, did you not think anyone would notice that you're acing all your tests?"

She huffed and crossed her arms in front of her. "What? So some teachers see a Mexican girl getting A's, and suddenly they're all suspicious? That's BS."

"No," he said, his brow furrowing. "Some teachers see a student with a shoddy academic transfer record, who doesn't show up to class with so much as a pencil, suddenly start to get a perfect score on everything she touches. *Then* they get suspicious." Cassandra sank a little lower in her chair.

"Some of the blame for this falls on me," he continued, looking straight at me, "as I should have alerted you to your true identity as soon as your kinesis activated."

"Yeah," I said, sitting up straighter and seizing my opportunity, even if I didn't totally know what that opportunity was. "This is your fault. What's wrong with you?"

He leaned forward, an elbow on his desk and his forehead in his hand, and sighed. "This season is killing me," he said. "Have you see our schedule? Every week, we're up against a top-tier school. Jimmy Rodriguez has an arm like Tom Brady, but he got caught smoking weed behind the Dairy Queen. Twice. I was able to get him out of it the first time, but—"

"Who is Jimmy Rodriguez?" I asked.

"He's our quarterback. He could definitely go D-1 and lead us to top in the city if—"

"Wait," I said, interrupting him. "You're trying to tell me that Cassandra and I had to figure this stuff out for ourselves because you were distracted by . . . sports?" I spat out the last word like it was a wad of flavorless gum.

"Like I said," he said, straightening up and dusting a speck of invisible dirt off his track jacket, "I'm sorry."

"You actually didn't say that," Cassandra said.

"Well, I meant it," he said. "And technically, I am only Esme's Counsel. We were not aware that you were a Sitter,

Cassandra, until you showed up. Besides, it's no big deal if we got a bit of a delayed start on your training, as the Synod's seal will hold until the end of the season." He cleared his throat. "End of the year, I mean."

My head was hurting from trying to keep track of everything he was saying. Counsel. Sitter. Synod. Freaking football. While I was trying to figure out the best way to formulate a question, Cassandra got straight to the point.

"What the hell are you talking about?"

To my surprise, Brian actually smiled. "My apologies," he said. "In my anger, I forgot how little you actually know." He got up, nylon shuffling, and walked to the side of the room with all the pictures. "You have a very proud lineage," he said, gesturing at all the photos on the wall, "one that has kept our world safe for thousands upon thousands of years."

Cassandra leaned forward and rested her elbows on her knees. She closed her eyes and pressed her palms into them. It was a gesture I'd never seen her make before, like she was stressed, and I realized I'd never seen her look stressed. "Maybe it's because I'm a transfer student with a shoddy academic record, but I'm still not following you," she said. "At all."

"These are all the Sitters who came before you, or who are currently protecting other Portals around the world." I opened my mouth to point out that he was still talking about stuff we didn't understand, but he kept going. "The Synod is our governing council, and I report directly to them and keep them apprised of all activities here in Spring River."

"Activities?" I said. "You mean like yearbook club and musical theater?"

"No," he said, "I'm not talking about high school. I'm talking about magic."

I was starting to feel like that time when I accidentally took a double dose of Mucinex and filled in *all* the bubbles on my multiple-choice math test. I needed Brian to pump the brakes and slow down, because nothing was making sense. "I think maybe you should start at the beginning," I said.

He tried to stifle a grin as he reached into a drawer and pulled something out. "They said I'd never need this Power-Point," he said under his breath, almost as if he were talking to himself. "But I knew it would come in handy."

I stared, dumbfounded. Was he really about to show us a PowerPoint? Then I saw what he had in his hand. It was a remote control. The wall behind Brian shimmered and became a giant screen. Then words swam into view. "Congratulations! You're a Sitter now!"

He looked at us, and when he registered that we were just as lost as ever, the smile fell from his face. "You should be taking notes," he said.

I nodded quickly, dug into my backpack, and pulled out a spiral-bound and a pen. Cassandra, of course, had nothing, so I ripped out a sheet and handed it to her, along with a spare pencil.

Brian clicked his remote, and a Venn diagram appeared. The circle on the left said "The Negative," the circle on the right said "The Definite," and the space in the middle said

"The Sitters." The middle space had a drawing of a girl that looked like it had been done by a third grader.

Brian's remote was also a laser pointer, and a tiny red dot made circles over the area that said "The Definite." "This is our dimension," he said, then moved the red dot over to the circle that said "The Negative." "And this is a dimension that runs parallel to ours. The two are connected through inter-dimensional gates, called Portals, that are protected by Sitters.

"The Negative sucks positivity from the Definite," he continued, clicking through to the next slide. "In addition to spawning actual demons, the Negative breeds emotions that allow evil to blossom and fester." Behind Brian, the screen filled with words—"innocence," "enthusiasm," "coopera-tion," "encouragement," "community," "inspiration"—that were soon eaten up by a new set—"indifference," "unhappi-ness," "ennui," "boredom," "selfishness," "passivity." And on and on. Then, with a poof, they all vanished, and "THE NEGATIVE" filled the screen in heavy block letters.

I could see why Brian was so proud of his PowerPoint. It was pretty good, and what was more, I was starting to follow him. From the way she leaned forward in her seat, rapt, eyes on the screen, it seemed like Cassandra was too.

"The natural order of the Negative is to seep into the Definite, and it is the Sitter's role to minimize the effects of that. Sitters must protect the values of the Definite, remedy the evil that is the result of the Negative, and Return any en-tities that manage to breech the Portal." The screen behind him filled with a crude animation of a girl whacking a ghost with a stick. Apparently there was a reason why Brian taught gym and not art.

Cassandra raised her hand, which I'm sure she never did in class, and Brian pointed at her. "Who are the Sitters?" she said.

"I'm glad you asked," he said, clicking the remote way more dramatically than he needed to. Sure enough, the slide that appeared said "Who are the Sitters?"

Brian kept clicking, and a list started to appear underneath the question:

- Female
- Young
- Responsible
- Highly trained
- Protective

Something clicked, and I sat back in my chair, flabbergasted. It had just hit me. "Oh my God," I said. "When you say 'Sitter,' you mean—"

"In a sense, a babysitter," Brian said. "You enforce the rules and make sure no one gets hurt."

"But instead of a couple of kids, we're in charge of . . ." I trailed off.

"Humanity," Brian said, finishing my sentence for me.

As I sat there letting his words sink in, Cassandra jumped

up and ran over to the wall of photos. She pointed to a picture of a redhead brandishing what looked like a bear trap. "So my mom's note that said 'Find the babysitters,' this is what that was about?"

Brian nodded. "Yes, exactly," he said. "Your mother was a smart woman, and she must have coded the note on the chance that it might fall into the wrong hands. The secrets of the Sitterhood are highly guarded."

"Wait," I said, still reeling. "So all those horror movies about babysitting, like *Halloween,* there's something behind that idea?"

Brian nodded. "Normies do not know about the Sitterhood," he said, "but occasionally an intuitive one picks up on something and a bit of Sitter mythology makes it into the culture of the Definite. When it comes to true evil and destruction, the traditional normie channels of protection are rather ineffectual. The police don't have a clue, and governments are useless, but Sitters get it done."

My head was spinning at the revelation that my being a Babysitter was about way more than just sitting for babies. "I always thought I liked horror movies because being scared made me feel something," I said, and Brian shook his head.

"It is likely that you were subconsciously drawn to them," he said, "because the female protagonists reminded you of your mother." I hated the idea of being psychoanalyzed by a guy wearing a whistle, but I had to nod. What Brian was saying made perfect sense.

"So if Sitters are female," I said, "where do you come in?"

"Like I said, I am your Counsel. I am a part of the Sitter-hood, but not a Sitter. I have access to information, but I have no inborn kinesis of my own. All the powers I possess have been granted to me by the Synod."

"Wait," I said. "Does this mean that Janis is a Sitter too?"

Brian shook his head. "Janis is a babysitter but not a Sitter," he said. "Janis's path to babysitting was more traditional. For her, it was a choice. For the two of you, it is destiny."

"And Janis's destiny is Central Saint Martins," I said mournfully, before realizing that the words meant absolutely nothing to Cassandra and Brian.

But Cassandra wasn't paying attention to me anyway. "I've only babysat once in my entire life," she said.

"And she sucked at it," I added, causing her to shoot me some serious side-eye.

"Don't get caught up too much in the literal," Brian said, "as you are most definitely a Sitter."

"But you and your Synosh, or whatever it is, didn't know about me?"

"Synod," he corrected her. "And no, we didn't."

Cassandra got up and walked over to the photo wall. "But my mom was a Sitter." She pointed to a teenage girl with bruise-colored lipstick and long, dark hair pulled into a messy ponytail. She wore denim overalls that had one leg shredded entirely, and one of her arms was in a sling, but her smile was wide and genuine. "This is her, right?" Cassandra asked.

Brian nodded. "Sitting sometimes skips a generation,

though," he said. "And when you were born, your mother was under the impression that you did not have powers. After her death, your custody was treated as a family matter, and not one in which the Synod should intervene. No one knew that you were a Sitter until you showed up at Spring River High and set the girls' bathroom trash can on fire."

Cassandra smirked. "You knew that was me?"

"I figured it out," he said. "Even the can was incinerated."

I expected Cassandra to keep pushing for more info, but instead she just nodded and changed the subject, turning back to the picture of her mom and pointing. "Why does she look like she just got the crap smacked out of her?" she said.

"That picture was taken right after her first Return," he said. "She would have been just about the same age that you are now." He walked down to the opposite end of the wall. "Esme, here's your mother."

I got up and walked closer to the picture that he had pointed out. It was teenage Mom, all right. Though, unlike the photo of Cassandra's mom, she didn't look like she'd just been through a werewolf car wash. She was sitting on a picnic table, leaning forward toward the camera, and didn't have a scratch or bruise on her, though her smile was a little lopsided. "Don't let that picture fool you," Brian said. "She'd just been through one of the most dangerous battles in modern Sitter history. It wasn't physical, but entirely mental, and she nearly lost her mind."

"A hint of what was to come, I guess," I said. Brian looked

away and cleared his throat. "So you were a friend of my dad's, but you also knew who my mom really was?"

"Not exactly," he said. "As your Counsel, a friendship with your father was the most likely cover story that would allow me to keep tabs on you without raising suspicions."

I was reeling. I'd always felt like there was something off about their friendship, but I never would have imagined it was as nuts as this. "So you two never even played on the same team, or whatever it is that Dad always gets nostalgic about?" I asked, picturing the look of contentment on Dad's face when he would tell me stories about how long he and Brian had known each other.

Brian shook his head. "I'm afraid those memories were implanted in him to create a bond. I used to be an interior designer." So that explained the pillows, but it also made my heart break a little bit for Dad. Brian continued. "I don't even like football, but now it consumes me. Or, to be precise, our offensive line consumes me. Those idiots couldn't hold on to a ball if it were covered in glue—" He caught himself. "Sorry. We're not here to talk about football."

"Wait," I said, still not sure I was hearing him right. "If you don't even like football, how did you get a job as the coach, then?"

"The Synod used a few spells on me. At the time I came to Spring River, football coach was the only job available that would allow me to be nearby when you faced your Changeover."

"Changeover?"

"Your seventeenth birthday. Your onset of powers and the assumption of your new role. I didn't realize it would happen right in the middle of one of the toughest seasons of my life." He groaned and cracked his knuckles, a faraway look on his face.

"So as our Counsel, you're like our . . . coach?" I said.

Brian nodded. "I will be your trainer and guide as you navigate your Sitter duties."

Cassandra had now moved over to the other wall, and took down a pair of handcuffs that seemed to be made out of very expensive barbed wire. With a flick of her wrist, they snapped open. I grimaced, waiting for her to cut herself.

"So basically, we're like Slayers, and you're our Watcher," I said.

"Excuse me?" Brian said.

Cassandra put the handcuffs back and tried to open a thing that looked like a high-tech, and very expensive, blow dryer.

"You know, like Buffy," I added.

Brian still seemed like he had no idea what I was talking about as he crossed the room, took the grabber from Cassandra, and put it back in the case.

"*Buffy the Vampire Slayer*," I said finally. "The TV show."

"I wouldn't know," he said. "I've never seen it."

I raised an eyebrow. How could someone like him have never seen that show?

"It's about a teenage girl who lives on a Hellmouth and

kills vampires," I said, trying to bring him up to speed in as few words as possible. "And she has a Watcher who's a librarian."

"Ah, yes," he said, nodding. "I have heard of that show. And you're not wrong for thinking that there are some similarities. But it is the differences that are the most important."

"And what are those?" I asked.

"One: a Sitter's job is to protect, not to kill. A Sitter only kills as a very, very last resort, and even then there are consequences," he said. "And two: Buffy was a fictional TV character, and you two are real."

As if to illustrate his point, Cassandra was now bleeding, having finally cut herself on what looked like a lethal blender. Brian handed her a tissue, which she wrapped around her finger before using the sole of her shoe to smudge a drop of blood into the floor. With a last glance at the weapons on the wall, she came over and sat back down.

"And, Cassandra, you are no longer unassigned, as I will be acting as your Counsel as well. So we had better get started on your training. Better late than never." Brian walked over to his bookshelves and pulled out a large, ancient-looking volume. He carried it back over and dropped it on his desk with a thud. He tapped its cover, then pointed at several more just like it that were still on the shelves. "A Sitter never stops training, and eventually all of the material in these books will be inside your heads."

Ouch, I thought. They were really big books.

"You have already gotten a taste from the notebook that

Cassandra's mother left, but this is volume one of the spells that are available to a Sitter," Brian said, taking a book off the shelf and opening it to a page in the middle. The pages were yellowed and thin, and the words on them were written in thick, inky script. It was like someone had taken the Bible and an encyclopedia and mashed them together. Intimidating, to say the least.

Cassandra seemed to have the opposite reaction—not intimidated but empowered. She drew in a breath as she flipped from page to page. "We can learn to do anything we want," she whispered, in the same kind of voice kids use when they've been told that they can pick out some candy.

"These spells are just like your kinetic powers," Brian said, snapping the book shut and pulling it away from her. "They are to be used to protect the innocent, and for Returns, not used to get out of tests or defeat a slighted cheerleader."

"What's a Return?" I asked.

"It is the Sitter's greatest responsibility," he said, flipping to a page that was filled with what looked like an illustration of a black hole, or a giant clogged drain. "The Portal is where beings can pass back and forth between this dimension and the Negative. Fortunately, we won't have to worry about that for a while. The Spring River Portal was sealed by the Synod many years ago, which means that, for our purposes, it does not exist for the time being. This is another reason why I was a bit lax with your training, as we have plenty of time to get you up to speed before anything comes crawling through."

I shivered. "Things crawl through?" I asked, and Brian nodded. "Like what?"

"Demons. Monsters. Nightmares. Evil," he said. "Anything that wants to wreak havoc on our world. When that happens, it is the Sitter's job to capture and Return them."

"You mean, like, put a stake through their heart?" Cassandra asked, and Brian shook his head.

"No, I mean send them back to the Negative." His voice was stern. "Like I said before, Sitters don't kill. We protect. I'm glad I have plenty of time to drill that into you before you're actually faced with the task."

I jolted forward as if I'd been shocked. "There *are* demons!" I said. "The seal, it's broken!"

"No, it's not," Brian said. "We have instruments to measure that, dozens of them. If the Portal opened, we'd know almost immediately."

I stood up, my mind racing as I started to pace back and forth. "But the Goblin King and Voldemort." I looked over at Brian, who was squinting at me, and backtracked. "I was babysitting last week, and someone, or something, dressed as the Goblin King came in and tried to kidnap Kaitlyn," I said. "I thought it was a nightmare, but then the same thing happened to Janis, with Andrew, just last night! Only this time, they were dressed as Voldemort. It had to be a demon. I can't believe I didn't think of it until now, but, uh, a lot has happened in the last twenty-four hours."

Brian nodded, urging me to go on. I told him how I had

felt, and everything that Janis had said, and how she automatically called me, instead of dialing 911. The look on Brian's face grew less confused and more worried.

He sat down at his desk and punched a few keys into a keyboard, and the last slide of his presentation disappeared and was replaced by something that looked like a weather map, with swatches of blue, yellow, and green. "That's so strange," he said. "The Portal is most definitely closed." He clacked a few more keys. "There's been no sign of Portal activity at all."

I waited for him to say something else, but he didn't. "So?" I asked. The weather map disappeared from the wall and the screen went blank again. "What do we do about it?"

"I will bring it up to the Synod when I speak to them next," he said. "And we will proceed with caution. Needless to say, we'll start your training sooner than I planned, just to be on the safe side."

Brian's tracksuit pocket started to buzz. Apparently cell phones worked in the closet, even if our kinesis didn't. He glanced at his phone, then slammed the book shut and put it back on the shelf. "I hate to cut our getting-to-know-you session short," he said, "but practice starts in twenty minutes, and I have a defensive coordinator who can't even lead stretches without my direction." He let out the most FML-ish sigh I'd ever heard a grown man make, and it took me a second to realize that he was staring at us because he was waiting for us to leave.

I started to gather up my stuff, but Cassandra stood motionless. "I have so many questions," she said.

"I'm sure you do," Brian said, putting a hand on her shoulder and turning her around toward the door. "I will answer them. Six p.m. tomorrow in the gym. We'll start practicing for Returns. Until then, if either of you is babysitting, I suggest you don't do it alone, and don't let Janis do it alone either."

"That won't be a problem," I said, "Janis doesn't want to babysit ever again. She quit the club this morning."

"I'm sorry to hear that, Esme," he said. "I know how much the babysitting club meant to you." I realized he was speaking as Brian, Dad's best friend, not as Brian, whatever the hell he was to me now. I looked at my shoes and mumbled thanks. Obviously, I had plenty to worry about—I'd gotten into a fight, used supernatural powers to get out of it, and was now sitting in a high-tech closet with my dad's best friend, who wasn't at all what he'd seemed. But still, the demise of the babysitting club hurt. It had been over for less than a day, but I already felt a best-friend-sized hole where the club used to be.

Cassandra still didn't move, but when Brian gave her a little shove, she reluctantly started walking.

The closet door noiselessly slid shut behind us, and before we knew it, we were outside, standing on his front porch as he locked the door and then hurried to his car. He climbed in and started the engine, and it took me a second to realize he wasn't going to offer us a ride. I walked over and knocked on the window, and he rolled it down a crack.

"So, wait, what are Sitters responsible for again?" I asked.

"Protecting the world," he said, then threw the car in reverse and zoomed out of the driveway.

"Huh," Cassandra said. "Not as important as football, I guess."

"Not in this town, at least," I said.

CHAPTER 17

"So," I said, looking at Cassandra, not knowing where to start. "We're Sitters."

"Hell yeah." She grinned, opened her flannel, and pulled out an ornate dagger that looked like it had been carved out of a single piece of jade.

I gasped. "You stole that? There's no way Brian won't notice that it's gone!"

"Relax," she said. "I'm only borrowing it. And if he hadn't wanted me to take it, he would have kept it out of my reach." She slid the dagger through one of the belt loops in her jeans and closed her shirt back over it. "Besides, there's no way he's going to rat us out to the Synod. We can do whatever we want."

"How are you so sure?" I asked. She had started walking down the street, and I had to practically run to keep up with her. "We don't even know what the Synod is."

"Yeah, but we know it's his boss, and old Coach here has been too busy with a stupid ball to pay much attention to us."

"It's not his fault," I said. "Football is a big deal in Spring River, and like he said . . ." I caught myself. Why was I defending him? Cassandra was right. I loved Brian as much as any interior designer pretending to be a football coach and my dad's best friend, but he *had* been neglecting his duties.

Besides, football was dumb. "So if we can do whatever we want," I asked, "what do we want to do?"

"Everything," she said. "But for now, let's start with shopping." Cassandra screwed up her nose when I suggested we hit the Salvation Army, and was equally displeased when I offered up my favorite secondhand store. "I don't want someone else's sweaty clothes," she said.

"Okay," I said. "Well, if you want new clothes, you can get them at Costco, like everyone else in this town, or Norman's."

"What's Norman's?"

"It's like a department store that has expensive jeans."

"Good," she said. "Let's go there."

Norman's had been a Spring River institution since the sixties, and I was pretty sure we were the only people in the history of the store to have ever taken the bus there. When it squealed to a stop in front of the main entrance, Cassandra got off and stared at the window displays with a look of satisfaction on her face.

"This place is perfect," she said.

"This is bougie boring-people clothing," I said. "I could spend all my babysitting money here and buy, like, one gray T-shirt." Cassandra was marching toward the door, and something about the look of determination on her face made my stomach turn. "Cass, there's no way we can afford to buy anything here."

"Good," she said, giving the heavy glass revolving door a shove, "because we're not buying anything."

"But you said we were going shopping." In my confusion, I jumped in the door right after her, causing both of us to take awkwardly tiny steps as she pushed it around.

"When I said 'shopping,' I meant 'shoplifting,'" she clarified.

Of course. I should have known. As soon as we were inside, Cassandra looked around, a grin on her face, and across the store a rack of scarves went up in flames, nearly scorching the shellacked bouffant of the sales associate standing next to it.

"Oh my God, a fire!" Cassandra screamed, sending everyone in the store into a panic. Before they knew it, several yards away a table display of Uggs was aflame, and while it was a gratifying sight, this was making me super nervous.

"Cass," I hissed, "cut it out. Somebody could get hurt."

"Chill," she said, making a beeline for the juniors section. "I won't let that happen. I'm keeping the fires small on purpose. If they get out of control, I'll put them out." She stopped and looked around, and then focused her gaze on the ceiling. A security camera started to smoke, filling the air with the smell of melting plastic as Cassandra made her way through the racks, pulling out jeans, sweaters, and T-shirts. The fire alarm started shrieking, an earsplitting pulse punctuated with a blinding flash. Cassandra strolled behind the register, grabbed a large shopping bag, and stuffed it full of everything she had in her arms.

I was sweating rivers, and could feel that my pits were soaked. Cassandra started toward the door, all the security cameras in her path crackling and smoking as their lenses shattered from the heat. Most of the other shoppers had fled the scene, and the only people left in the store were employees and a few voyeurs recording everything on their cell phones. Outside, a screaming siren was getting closer and closer, and behind us, flames started to crawl down the Clinique counter.

"So you've destroyed a store," I said to Cassandra, "but all that stuff has security tags, so it's not like you can get it out of here anyway."

The words were barely out of my mouth when the alarm panels flanking the door caught fire. Cassandra smiled at me, then strode between them and right out the door.

At home, I shampooed twice and still felt like I couldn't get the smell of burning Coach bags out of my hair. The next morning, the "electrical fire" at Norman's had made the front page of the paper. I read every word, and fortunately there was no mention of two teenage girls who remained suspiciously calm while everyone else freaked out.

Cassandra was wearing some of her new clothes at school, and there was a frayed slit in the back of her new denim jacket where she'd had to rip the security tag out. I was on edge through all my classes. My breath caught every time a classroom door opened, as I expected it to be someone coming in to call me to the principal's office, where the cops were surely waiting to arrest me for being an accessory to looting. But nothing happened, and no one ever came calling. It appeared we'd gotten away with it.

I wondered if Brian would take one look at us and know, like we were some sort of magical bank robbers and the improper use of our powers had marked us with invisible ink, but when we ran into him after lunch, he seemed preoccupied, as usual, and reminded us of our meeting that night.

As if we could somehow forget.

The day dragged on, and, as I was starting to do almost every day now, I got a bathroom pass to kill some time during history. As I redrew my eyeliner, I realized that my subconscious must have played a role in my choice of outfit today, which was Coco Chanel at her country house. My Breton shirt could definitely have doubled as convict stripes.

Behind me, the door to one of the bathroom stalls flew open with a clang, and my breath caught when I saw that it was Stephani Riggs, her split ends cemented into a bun on the top of her head.

I wasn't ready for another confrontation already. I wasn't ready for another confrontation ever, and I was straightening up, bracing myself, when our eyes met in the mirror. But she looked straight through me, like she'd never seen me before in her life, and walked right out the door, *without* washing her hands. My eyeliner wings were still slightly uneven, but I grabbed my stuff and booked it back to class as quickly as I could. The whole non-interaction made me cold.

After school, I went home and hung out with Pig, then took the bus back to campus to meet Brian. The sun was setting earlier and earlier now, and the sky was already dark as I walked up to the building. Floodlights illuminated a few strands of toilet paper still flapping in the tops of the trees, but the campus was empty as I headed into the gym, and my footsteps echoed down the hall. Cassandra was already waiting on the bleachers when I walked in, and neither of us said anything as I sat down next to her.

A few minutes later, the double doors at the opposite end of the gym opened, and Brian walked in, pushing a dolly with two very large, very old-looking boxes on top of it. The rubber wheels squeaked on the wood floor, but as he got closer, I noticed that Cassandra sat up straighter, and without meaning to, I followed suit.

He stopped in front of us, then held out his arm, palm out, like he was telling someone to talk to the hand, and then spun in a slow clockwise circle, mumbling something

I couldn't understand. I felt a slight cool breeze as his eyes moved over us. When he was done, he sighed.

"Are you, like, praying or something?" Cassandra asked.

"No," he said. "I'm sealing the space so no one else can get in."

"So you're locking the doors."

"It's more complicated than that," he said, sounding slightly annoyed. "The doors will be unlocked, but if anyone looks in the windows, the gym will appear empty. Even if they came here to enter the gym, they will lose all interest as soon as they touch the door. No matter what happens in this room, no one on the outside will see or hear anything."

Then Brian bent down, popped the latch on the biggest box, and lifted the lid. He reached into the box and pulled out something that looked like a barbell, with a smooth rod in the center and spiked spheres on the end. Without saying anything, he turned and threw it at me.

I closed my eyes and braced for broken bones, loud noises, pain, everything that would overwhelm me when it hit me and then crashed to the floor. Instead, there was silence and the feel of smooth metal in my palm. I opened my eyes to see that I had caught it, right in the center, right where I was supposed to.

I had expected it to be heavy like a bowling ball, but it was light, and holding it felt as natural and easy as holding on to my phone. Without even really thinking about it, I tossed it into the air and caught it with my other hand.

What the . . . ?

I had flashbacks to every tetherball that had ever hit me in the face, every humiliation I'd ever endured in this very room, every time Dad had said "Catch" and I'd closed my hands over air instead of the keys or remote control or can of soda he was trying to throw to me.

I looked up to see Brian full-on grinning. He reached back into the box and pulled out a long, sharp-tipped spear. He hurled it into the air so that it was spinning end over end. Cassandra stuck her arm out and, like it was the biggest NBD that had ever been dealt, caught it a second before it plunged right into her thigh.

"The skills needed for a Return are innate," Brian said. "They don't need to be taught, since they've been inside you since the day you were born and activated at your Change-over. The most important thing is to trust your instincts. If you can learn to block out the noise that surrounds you in daily life, you will inherently know what to do, and you will do what is right." I cast a side glance at Cassandra, since I was pretty sure that setting fire to a department store and stealing skinny jeans did not count as doing what was right.

"So," he continued, "after trusting your instincts, the second most important thing to remember about a Return is the Sitter law of 'do no harm.' When a Negative demon manages to get into the Definite, you don't want to kill it. You just want to send it home."

"When you say 'demons,' you mean actual, literal monsters?" I asked, and Brian nodded. He turned, held his palm up, and mumbled again. The air in front of him shimmered, and then tiny monsters began to appear, none larger than a penguin. There was something that looked like a cross between a banana slug and one of those blow-up tube men that dance outside car dealerships, and another that looked like a water balloon of maggots.

"Mind you," Brian said as a whole carousel of creatures swirled into view in front of us, "these are not actual size. Some can be several stories tall."

I gulped.

"I've never seen anything like this," Cassandra said, and I nodded in agreement.

"Me either," I said, "and I've lived here my entire life."

"That's a good thing," Brian said. "It means that the Synod's seal is working. When a Portal is not sealed, demons are burped up into this dimension on a fairly regular basis."

"So why doesn't the Synod just keep the Portal sealed all the time?" I asked.

"A Synod seal is the nuclear option," he said, "and as it's a major drain on Sitter magic. It is only deployed in drastic circumstances. To renew it would deplete our powers past the point of replenishing."

"What happened here, then, that made them seal up this Portal?" Cassandra asked.

"I'm not privy to that information. But I know it wasn't good," he said, not looking directly at us and clearing his throat as he bent toward the smaller box on the dolly. Using his foot, he nudged it onto the floor and scooted it until it was directly in front of us.

"Now the whole reason we're here," he said, straightening back up. "To practice."

The box coughed, then started to jerk back and forth and emit a sound like a pack of coyotes going ham on a rack of lamb. Cassandra was looking at it just as warily as I was.

"Why do these things seem so deadly if we're not supposed to harm them?" Cassandra asked, holding up the spear so that the harsh fluorescents of the gym glinted off the sharp tip.

"Oh, I didn't say they weren't deadly," Brian said. "They most definitely are, and even if you're not supposed to harm them, they will try to harm you." And with that, he gave the howling box a sharp kick so that it tipped over onto its side. I was no expert, and I'd never seen one before, but I was pretty sure that what came spilling out of the box was a demon. "This is Kevin," Brian said. "Now catch him."

Kevin was pissed. He was also green and drippy-looking, with one giant eye in the middle of his forehead and another one off-kilter, kind of slightly above his ear, like it had just accidentally drifted over, gotten stuck there, and stayed. Kevin was about three feet tall, with long, slappy feet like they were made from Silly Putty. He sputtered and looked around the room. The eye in his forehead fixed on Cassandra, and the one above his ear looked right at me. He left a trail of slime when he moved, and his feet made squeegee sounds peeling off the floor. He was so gross that he was almost cute. Almost.

"This is our demon?" Cassandra snickered. "He's not scary. What's he going to do? Slime me to death?" Kevin gave her the side-eye, literally, and then almost smiled, one snaggletooth spilling out over his bottom lip. With a gurgle, he started to move toward her, and two arms sprouted out of the goo of his body, the fingers on each hand long and skinny, like pieces of sour-apple licorice. "Still not scary, dude," she said. She stuck out a leg, meaning to nudge him with the toe of her shoe, but as soon as her foot was in reach, Kevin moved as quick as lightning and wrapped a sticky hand around it. Cassandra kicked, trying to shake him off, but Kevin was stuck, and very happy about it, his one rotten tooth on full display.

"My foot is getting hot?" she said, almost as if she were asking a question as she swung her foot through the air, Kevin's gloppy body dragging back and forth across the floor. Then, in an instant, all traces of amusement vanished from her face, and she started to scream. "Esme, it burns, it burns! Get him off! Get him off!"

I tried to grab Kevin with my kinesis, but as soon as my powers made contact with his skin, a jellyfish-like sting ripped through my entire body. I turned, and in one big step, I was at the big box and digging through it, carefully, so that I didn't cut myself on any sharp edges. I couldn't bang at Kevin with the barbell, or throw a spear at him, without risk of hitting Cassandra too. I tossed aside a sword, a dagger, and a flamethrower. Finally, at the bottom of the box, I found it—a platinum trash grabber.

I ran back to Cassandra, opened the pincers, and then closed them around Kevin's midsection. I started to pull, but he had a tight grip on Cassandra, whose screams were getting louder. Still holding on to the trash grabber with my hands, I used my kinesis to empty out the rest of the box of tools, but that was useless, as everything that flew out was sharp or pointy and looked like it would get rid of Kevin by slicing Cassandra's foot right off.

"Brian!" I screamed. "Help me! He's hurting her." In response, Brian crossed his arms and didn't move an inch.

Frantically I unzipped my hoodie and pulled it off, then used my powers to fly it through the air and wrap it around Kevin's face. He howled as his world went dark. With my kinesis, I gripped the trash grabber again and yanked with all my mind's might at the same time that I used my powers to grip Kevin's head through the sweatshirt, digging my thumbs into his big gross eye. He shrieked and let go of Cassandra to try to defend himself. I sprang back and out of his reach. The trash grabber still had a hold of his middle, so I gave it a spin and then released Kevin midair. He arced through the air and landed on the gym floor with a splat. A box of flames sprang up around him, and with a harrumph, Kevin admitted defeat and sank into a puddle.

Cassandra was right beside me. "You okay?" I asked, and she nodded.

"One question," she said, turning to Coach as she caught her breath. "That thing is named Kevin?"

By the end of the night, we had Returned Kevin so many times that I almost felt sorry for him when Coach put him back for the last time. Almost, because as soon as the thought crossed my mind, Kevin leaned over and hocked up a loogie down the side of his box, and I was completely disgusted again.

"So he just lives in your house?" Cassandra asked.

"Kevin works for the Synod," Coach said, fastening a buckle on Kevin's box and not really answering the question. "He has helped train generations of Sitters."

"Does he get paid for this?" I asked, and Coach nodded. I snickered. "With what? Venmo?"

"Rodents, mostly. Worms too, if we can find a good varietal. He's rather picky." I shuddered, hoping I was long gone when it was time for Kevin to collect his wages.

Cassandra and I followed as Coach pushed the boxes back toward the locker room. When we got to the door, he held his hand up and turned in a circle again, this time counterclockwise, to unseal the gym.

"How many people know about us?" I asked. "Not me and Cassandra, but Sitters in general."

"Non-magical people?" he asked, and I nodded.

"We like to keep that number at zero," he said. "Normies

don't believe in magic, so if one is accidentally exposed to it, like during your tussle with the cheerleading squad yesterday, we like to take care of it as quickly as possible." I shivered a bit, remembering the blank look on Stephani Riggs's face when I'd run into her in the bathroom.

"So you just, like, muddle up their mind until they don't remember?" Cassandra asked.

"It sounds harsh, but yes," he said. "Knowing about the Sitters only puts people in danger. You are protecting people by not sharing your true identity." He stopped for a minute and looked back and forth between the two of us. "Who knows about you?"

I was about to say "Janis and Dion," but Cassandra spoke first. "No one," she said, and said it definitively. Before I could stop myself, I shot her a look of surprise, then hoped that Brian hadn't caught it. I'd have to wait until we were alone to find out why she'd lied.

I had one more question, something I'd been wanting to ask all night. "Did being a Sitter make my mom like she is now?"

Brian shifted in a way that made his tracksuit rustle. "I wish I knew, but I don't. It could be that the stress of being a Sitter eventually broke her," he said, "or it could have nothing to do with being a Sitter at all."

Cassandra stepped in. "And my mom? She battled demons and protected kids and did all sorts of stuff, then just died in a car wreck like she was a telemarketer or something?"

Brian looked down and scratched a spot above his elbow.

I could hear the rasp of his fingernails on the nylon. "I'm sorry," he said. "I know that it's hard to believe for both of you, but even in our world, magic isn't everywhere. Sometimes Sitters have breakdowns, or are just in the wrong place at the wrong time. Even superhumans are still human."

Cassandra stared at him, her dark eyes obsidian marbles, and finally Brian cleared his throat. "Good job tonight," he said, looking back and forth between us. "There's a lot of hard work and practice ahead of us, but we're off to a promising start."

Cassandra was quiet as we walked back across campus. "Hmm, seems like we're the ones doing the hard work and practice," she finally grumbled, "He just stood there."

"Why'd you tell Brian that no one knows about us?" I asked. "Dion knows, and Janis knows too."

"He's not telling us everything he knows, so why should I tell him everything I know?" She was heading to the parking lot, and without thinking, I followed her.

"He's the only person who's told us anything," I said, playing devil's advocate, even though I knew exactly what she was talking about. "Besides, we're going to be training for a long time, so this is just the beginning of what we're going to learn." I wasn't sure I really believed what I was saying. I just wanted to hear her confirm what I was already thinking.

She pulled her new jacket tighter around her. "He's

lying," she said. She fished a stick of gum out of her pocket and folded it into her mouth, then crumpled up the wrapper and dropped it to the ground.

I groaned and picked it up, then held the wrapper out to her. "What do you mean, he's lying?"

"About our moms. Esme, think about it. He's sitting there telling us how everything in our lives in predetermined, and yet somehow we're supposed to still believe that my mom just died in a car wreck and your mom just snapped? And right around the same time?" She smacked her gum. "I don't buy it. I mean, the guy has a Bat Cave hidden in his closet, and this Synod sounds like the Illuminati on Adderall, but when it comes to our moms, they're just like, 'IDK, coinkydink?'" She held up her hands and raised her eyebrows in mock stupidity.

"I know," I said. "I actually think you're right. Only, I don't know exactly what he's lying about." I was still holding the gum wrapper, but she wasn't taking it, so I put it in my pocket.

"I'm going to find out," she said. "Though I assume you're just gonna do you and do whatever he tells you?" she asked.

"No. Not exactly, at least. But I'm also not trying to rebel against something I don't even understand yet."

"I'm not either," she said. "I'm just trying to be careful. Until we understand what's really going on, I think it's safer to leave Janis and Dion alone. They know you can move stuff and I can start fires, and we can just leave it at that. We don't have to tell them about the spells, or the Portal. I don't want their brains turned to peanut butter, okay?"

I didn't like lying to Brian, but she had a point. The last thing I wanted was to do something that could get Janis in even more danger.

"Are you going to take the bus?" she asked.

I shook my head. "I'm going to walk." I started to walk away, but turned around when she grabbed my wrist and pulled me back.

"Esme, this is bigger than us, but it's also about us," she said. "We're seventeen, and up until now, our lives have pretty much sucked."

"Speak for yourself," I said automatically, but I knew I wasn't being completely honest. So did Cassandra, and she rolled her eyes.

"Trust me, I want to do all this rad stuff Sitters do, and I am going to fulfill all my responsibilities, but I'm also going to have some fun with it. And you should too."

"Because we deserve it," I said.

She nodded. "And because we can. We're powerful," she said. "You are powerful. Don't forget that."

I figured I'd just go home, but my feet had a mind of their own. They were headed to see Mom, and were taking the rest of me with them. Usually when I walked, I put my headphones on and zoned out, imagining I was someplace far away doing something very different. Today, though, after everything that Brian had told us, I had an urge to stick my head down drains and peer in dark windows.

Cassandra's words echoed in my mind. Yeah, so maybe she was a rule-breaking, fistfighting shoplifter, but maybe she was also right. You are powerful, I said to myself, then repeated it again and again like it was my mantra. As I walked down the block, I almost wanted someone to jump out of the shadows to screw with me, just so I could show them who was boss. It was me. *I* was the boss. When I got to an intersection, I crossed the street without even waiting for the light to change. At the facility, I signed in to the visitors log and was escorted into her ward.

In Mom's room, the TV was on, some game show with the volume turned down, and she was sitting on the bed, just staring straight ahead at the pictures I had taped to the wall. There was one of me, Dad, and her from my first birthday, grinning and gathered around what easily could have been a big cookie cake from the same cart where Janis would someday work. One of me and Dad from my fourth-grade Christmas recital, where I'd played a camel. One of young Mom on a beach. One of young Dad riding a bike. And the most recent pic was from Thanksgiving last year, all three of us looking like we'd rather be someplace else, Mom focused up and off to the right, not looking toward the camera.

A few years before, I'd bought her a whole bunch of clothes from the thrift store and brought them in, but one of the nurses had told me that they didn't have time to dress the patients in "outfits." In all the before pictures I'd seen of her, she had dressed cool and creatively, like she had set trends instead of followed them, but now she was wearing sweatpants with dirty hems, and some slippers that had probably come from the dollar store.

I sat down in a chair across from her and started doing what I normally did—talking. Only, instead of the normal nothing I used to fill the air with, this time I talked about how I'd felt currents of power run through me when I dangled Stephani Riggs in the air by her ankles. How Cassandra's recklessness was scary and exciting at the same time, and how I could feel myself changing by the day. After about five minutes, I realized that something felt different. I wasn't just talking. She was listening,

Mom didn't take her eyes off me the whole time I was speaking, and when I finally stopped, we sat there in silence, looking at each other. Then she got up, walked over to her dresser, and opened the top drawer, the one filled with what Dad and I referred to as her collection. She reached down and scooped up an armload, then came back and dumped it into my lap. Glue sticks, plastic barrettes, souvenir key chains, glitter gel pens, jars of spices, eyeshadow quads, dog biscuits, balloons, goggles, fruit-shaped erasers, and more. I looked up at her, and she uttered the most coherent sentence I'd heard her say in years.

"Been saving." With her teeth, she bit off one of her fingernails, then spit it out. "For you." She pulled at her ponytail, strands of her hair tangling in her fingers. "Esme." Then she turned and went back to being absorbed in an infomercial for leggings that zipped off into underwear.

Her back was to me when I started to cry.

When visiting hours ended, I said goodbye to Mom and started my slog home. I'd walked there because I'd wanted the space to clear my head after Returning Kevin so many times, but now I had no desire to walk anywhere. I would walk, though, because it was late enough that the bus only ran twice an hour, and calling Dad for a ride would only lead to unwanted questioning about where I'd been and what I'd been doing. He'd texted me earlier telling me there was pizza, but I'd been too busy to respond. Now if I just showed up at home, he'd assume I'd been out babysitting again or that Janis had dropped me off.

I wearily started down the block, and did a double take when a familiar van pulled up at the corner. It idled there, and then the window cracked. "Esme?" called a voice.

"Dion?" I called back, even though I was sure it was him because no one else in Spring River drove a car like that. No one else in the world drove a car like that.

"Where are you going? Do you want a ride?"

"I'm just heading home, and yes, I do. What are you doing down here?"

"I could ask you the same question," he said, helping me open the door so that I could climb in.

"I was visiting my mom," I said. "You?"

"On my way home from work," he said. "The condos are behind schedule, which means more overtime for me." He seemed stoked about this, and rubbed his thumb and forefinger together in that universal sign for gimme-dat-cash.

"Did you get the walls dry?" I asked, and the confused look on his face told me I had gotten it wrong. "Never mind," I said quickly. "What are you doing now?"

"I was trying to find a place to get something to eat, but it looks like the only place open is McDonald's, and that's what I had for breakfast. And lunch." In the glow of a stoplight, I could see his smile.

We made small talk about his job, where he'd been putting up the drywall, not drying the walls, apparently, and about Spring River's lack of culinary options, and before I knew it, we were in front of my house. Once again, the drive had gone by way too fast.

Dion parked, and a low grumble filled the car. "Was that my stomach or yours?" he asked, making me realize I hadn't eaten anything since lunch.

"Let's assume it was both." I continued, "Do you want to come in? We have pizza." As soon as the words were out of my mouth, I bit my tongue in surprise. Who was this bold new person inviting a hot guy to come into her home? But I had no time to reconsider, as Dion was nodding and unbuckling his seat belt.

Thankfully, Dad had gone to bed, so I didn't have to do any awkward introductions, at least between humans.

Normally a cuddle monster, Pig chose tonight to act weird and protective. As soon as Dion came in, she went to her bed in the corner, but instead of lying down to snooze, she just sat there, staring him down.

"I think your dog is mean-mugging at me," he said.

I tried to send Pig a mental message to help me out here, but instead I could just hear her farting, which made me glad she was on the other side of the room. "Ignore her," I said. "She thinks this is her house."

I could count on my chin the number of times I'd had a guy over—one. This one. So I wasn't sure what to do. Did I put pizza on plates? Should I ask him if he wanted a fork? Though who ate pizza with a fork?

Telling my brain to shut up, I just grabbed the box and a couple of paper towels, then went back into the living room, where Dion was sitting on the couch. "It's cold," I said, "and TBH, it probably wasn't that good to begin with, but it is food."

"That's all that matters," Dion said, helping himself to a slice. I did the same, and we chewed in silence. I flipped on the TV, then flipped it back off as soon as I realized it was a *Grey's Anatomy* make-out scene.

"So," I said, casting around for something to talk about. "How's the house going?"

"Expensively," he said. "At the rate I'm going, I should be able to add two or three tiles to the bathroom every other week. It's going to take forever." He gave a little smile. "I asked Cass if she couldn't just use one of those spells you guys have to conjure up a Home Depot gift card, but she wasn't having it."

I almost choked on my crust. This was a surprise. I'd thought she wasn't going to tell him about the spells. Also, using spells to get stuff for free was exactly the kind of thing that Cassandra was all about.

"Oh, she told you about that?" I asked, trying to sound casual.

He shifted and crossed his legs, his body turning now so that it was slightly facing me. He was just close enough that I had to remind myself to breathe, and to make sure I didn't have any food on my face. I dabbed at my lips and chin with a paper towel.

"Yeah, all that stuff is crazy. It's like you two can do whatever you want." Now, that did sound like how Cassandra would have explained it. Dion was looking at me so intently that I couldn't hold his stare. Instead I started an intense examination of the chipped polish on my thumbnail.

It was quiet enough in the room that all I could hear was breathing. His. Mine. Pig's. Still, there was something funny about the tone of his voice. It was like he thought Cassandra and I had somehow been given a free pass for everything. He sounded almost envious. "It seems like a lot of responsibility too," I said, trying to get him to understand. "It's kind of overwhelming. I mean, look at my mom, and your parents. Though Brian says that being a Sitter had nothing to do with one of them ending up on another planet and the other ending up dead."

"Brian?"

"Oh," I said. I'd figured that if Cassandra had told him about the spells, she'd also told him about Brian. If she hadn't, it now seemed too late for me to backtrack. "Brian is just like an old dude who's supposed to teach me and Cassandra stuff. He's the football coach at Spring River and one of my dad's friends. Or, I mean, my dad *thinks* they're friends. It's kind of complicated. . . ." I was talking in circles, and realized that I had just made it sound like Dad and Brian were in an on-again, off-again relationship.

Fortunately, Dion seemed to have already moved on. "Did Cass tell you what I found in the basement?"

Huh, I thought, shaking my head. She hadn't, and I was starting to think that there were a lot of things Cassandra wasn't telling me. Dion pulled out his wallet, and from the section where the bills were supposed to go, he pulled out a creased photo and handed it to me.

"That's my dad," he said, then corrected himself. "*Our* dad—Mine and Cassandra's. It's the only picture I have."

I looked at it closely, and it certainly looked like Dion took after his dad. They had the same chiseled features, the same dark hair, the same gaze like a controlled burn. I handed the picture back to him. "He looks cool," I said, thinking back to what Dion had said a few days before, about his dad being in a band and everything.

Dion nodded and looked down at the photo. "I was going through a bunch of old junk in the house and found his journal from right before he died. He wrote songs and poems and stuff, and a lot of it was pretty good," he said. "But he also wrote about their life." He sighed and pushed his hair off his forehead again, the gesture that always made me catch my breath. "It, uh, doesn't sound like our mom was the nicest person," he continued. "It seems like, with all the Sitter stuff, she pretty much treated him like a servant, and I guess she was messing around on him. His last entry was the day that they died, and it looked like they were fighting."

I couldn't read him, and couldn't tell what he wanted me to say to this revelation, but I understood where he was coming from. I'd been there with Mom a million times, scrutinizing any little thing of hers, trying to piece together a picture of who she was and what her life had been like. If I'd ever found a journal, it would have been like hitting my own personal jackpot, though I could also imagine that finding out that his parents didn't get along wasn't exactly the kind of info Dion had been hoping for. "Why would he hide his journal in the basement?" I asked.

"I guess he really wanted to make sure she didn't find it." Dion fidgeted again, and from her dark corner, Pig gave a small grunt. "To be honest, his side of the account sounds pretty accurate to me," he continued. "I don't remember much, but I do remember how everything was always about my mom. That had to be hard on him, you know? I think Cass is a lot like my mom, and I'm probably like my dad, so it's no wonder that we don't always get along. She really sees Mom as this perfect superhero, which maybe she was, but she was still human."

Wow. After telling me she wasn't going to tell him anything, it looked like Cassandra had pretty much told Dion everything.

"So why do you worry about her? Cassandra, I mean," I asked. "She seems like someone who can handle herself."

"I guess it's just that . . . if she thinks our mom could do no wrong, then what if she thinks that about herself too? And maybe it's the older brother in me, but it seems like there are a lot of ways things *could* go wrong." He paused for a beat. "A lot of ways that she could make things go wrong. I've been cleaning up Cass's messes my whole life, and I don't expect anything to change now that she's a firestarter."

It felt weird to be talking about her behind her back, but I had to admit that I felt the same way about Cassandra. That day behind the annexes with the cheerleaders, she hadn't given anything a second thought. She hadn't given me a second thought. She'd just straight up gone for it, consequences be damned. Same with her shopping trip. She had a level of confidence in herself that I'd never seen in anyone else. It went past confidence, even, to hunger. She didn't doubt, for a second, that she deserved to get what she wanted, no matter what she had to do to get it.

Dion sighed, then smiled at me. "Let's stop talking about my sister," he said. "Let's talk about you. How do you feel about all this? Ready to save the world from evil?"

I groaned and rolled my eyes. "I have no idea. Most days, I don't even feel ready to get out of bed. It's weird knowing something can choose you even if you didn't necessarily choose it."

"I can't imagine," he said. "I'm the opposite of chosen. As unchosen as you can get."

I coughed, thinking that if I were a different kind of person, now would be the time when I'd say something coy about how I'd choose him. The thought of me being that kind of person almost made me laugh, so much so that Dion looked at me. "What's so funny?" he asked.

"Nothing," I said quickly, then tried to change the subject. "Want to watch a movie?" It was the first thing that popped into my head, and it wasn't a real suggestion, as I thoroughly expected him to use that as a cue to stand up and say he had to get going. I was prepped for the rejection when he surprised me and nodded.

"Something funny that I've seen a million times before," he said. "I know you probably like smart movies where people talk about how complicated life is, and I'll watch those with you sometime, but right now, I don't want to think." Had I heard him right? Had he just insinuated that this was the first of several movies we were going to watch together?

"I'm flattered, but you give me way too much credit," I said, trying to keep my cool. "My desert island pick would probably be *Mean Girls*."

He started laughing. "But that's serious cinema. So," he continued, a note of teasing in his voice, "are you more a Cady Heron or a Regina George?"

"Wow," I said. "That was a question specifically designed so that you could do some impressive name-dropping."

"Well, were you impressed?"

I nodded. Dion was definitely the Aaron Samuels of the situation, but I wasn't going to just volunteer that information. "I'd probably want to be the Janis Ian," I said. "But that would go to Janis, for the obvious reasons. So I guess I'm . . . Ms. Norbury?"

He wiggled his eyebrows. "I have always had a thing for girls in glasses." It came off as deliberately sleazy, and I leaned over to punch him in the shoulder. As he rolled away, his arm shifted so that I could see the smooth underside of his forearm, the one that was marked with the thick, runny lines of his tattoo. Without thinking, I reached out and traced one of them with my index finger. It was slightly raised, like a scar.

He groaned and clamped his hand down on top of mine, pinning my fingers to his arm. "Don't look at that," he said. "It's embarrassing." I shrugged his hand off, and then leaned over so that I could do the opposite and see it better.

The idea itself wasn't atrocious. It just looked like it'd been done by a middle schooler with a sewing needle and a Bic pen.

"You really hate it, don't you?"

"Yeah." He nodded, looking not at the tattoo but at some point on the floor. "It reminds me of everything I don't like about myself."

It was funny to hear him say something like that. If any-one ever asked me what I didn't like about myself, I'd ask them how much time they had to listen to my answer. I could start with my baby-fine hair, which ended up plastered to my head no matter how much product I used, and end with my feet, which had not gotten the memo that toes are supposed to decrease in size as they go down the line.

But right now I was close enough to Dion to see his chin stubble, and I could attest to the fact that he was actually physical perfection. Except, of course, for the tattoo. Maybe that was why he hated it so much.

"What do you mean?" I asked.

"Just, like, another grand idea that turns out kind of stu-pid. I'm starting to think that maybe moving into this house was another one. Even if I dump every penny I earn into it, it'll never be nice. . . ." He opened and closed his fist, mak-ing the eagle and cactus shimmy as his muscles contracted. "Man, I just keep bringing up the happy topics with you, don't I? Sorry. I swear I'm not usually this negative."

A fully formed idea popped into my head. "Wait here," I said, getting up off the couch. "I have an idea."

I flipped through the stack of papers until I found the one I was looking for, a spell that until this moment, I hadn't known what to do with.

I wasn't going to say anything to Dion until I was sure I

had everything I needed. There was always the possibility that he would reject my offer flat out, but on the chance that he was enthusiastic about it, I didn't want to get his hopes up unfairly.

Melani, for melanikinesis, the power to manipulate ink. I needed an eraser. Mom had given me several as part of her collection, and the spell didn't say anything specifically about how it needed to not be shaped like a fruit, so I chose the bunch of grapes.

Calendula flowers—I had a face toner that had petals and buds floating in it. I went to the bathroom and used tweezers to pull some out, then patted them dry on a Kleenex. Yellow jasper—again, thank you, rock collection, and thank me, Esme, for never throwing anything away, even when I'd long outgrown it. Finally, a paintbrush. That I did not have, but I had dozens of eyeshadow brushes, so same-same.

When I went back into the living room, Dion was standing looking at our bookshelves, which mainly held Dad's DVD collection, but he quickly sat back down when he saw me. I sat next to him and put the four items in a row in front of us on the coffee table. "I think I can fix your tattoo," I said, and the look on his face made me smile. "Not with needles but with magic."

"Oh," he said, leaning forward and looking at the stuff on the table. "Really? You could do that?"

"No guarantees," I said. "But I can try. What would you want it to look like?"

"Just better," he said. "Like it was done by someone who

knew what they were doing. Thin lines. Brighter colors. An eagle that looks more majestic and less . . ."

"Like a bald rooster?" I asked, and he nodded.

"No guarantees," I said again.

"I know," he said. "I trust you."

I happened to look up at him right when he said that, and our eyes met in a way that made me want to lick my lips, and not just to check for crumbs. I held his gaze for as long as I could without blushing, then cleared my throat and got serious.

I sat cross-legged on the couch, facing sideways, and Dion mirrored me, so our knees were touching. Then I arranged the four items around us and had him hold out his arm. He rested his elbow on his knee and his hand, palm up, in my lap.

I held my hand out over the tattoo and said the word, letting everything else but the image on his skin fall from my mind. Aside from trying to make Cassandra fall asleep—when I'd managed only to make her sleepy—I'd used the spells only on objects or Pig, never another human. Now I felt my hand getting hot, and it felt like it was held over Dion's arm by magnetic force. My fingers trembled slightly, and my heart was pounding. I could hear his breathing speed up, and I wondered if it hurt him, like a burn, or if he felt anything at all.

The skin on his arm started to swirl like oil paints dripped in water, and as I moved my hand slowly up and down, from his wrist to his elbow, I could feel the space between us crackle. I almost panicked when the colors blended together in a sea of muddy brown, but I forced myself to keep my hand steady. Slowly they separated and differentiated themselves, as if red, yellow, black, green, and brown all knew exactly where they needed to go. The cactus filled in first, then the eagle, starting with its claws and ending with the feathers at the tips of a grand wingspan. The snake in the eagle's beak looked like it was ready to thrash right off Dion's arm, and the crown of laurels made the eagle look immortal. The whole thing was so detailed, it looked like it had been painted with a brush the size of a straight pin. It was beautiful.

I stayed totally still until the fizzy feeling beneath my fingers faded, the sparkles on my palm first, until it was just my fingertips, then nothing. Slowly I pulled my hand away and put it in my lap. My heart was pounding, and I could feel that sweat had gathered on my hairline. I was embarrassed to look up at Dion, scared that he might not like it. The only sound in the room was the rush of air through his nostrils. I wasn't even sure I was breathing. He held his arm out, bending it away and then back toward him, flexing and wiggling his fingers.

"Oh my God," he said, looking up at me. "You're amazing. . . ."

Down the hall, a light flickered on. The clunk of a door swinging open into the wall. Dad's door. Seconds later, his voice. "Esme, are you still up?"

Ugh. The *Mean Girls* would have to wait.

CHAPTER 18

I woke up with a smile on my face and got dressed accordingly, in my yellow happy-face sweater, which I typically wore only ironically on days when I was in a really bad mood, and my lavender corduroy skirt. My happiness had nothing to do with Kevin and everything to do with Dion. I had very little experience with guys because there had never really been anyone worth having experience with. Dion was different.

Part of having a "crazy" mom meant there was always this block of ice between me and anyone who came from a family that was even remotely normal, and I couldn't imagine how much energy it would take to melt that ice. Janis was—or at least had been—my BFF, and even with her, I'd hardly talked about Mom because I didn't want Janis to think I was too much of a downer. But I'd never met anyone like Dion. It wasn't even that he and I had talked about Mom. It was just that I got this feeling like I could and it would totally be okay. He brought up serious stuff all the time. Also, even though he'd been joking about Ms. Norbury, I was pretty sure he'd meant it when he'd said he liked girls with glasses.

My high lasted until I got to school and saw Cassandra waiting for me at my locker. Then it was replaced with guilt. Did she know? Did she care? I mean, nothing had happened yet, so what was there even to say or tell her? She'd said he was a real jerk, but didn't everyone with a brother think that? He could have just been a real jerk to her.

"Hey," I said, shooing her aside so that I could get to my lock. As she moved, I saw that she was once again carrying zero school supplies. "No homework?" I asked. Granted, the only thing I had studied the night before was the curve of Dion's ear, but I had still dutifully packed up my textbooks and hauled them around.

She crossed her arms and gazed over my shoulder, down the hall toward the gym. "None that I'm going to do," she said. "Brian said we should only use our powers for necessary purposes. Not my fault if his definition of 'necessary' and mine aren't exactly the same."

I rolled my eyes and pulled my locker open.

My chemistry textbook had fallen sideways in the bottom of my locker, and as I struggled to get it out, Cassandra took a step back and looked at me. "What's up with you?"

"What do you mean?"

"You seem happy," she said, "but also not."

I gave the book a good hard tug and almost fell backward

into a passing pack of freshmen. "Well, last night was weird. Even you have to admit that."

"Yeah. Weird and awesome," she said. "Kevin was kind of small change, though. I want to train with something that's really scary."

I'd finally gotten the book out, and I stood up. "Cassandra, you say that now," I said. "But last night, you were screaming your head off when Kevin was stuck to your foot."

She got a pouty look on her face. "Well, he was stingy. Just not scary." She bit her lip. "I wonder what happens if you accidentally kill something. Is that going against Sitter code if you don't mean to do it?"

"Tell me you do not want to kill Kevin."

Now she looked offended. "Of course not! Kevin's been through enough." Her face brightened at something over my shoulder, and I turned to see Brian swishing down the hallway looking like he had a bee in his jacket.

As he passed us, Cassandra fell into step beside him, and I followed, half-panicked that Brian's look of total displeasure meant he somehow knew I'd used my powers to alter Dion's tattoo.

"What's up, Brian?" Cassandra said. "What's on the agenda for tonight? Are you going to show us the hole?"

Brian didn't miss a step, and didn't look at her. "You shouldn't be talking to me at school," he said out of the side of his mouth, "and you definitely shouldn't be talking to me about *this* at school." I put a few steps between us so it would look like we were maybe going to the same place, just not together, but Cassandra kept pace right next to him.

"Whoops, my bad," she said. "So, are you going to show us the hole?"

Now he stopped and turned to her. "What did I just say?" he said. "Also, please do not refer to the Portal as a hole. It's diminishing language." He resumed his stride. "We're not practicing tonight. Haven't you seen the news?"

"The viral video where the cow does ballet?" I asked. "It was all over my feed this morning." Brian shot me the most withering of stares.

"No," he said. "Actual news. Bishop Ward beat Pawnee East, which means if we don't win this Friday's game against West Mission, we can kiss our shot at state goodbye."

Cassandra stopped walking. "Of course. Football," she sighed. "You consider that news."

Brian made a flustered noise. "I've got to call double practices for the rest of this week," he said. "We'll resume your training next Monday."

"Are you serious?" Cassandra asked. "Tomorrow is Halloween. Isn't that like demon spring break?"

Brian glanced nervously up and down the hall as students and teachers flowed past us. "Even if the Portal hadn't been sealed by the Synod, Spring River has never seen much activity on Halloween. Most of the demons travel to hot spots like Disneyland."

"Disneyland?"

Brian nodded. "All those kids in one place, and people

in costume. Keeping the demons out of there is like playing Whac-a-Mole. I'm always thankful I wasn't assigned Anaheim." Brian nodded at a passing administrator, then looked back at us. "I really have to go, okay? We'll go full speed ahead next week. Until then, I promise there's nothing to worry about. If you're really itching for something to do, I can see if Kevin's available."

"Don't bother," Cassandra said. "We'll just go trick-or-treating with the normies. Maybe we can catch someone trying to smash a pumpkin or steal a Baby Ruth."

"Did you talk to the Synod?" I asked, not wanting to let him go. "About the Goblin King and Voldemort?"

He glanced up and down the hall, more impatient with each second. "I did," he said. "And they confirmed that there has been no Portal activity in Spring River. Nothing has passed in or out, and they suggested that the next time someone breaks into a house while you are babysitting, you do not handle it yourself and instead call the police."

"Ha," Cassandra scoffed. "You yourself said they were useless."

"Against demon activity, yes, but that is still the protocol with . . . uh . . ." He paused and seemed to cast about for the right word. "Perverts," he said finally. "I really have to go. The only way we can get away with this much interaction at school is if you two decide to manage the football team."

"Gross," I said at the same time Cassandra said, "Never."

"That's what I thought," he said. "Now bye."

"Maybe I should just burn down the football stadium,"

Cassandra said as he turned the corner out of sight. "That would get his attention."

"I have to babysit tomorrow," I said. "You should come with me."

Cassandra smiled. "Perfect," she said. "I'm excited. I don't think Sitter do-no-harm rules apply to human kidnappers."

I nodded, but hoped that Cassandra wasn't going to get to test her theory, even though I had to admit that I had a feeling too. Babysitting on Halloween—what could not go wrong?

In spite of the existence of the movie *Halloween*—basically the blueprint for the let's-torture-the-babysitter genre—I'd never been freaked out about babysitting on Halloween. Until now. Cassandra had a point. What better way to catch a kidnapper than being with a kid? I wasn't even sure we were actually trying to catch a kidnapper. It just kind of seemed like, well, what else were we supposed to do, now that we knew we had superpowers but the only person who could tell us what to do with them was busy with a bunch of androgen-addled primates who only knew how to drink water when it was squirted directly into their mouths?

As I waited for the bus after school, I pulled out my phone, took a deep breath, and then hit one of the two numbers in my favorites. I grew more nervous with each ring. Janis and I hadn't talked much since the night at the Reynoldses'. Even a week ago, it would have been inconceivable that I would hang out with a guy and *not* rehash every second and dissect every detail with her. But I hadn't even told her about Dion yet, and that wasn't what I wanted to talk about now.

The call went to voice mail, and I hung up without leaving a message. I was about to put my phone back into my bag when she called me back.

"Hey," she said, and I could tell she was driving.

"Hey," I said.

Silence.

"What's up?" I added.

"I was going to call you," she said. "I don't think I'm going to dress up tomorrow. My mom accidentally washed my wig and now it looks like crap, and I kinda already wasn't really feeling it."

"Okay," I said. Janis's wig was a frizzed-out red triangle she'd ordered from Amazon weeks before, so if she said it looked like crap now, it must have been really bad. We'd been planning on going as our redheaded fashion heroines. She was going to be Grace Coddington, and I was going to be Vivienne Westwood. It was an idea that had been sparked by a pair of knockoff pirate boots I'd found at the end of the summer. My outfit was going to be perfect.

"Oh yeah," I said. "No worries. I'd kinda forgotten about it anyway."

"Cool," she said. "I'm glad you're not mad."

I saw the bus round the corner, and I pulled out my card to get on. "I wanted to ask you about that night you were babysitting."

She responded with nothing.

"You remember that night that someone came into the house dressed like Voldemort?"

"Yes, Esme, I remember the most terrifying night of my life. What about it?"

Ugh. I wanted to kick myself. I couldn't believe I'd said something that stupid.

"I wanted to ask you about what you saw. What did it look like?"

"You've read the books. You've seen the movies. You know what Voldemort looks like. Black cloak, botched nose job. The whole deal."

I swallowed. "Did it look human?"

She was quiet again, but even through the phone, I could tell that it was a different kind of quiet.

"Kind of," she said. "Yes and no. It gave me a weird feeling, like I was hyper and pissed off. You know like when you drink too much coffee? It made me feel like that."

I nodded, even though she couldn't see me. That definitely sounded like a demon from the Negative.

"But I saw its shoes, and those were definitely human."

"Janis! You saw its shoes, and you're just mentioning this now?"

"I was scared out of my mind, okay?"

"Okay," I said. "I know. But what kind of shoes were they?"

"They were like that kind of boot that Aaliyah wore, and then they did that Off White collab . . ." I was dumbstruck, and I didn't know which was more mind-blowing, that the kidnapper had worn Timbs, or that Janis appeared to have forgotten what they were called.

Halloween was my favorite holiday, but I woke up with a sense of dread that even the smell of fake blood in the air couldn't dispel. I dragged myself out of bed and stared at my closet. Janis or no, I couldn't let Halloween pass without a costume. This was the only day all year when I almost didn't hate my school, because on Halloween, the halls are hyped on horror and sugar, and even the teachers get into it. You can find Freddy Krueger teaching math and Norman Bates giving a sex ed lesson, and the cafeteria just gives up on cooking and passes out Tootsie Rolls and peanut M&M's. I had to figure out what I could pull together from the clothes I already had, since rolling solo as Vivienne made me too sad. When my eyes settled on a tan, cable-knit cardigan, I knew exactly what I was going to wear.

Fifteen minutes later, in a forest-green mock turtleneck, said cardigan, knee-length floral skirt, cream-colored tights, and penny loafers, I, Esme Pearl, Babysitter on Halloween, left for school dressed as Laurie Strode, babysitter in *Halloween*.

No one got it. Oh well.

• • •

Even with the costumes and the candy and the girls screaming bloody murder to stoke the ego of every idiot in a hockey
mask, the day was a drag. Janis didn't dress up, and Cassandra was nowhere to be seen, and the cafeteria made a
big deal about a "two-per-person limit" on the Tootsie Rolls,
even though they were, like, the smallest size possible. Finally,
I set out for my job, starting to regret that I'd said I'd do
it, even though I definitely needed the money.

The thing about MacKenzie McAllister—or MacMc, as
Janis and I sometimes called her, but never to her face—was
that I wasn't sure that I liked her. Or, more specifically, I
wasn't sure that she liked me. She was well behaved and
caused no trouble, but it was like she'd been a grown-up
since she was seven years old. She didn't laugh at any of my
jokes. She thought most stories were silly ("I prefer non-
fiction," she'd said to me once when I'd suggested a book
of fairy tales), and she considered all games except chess a
waste of time. But as long as I could put aside the fact that
MacKenzie was probably smarter and more mature than
me, she was the easiest money I could make.

Mrs. McAllister left a large plastic pumpkin of candy for
us to pass out to the trick-or-treaters. She and Mr. McAllister were headed to a costume party, dressed as Princess Leia
and Han Solo. MacKenzie was clearly unimpressed with her
parents, but I had to admit that Mrs. McAllister was really
rocking that sex-slave-in-a-precious-metal-swimsuit look. I
guess her eighty-dollars-an-hour Pilates lessons had paid off.

As soon as they'd pulled out of the driveway, MacKenzie

turned off the porch light. "Let's just pretend we're not home," she said. "I'm not in the mood to coo over some half-hearted re-creations of commercial icons taped together by parents who couldn't really be bothered."

"Ooohhhh-kay," I said. "More candy for us, then. What do you want to do tonight?" I still had two hours before MacKenzie would put herself to bed.

"I'm configuring my new phone," she said, holding up the shiny, brand-new device that I'd seen on the counter and had just assumed belonged to one of her parents.

She quickly typed in a password, then looked up at me. "We should have each other's phone numbers, just in case," she said.

I bit my lip to keep from smiling, then recited my number for her. The instant I was done, my phone dinged. Her full contact information, complete with email address and home number. In the company field, she'd entered "Sunrise Elementary, fifth grade."

I trailed after her into the family room, where she sat down on one end of the couch, barely looking up from the screen. I sat down on the other end and started to pull out some of my homework. Then my phone dinged with a text from Cassandra.

omw

Crap. I'd forgotten to clear Cassandra's presence with Mrs. and Mr. McAllister before they'd left, and now I was in the position of having MacKenzie see me break the rules.

"Hey, MacKenzie," I said, "do you mind if my friend Cassandra comes over to hang out tonight?"

She looked up at me, genuine wonder in her face. "Why?"

I could have said for a school project or to study for a test, but I knew that Cassandra wouldn't bring any books, and that MacKenzie would see through that in a second. I settled on the truth. "Because it's Halloween," I said. "And two babysitters are better than one."

"Does my mom know?"

"I forgot to ask her. You can say no if you want, or if you don't like Cassandra, she'll leave. We won't bother you."

She stared at me for a few moments, brown eyes big and serious under heavy brown bangs that set off a smattering of cocoa-dust freckles across her nose. "Okay," she said, turning back to her phone. It looked like she had the stocks app open, probably tracking the progress of her college fund. "That's fine." Which was good, because two minutes later the door-bell rang.

Never underestimate the effect of beauty on guys, or kids. From the minute Cassandra showed up, MacKenzie was way more interested in her than she'd ever been in me. She asked Cassandra all kinds of questions, like where she was from, and how we knew each other. She even played hostess, get-ting up from the couch and saying, "I'm going to get a snack.

Cassandra, would you like anything?" before heading into the kitchen.

As soon as she was out of earshot, Cassandra turned to me. "You're getting paid for this?" she asked. "Who's baby-sitting who here?"

I shrugged. MacKenzie returned with some potato chips on a plate. Cassandra and I watched TV and kept our conversation to a minimum, since it was clear that MacKenzie was listening to every word we said. We also helped ourselves to as much Halloween candy as we could stuff into our mouths, since the trick-or-treaters weren't getting it and it would have been a shame to let it go to waste.

"MacKenzie, here's a Starburst with two pinks," Cassandra said, holding it out. "You want it?"

MacKenzie shook her head. "I don't really like candy," she said. Cassandra responded by eating both pinks at the same time.

Finally, MacKenzie picked herself up off the couch and started getting ready for bed. I could hear her in the bathroom, brushing her teeth, and then she came out to say good night wearing a pair of red plaid pajamas. She was in her room with the door closed a full twenty minutes before her bedtime.

Cassandra and I watched a Lifetime movie about an evil doctor, called *Evil Doctor,* and I gave up trying to explain to her that yes, it was supposed to be this bad.

When my phone dinged, the sound was muffled and far away. I stood up and started picking up couch cushions, trying to find where it had fallen. It dinged again, and again. This time, I could clearly tell that it was coming from the recliner, and I fished it out from between the seat cushion and the armrest. I read the first two texts aloud before I realized what I was reading.

> Esme, it's MacKenzie.
> I think someone is trying to get in my bedroom window.

Cassandra's head snapped toward me, a Snickers raised halfway to her mouth. I swallowed and read the next one.

> I'm scared to move.

I turned and sprinted down the hall to MacKenzie's room at the same time that Cassandra jumped up and ran for the front door.

A few steps from MacKenzie's bedroom door, I slowed and turned my ringer off, then shoved my phone into my skirt pocket. I felt strangely calm, as if this were as routine as handling a kid who didn't want to eat their carrots.

At her door, I placed my hand on the knob and quietly gave it a turn. It was locked, so I held out my palm and focused my mind. As soon as I heard the click of it unlocking, I pushed it open with a bang, practically falling into the room. MacKenzie wasn't in her bed. I crossed to the closet and flung open the door. She wasn't in there either.

I turned, and stifled a scream as a face popped into the open window, framed like a ghost between the curtains billowing in the breeze. It was Cassandra.

"There's nobody out here," she said, hoisting herself up and in, before she turned and shut the window behind her.

Suddenly I wasn't so calm anymore.

"MacKenzie?" I screamed. I ran through the house, throwing open the McAllisters' perfectly organized linen closet. No little girl. Nor was she under her parents' bed, behind the shower curtain, or tucked behind the recliner in the guest room. I ran out the front door and pawed through the bushes and looked up and down the street. Most of the trick-or-treaters had gone home by now; the street was empty except for three skeletons doing skate tricks in a driveway.

I ran over to them, breathless. "Did you see a little girl out here? Eleven years old, with brown hair?"

"Hey," said the tall one, "don't you go to our school?"

"Shut up," I said. "Did you see her?"

"We haven't seen anybody," said the short one.

As I raced back to the house, I could hear one of them yell after me, "What'd you do, lose a kid or something?" I tore through the first floor and then went out the back door. There was a full moon, so I could see clearly that the backyard held nothing but an empty swing set making an injured-robot cry as it creaked in the wind.

Cassandra was right beside me. "She's actually gone," I said, turning to her. "There were two of us here, and someone took her anyway. So what do we do now?"

Cassandra opened her mouth to answer just as my phone buzzed in my back pocket. I pulled it out as fast as I could, but it was just Janis, so I hit decline. As soon as I did, she started calling again, so I hit accept. Her words were already pouring out as I put the phone to my ear.

"Oh my God, Esme, did you hear? Does your dad know? Are you okay?"

Normally this would have had my full attention, especially since Janis had been so distant the last couple of days, but now I was ready to tell her that I couldn't talk because I was currently wide-awake and living my worst nightmare. Then the words sank in and I stopped.

"Wait, what are you talking about? Does my dad know *what*?"

"Coach Davis was arrested today. I guess the school got a report about him having inappropriate relationships with a couple of female students. It's all over the news. People are freaking out. Mostly because they're worried about the football team, of course, and not whatever girls he's been fooling around with—"

"Crap, crap, crap, crap, crap . . ." My voice cracked, and I stopped talking. I had no idea what to say or do next.

"Esme," Janis said, her voice softening. "What's going on? You sound like you're about ready to cry."

Hot tears were gathering in the corners of my eyes, and one spilled out onto my cheek. "I'm at MacKenzie McAllister's with Cassandra," I said, taking a deep breath. "Except MacKenzie's not here."

"Well, where is she?"

"She's been kidnapped." My voice was barely a whisper, like I was just muttering under my breath to myself.

"Wait, what? I can't hear you. She took a catnap?"

"Kidnapped," I said, more loudly this time. "She's been kidnapped."

A beat of silence. I wondered if Janis could hear my hands shaking through the phone. "Esme, you're kidding, right?"

"No," I said, choking out an answer, the tears building up in my eyes.

"You and Cassandra, though, you know what to do if something like this happens, right?" Janis said with hope, a hope I was about to shred.

"Not really," I said.

I looked at Cassandra, who was staring at me. Each of us was waiting for the other to do something. Evidently it was my turn to step up. I didn't know what to do, but I did know that Cassandra and I couldn't just stay in this house doing nothing. At the very least, we had to look for her. "Janis," I said into the phone, "I know you're mad at me and I'm really sorry that I've kept things from you, but I need a favor and I will never ask you for anything ever again and will give you whatever you want out of my closet to keep permanently." I took a deep breath. "But right now, I need to borrow your car."

"No way in hell, Esme," she said. "But I *will* give you a ride."

CHAPTER 19

Waiting for Janis to get there felt like forever. It wasn't that chilly out, but I was shivering as we stood in front of MacKenzie's house.

"Did you find your kid?" yelled one of the skeletons from down the block, and Cassandra responded by flipping him off.

"We need Brian, right now," she said, and I almost slapped myself in the face. I'd forgotten to tell her why Janis had called in the first place.

"He was arrested," I said, still not believing that this was all actually happening. "That's why Janis called. Someone accused him of having an inappropriate relationship with some students." Something hit me, as I was too upset to have thought of it earlier. "Oh my God, what if people think it's us?"

"They don't, or else we wouldn't be here," Cassandra said

logically. "And that is obviously a lie. I don't totally trust him, but spend five minutes with the guy, and you know 'pervert' is not his thing."

"Someone wanted to make sure he was out of the way," I said. "Out of *our* way, at least." From down the block, I heard tires screeching, and I looked up to see Janis's Honda rounding the corner on two wheels. It slammed to a stop right in front of us, and Cassandra gave a little smirk. "At least you have friends who know how to drive." She started toward the car, but I felt rooted to the sidewalk. We didn't even know where we were going.

Cassandra must have noticed me lagging, because she turned and grabbed my sleeve. "Try to relax," she said, "MacKenzie is going to be fine, and so will we. This is what we were born to do, remember?"

"We don't have much time," I said. "We have to get her back before her parents get home."

"That's plenty of time," Cassandra said. "If you stop standing there."

Cassandra opened the front passenger door and took shotgun, and I climbed into the back seat. In the rearview mirror, my eyes met Janis's.

"Hi, Janis," I said. "Thanks for coming to get us." These words felt very small, and very inadequate for the colossal levels of relief and gratitude that I felt for Janis at that moment.

"No problem," she said, slamming the car back into drive. "You're my best friend. I'm not going to leave you hanging."

Then she smiled. "But if you get me killed, I am going to be so, so pissed. Where am I going?"

"I don't know."

"You don't know? You want me to just, like, drive around the block and hope that MacKenzie's waiting on a corner?"

"I haven't had time to think," I said. Then I did the only thing I could think of to do: I picked up my phone and tried to call MacKenzie. It went straight to voice mail. Of course it did. I disconnected, feeling stupider and more desperate than ever. Cassandra and Janis were watching me.

"Well?" Cassandra said. "Did you leave a message?"

"Of course I didn't leave a message!" My voice was rising. "She's been kidnapped. She's not just in the bathroom!"

"If she was in the bathroom, wouldn't she have her phone with her?"

"Cassandra!" I wailed. "That's beside the point. What are we going to do?"

Then I got a text. I looked down, and my heart leapt.

"Oh my God," I said. "It's her."

> Hey, Esme. It's MacKenzie.
> Sorry I didn't answer.
> I put my phone on silent because I don't want him to
> know I have it.
>> R U OKAY?
> Well, I've been kidnapped. I'm in a car.
>> we're going to find u
>> keep texting.

Then I added something as an afterthought.

> don't be scared. you're very brave

I had forgotten who I was texting with.

> I'm not scared, just annoyed. I'm going to be so tired
> for school tomorrow.
> We're moving again. I'll send you a pin.
> *Ding.*

And just like that, we knew where she was.

Her pins were coming every few seconds, and as fast as Janis drove, we were quickly closing the distance between us. The sharp turns combined with my already nervous stomach were making me carsick, so I passed my phone up to Cassandra, who held it with one hand while she kept the other on the door handle, maybe so she could throw it open and jump out at any moment.

"Turn left," Cassandra called out to Janis, who sailed through a yellow light. The route was taking us by the university, and the streets were filled with college kids, all in various stages of Halloween partying.

"Do you think Brian used his one call to get in touch with the Synod?" Cassandra asked. "If they can create and erase memories, then surely they can get him out of jail, right?"

Janis swung the car right, down a side street.

"No, no, keep going straight," Cassandra yelled.

"You said 'right'!"

"I didn't mean to turn. Sorry!" Janis swung around in a U-turn, illuminating in her headlights a pack of drunk girls dressed as various sexy animals. A frog in a bustier sat in the gutter, laughing, as a giraffe in garters tried to pull her to her feet.

"Learn how to drive!" yelled a very short-skirted penguin.

Cassandra leaned out the window. "Learn how to fly," she yelled back.

Janis jerked the car to a stop as a group of people dressed like the cast of *Jersey Shore* crossed the street in front of us. Snooki looked like she was barely able to walk, and the whole crew was staggering and taking forever. Janis lay on the horn.

"Oh my God," she yelled. "Get a relevant costume! It's not 2012 anymore!"

The second they passed, Janis hit the gas and peeled out, nearly clipping Pauly D in the butt. Cassandra banged her fist on the dash in support, and then a ding announced another text.

"'We've been stopped for a while,'" Cassandra read aloud. "'I can hear one person talking, but I don't know who he's talking to.'"

"Tell her to text us any detail that she notices," Janis said. "I saw that in a movie."

"MacKenzie gets a medal," Cassandra said. "How is she not scared to death?"

I thought about how well MacKenzie was keeping her cool, and felt bad about all the times I'd wished she were more kidlike. Another pin drop sounded, and Cassandra held up my phone and zoomed in. "'It's a big parking lot,'" Cassandra read. "'There's a big building. It almost looks like a mall.'"

Janis mashed on the brakes, ramming my seat belt into my chest and sending Cassandra, who wasn't wearing one, flying into the dash.

"The mall?" Janis said, her voice coming out as a helium-esque squeak.

Cassandra struggled to right herself. "The mall? Spring River has a mall?"

"Not exactly," I said. "Spring River *had* a mall. There's nothing but a haunted house there now."

Now that we had a destination, Janis was really stepping on the gas. "If we get pulled over," she said, speeding up through a red light, "we'll tell the cops that Esme just got her period. That works every time."

I started to protest, wondering why I had to be the one to get her period, but I decided against it. "How about you just not get pulled over, okay?" I said.

I'd been to the mall a few times since it had closed. It was sur-rounded by a big, dark, empty parking lot, which made it a prime spot for my classmates to get their underage drink on. But tonight the parking lot was anything but empty.

"Oh God," I groaned as Janis pulled into the parking lot and had to nose her way around crowds of people tailgating for the Mall of Terror. "How are we ever going to find them here?" Giant speakers had been set up to blast scary sounds across the asphalt, and I could pick out a few terrifying piano plunks through the din. Glitch static and choppy footage of a girl running were projected onto the side of a building, and masked men in blood-soaked coveralls strode up and down the line of people waiting to get in, stopping occasionally to breathe heavily in someone's ear. The wind had picked up and was whipping candy wrappers and beer cans into frenzied dust devils.

Janis pulled to a stop in what was definitely not a space, and parked her car. I followed her and Cassandra's lead and climbed out. "What do we do now?" I said. "They could be anywhere, and everyone's in costume! And we don't even know what the kidnapper is dressed like tonight."

Cassandra looked around, then walked up to a crowd of vampires. "Have you seen a little girl in red pajamas?" she asked the tallest one.

"I got your red pajamas right here," he responded, licking his fangs and grabbing his crotch.

"Ugh," Cassandra said, reaching up and giving him a quick, sharp punch right in the middle of the throat. "That doesn't even make sense." As we walked away, the vamp was still howling about what a bitch she was.

I tried to clear my head and think. Really think. If you were an evildoer, tonight was the night to get away with all your evil deeds. That was always happening in movies—the monster shows up and everyone just thinks it's their next-door neighbor in costume or something. I didn't think much of the collective intelligence of this parking lot, but I still doubted you could carry a struggling—or worse, unconscious—little girl through this crowd without someone getting suspicious. The mall was big enough that the haunted house couldn't take up all of it, so there had to be some part of the building that was still empty.

I took my phone back from Cassandra and zoomed in on the pin drop McKenzie had sent. "It looks like they're quite a ways away from here," I said. "We just have to figure out how to get in and get over there."

"Hmm," Janis said. "*That* is probably a good place to start." I turned to see what she was pointing at—a set of double doors with a giant hand-painted Entrance sign over the top.

I started weaving through the crowd, and Cassandra and Janis fell in behind me. "Dead Man's Party" came on over the loudspeakers, sending the crowd into a dancing frenzy. "This is so weird," Janis said as she jumped back to avoid a stumbling werewolf. "This is the most crowded place in Spring River tonight. If you were a kidnapper, why would you come here? Wouldn't you want to go someplace where no one would see you?"

I nodded but didn't say anything. I'd thought of that as soon as we'd pulled up and seen all the cars. We definitely weren't dealing with a run-of-the-mill creep, because this kidnapping had "Negative" written all over it. Synod-sealed Portal, my foot.

We'd reached the door to the mall.

"Hey!" some girl squeaked at us. "The line starts back there. You can't cut!"

"Relax! We work here," Cassandra shot back, and then walked confidently past two people taking money and checking tickets. Janis and I were right behind her. The inside was just more of the outside, crowds and spooky music that was played too loudly to be scary, and costumes that were really just monster masks paired with everyday bad outfits. I turned left, away from the Mall of Terror entrance, toward some rolling barricades that were separating the haunted house chaos from the rest of the mall. No one noticed as we slipped behind them.

It took my eyes a few seconds to adjust to the dark. Janis cleared her throat behind me. "Wow," she said. "Now, this is truly scary."

The old mall staples were still there, like a preserved monument of The Time Before Online Shopping: store signs, metal grates that came down when stores closed at night, and the once-cheery tile patterns that dotted the floors. Trash was all over the place, as were remnants of small bonfires and debris from where squatters had camped out. Some of the plants were still green, but when I got close enough to touch the leaf of a palm, I saw that it was plastic. Cassandra kicked a half-full-with-something soda bottle out of the way, which prompted a cascade of skittering sounds in the darkest corners.

I looked at the pin MacKenzie had sent. Now that we were in the mall, recognition clicked and I knew where we were going. "It's the food court, right?" I said. Janis took the phone from me, zoomed in, and nodded.

We started walking, and the screams and shouts of manufactured horror grew farther and farther away behind us. The mall was dotted with skylights, and light pollution and moonshine filtered in, so we could see a little bit. Everything was dusty from disuse, and Janis sneezed right as the food court came into view. There were still visible signs for Just Wingin' It! BuffaLow Wings, and PandaSub, a fast-food chain exclusive to Spring River that sold "Chinese food" on hoagie rolls, amongst other fusion atrocities. If anyone had ever wondered why this town had high cholesterol, they need have looked no further than PandaSub. Even their logo looked like it was about to have a coronary. There were plastic tables and chairs, some toppled onto their sides and others still set like they were just waiting for someone to sit down and dig into a plate of cheesesteak lo mein. I checked my phone again, and it looked like we were right on top of the pin MacKenzie had sent, but we hadn't seen anyone since we'd left the Mall of Terror crowd.

From several feet away, I heard Janis gasp. "Esme," she said, her voice soft and trembling. "What the crap is that?"

It took me a second to figure out what she was talking about, because it was all on the floor. Several of the tables had been pushed aside, and a large space had been cleared. There was a complicated circle, crosshatched with lines and symbols, etched onto the tile in what looked like pink chalk. As we got closer, I could see that the circle was dotted with objects, and with a chill, I realized how alike yet different they were from the things Cassandra and I used to cast spells. A decapitated teddy bear, with the head on one side of the circle and the body on the other; a ball of hair that could have been ripped from combs and scalps; and a half-deflated happy-face balloon that hovered just a few feet off the ground.

I was standing there, examining the shapes, trying to make sense of what they could mean, when something caught my eye over by a Dippin' Dots cart. It was an absence more than it was anything I could actually see—a dark shape moving, absorbed in a task—but I couldn't make out anything more than movement. Then it stepped out of the shadows into the pale cast of a skylight, and I saw what it was: Darth Vader. The black plastic frog-face helmet, and a cape that nearly swept the ground. Then it moved again, and I screamed.

MacKenzie had been hidden behind it, still in her red pajamas, sitting in a chair but looking as blank and lifeless as a cardboard cutout, clearly under some sort of spell, her arms tied together behind her. I started to run toward her, but as soon as I stepped inside the chalk circle, I felt like I'd been shocked. Everything in me burned, from my fingertips to my teeth. It was agony, and I screamed. My body twisted and jumped out of the circle, almost of its own accord, and Janis caught me by the arm as I tumbled into a table and almost hit the ground. If Vader face hadn't been aware of our presence before, he was now.

Cassandra took a step into the circle and yelped when her foot hit the floor. She tried to stand her ground but stepped back, her face twisted in pain. Vader strode toward us, his cape billowing behind him, swishing over the chalk lines, until he was standing face to face with Cassandra. In his hand, he held a Magic 8 Ball exactly like the one Janis and I used to consult on the daily in middle school. He shook it, looked down, and then looked back up and spoke.

"Oh, goody," he said. "An audience." His voice sounded dead and flat, two octaves below anyone's normal speaking voice, but there was still something familiar about it, something that struck a gong deep in my belly.

"We want the kid back," Cassandra said.

Again, DV shook the 8 Ball and appeared to read from it before he spoke. "Go get her," he said.

Skirting the chalk lines on the floor, I moved until I was standing next to Cassandra, and at the same time, she and I started to raise our hands. My intention was to yank his mask off and then send him sprawling onto the ground. I assumed Cassandra was going to torch his robes. But her hands sparked and fizzled, and mine barely emitted a breeze. Plus, it felt like my arm was made of lead. It took all my strength to lift it, and then it was barely up for a second before gravity pulled it back down.

"What the hell?" Cassandra said, her voice sounding like taffy, with her words all stretched out.

Vader laughed. Or, more precisely, he said, "Hahaha," but still looked at the 8 Ball before even saying that. "I see that our Sitters have not yet learned that their magic is not the only magic around here," he said. "How does it feel to be even weaker than your mortal counterparts? To be reduced to what you really are—just a couple of little girls?"

As odd and inhuman as his voice was, I still couldn't shake the feeling that I knew it. I had almost placed it when a scream burst through the silence.

Specifically, Janis burst through the silence, holding a food court chair above her head and swinging it with all her might at Darth Vader's helmet. I'm sure the real Darth Vader had a helmet made of something even stronger than titanium, but this was just a costume from Walmart, and it splintered and cracked. He let out a howl in response, bending over and holding his head, and I saw why his voice had sounded so familiar.

"You hit me with a chair!" Dion squealed, a part of the broken mask still dangling off his ear. Instinctively I glanced down at his feet. Not Timberlands, but construction boots nonetheless. He looked at Cassandra and me, seeming like he was lost, and then something washed over his face, and his eyes turned big and black like he was in the middle of a bad trip. Wordlessly he turned and started after Janis, who threw the chair she was still holding to the ground and ran. He took two steps after her but didn't follow any farther. "She's not important," he said, his voice returning to the cold gravel it had been previously.

"Dion," Cassandra said. "What are you doing? I don't understand this."

He walked over to her so that he was staring into her face, and consulted the 8 Ball before he spoke. "Dion is doing what should have been done a long time ago," he said.

"This isn't funny," she said. "If this is some kind of prank, you can stop now. You got me, okay? You got us."

"Dion is tired of everything in this family always being about you," he said.

"Why are you speaking in the third person?" she asked.

Every time I'd ever been with Dion, I'd studied his face. When I wasn't with him, I thought about it. Now, in the dim and dusty mall moonlight, I looked at it again. Something was different, and it wasn't just the shards of a Darth Vader mask that now hung around his neck, or the costume, which looked cheap and tacky up close. I looked at him, and then down at my shoes, the toes of which had edged up to the pink chalk. A line none of us was crossing. He was staying in, and Cassandra and I were staying out.

"It's not him," I said, looking over at Cassandra. "Something's using him, and that Magic 8 Ball is telling him what to say." I reached out and caught her as she started to step back into the circle. "And whatever that is, it drains us. That's why Janis could run through it when we got stuck." Janis. Crap. Where was she? I screamed her name and got no answer but my own echo. I was kind of thankful, as I hoped that she was hiding far away from whatever this was that was happening.

I turned to see Dion looking at me, his eyes like black rocks. As if on cue, he shook the 8 Ball and read from it. "The unattractive one is always the smart one," he said. Even though I knew it wasn't Dion who'd said that, the words hit me like a slap in the face.

Shake, read. "This is a delight." Shake, read. "Two Sitters for the price of one." Shake, read. "Double the power, double the fun." He walked over to me now.

"Your costume sucks," I said.

Shake, read, smile. "You played right into my hands." Shake, read. "Do you really think I would be . . ." It took forever to have a conversation with someone who had to read everything off a tiny triangle, especially because he seemed to be having trouble, and was shaking it again and again.

"Jeez," I said. "Haven't you ever played with one of these before? If you shake it too much, you get bubbles."

Finally he continued. "Dumb enough to let her keep her phone?"

He reached under his robe and pulled out an iPhone. MacKenzie's iPhone. "You douche!" I gasped. "She loves that phone." He tossed it, and I winced as it hit the tile and shattered. At that moment, as if she had been psychically connected to the phone, MacKenzie came to, saw me, and screamed my name.

"It's okay," I called to her. "We know him. It's just a prank. We'll have you out of there in just a minute."

"I said, it is not a prank," Dion said, still reading off the 8 Ball but with emotion this time. "You played right into my hands, and now I have you right where I want you." He turned and walked out of the chalk lines so that MacKenzie was the only one left inside the creepy circle, right in the middle.

There was no way this was good, and I knew I had to act now that Dion was out of the circle. Janis seemed to have had the right idea earlier, so I followed her lead and grabbed the nearest chair, but before I could smash it into his skull, a tiny flame burst forth in his hand. Nothing magic, just a match. He turned and tossed the match into the circle. It flickered, then went out as soon as it hit the ground. That was it?

I raised my hand again so that I could use my powers to grab a chair, but I didn't have to. Something else, something unseen, blasted Dion off the ground and up into the air. He landed with a thump and didn't move. I heard Cassandra scream.

The air around me started spinning, and within seconds, I felt like I was in a wind tunnel. Dust blew into my eyes, and a piece of trash wrapped around my leg. Cassandra was yelling and pointing at something above my head. A giant whoosh filled the air, and as I spun to follow Cassandra's finger, MacKenzie was sucked up into the air, chair and all, and disappeared.

CHAPTER 20

No one had to tell me that that was the Portal. I knew instantly, just by looking.

It was a giant, swirling pool of all the darkest colors of the rainbow, navy and purple and black and shades that I didn't even have words for. It looked like galaxies, or oil paints floating on water, swirling dark on dark like an endless whirlpool slipping down the drain. It cast a cold glow that illuminated specks churning in the air all around it. Cassandra was by my side in an instant. "Fuuuuu . . . ," she said, the vortex seeming to swallow up her words.

There was something almost beautiful about it, and it was certainly hypnotic. It felt like a part of my brain switched off, and I could have stood there and watched it forever. But the Portal was essentially a door, and now it was wide open. MacKenzie had gone in, and everything else was beginning to come out.

The demon that came through looked like a rhinoceros coated in grape jelly. It seemed to fall through the Portal and just landed on the floor with a splat. It looked around, then raised what passed for its face to the ceiling and let out a blast of fiery breath that smelled like a truck stop bathroom in July. Then it turned and started to walk on its creaky, slimy legs away from the food court, right in the direction of all the Halloween revelers.

I held out my hands, focused my power, and grabbed hold of it, stopping it in its tracks. Cassandra whipped around, and in an instant, she was running toward it, her hand out as an arc of flame leapt from her fingertips and smacked the demon right in the center of the chest. It caught fire and stumbled back. Without even thinking about it, I held both hands up and used my powers to give it a sharp tug off the ground and then launched it toward the Portal. It sailed right through the middle, and with an appropriate flushing sound, it was gone.

So that was a Return.

I tried to scan the space for Dion and Janis—Janis because I wanted to make sure she was okay, Dion because I wanted to make sure he didn't go anywhere. I thought I saw a billow of black plastic cape out of the corner of my eye, but before I could even make sure it was him, there was another demon. This one billowed like an amphibious cloud, like a sheet on a clothesline on a windy summer day. A terrifying sheet. It had no face, and the edges were blurry, as if my eyes couldn't quite tell where it ended. I held my palms up and used my powers to reach for the demon, but the sheet evaded my grasp with ease, rising over our heads, zigzagging quickly on its way toward the flashing lights and screams that were coming from the Mall of Terror.

"I can't grab it!" I yelled to Cassandra, panic rising in my chest. "It's getting away."

Cassandra ran after it, and then with one big leap jumped onto the top of a table and used that to launch herself at it. In midair, she hurled something at it, which hit it and pinned the demon to a plastic palm tree. The dagger she'd stolen from Brian's that first afternoon. I felt a smile spread across my face.

"Nice toss!" I called out to her. Something was coursing through my body, a feeling I'd never felt before in my life. It was as if I were on autopilot, but not because I was asleep. Because I was fully awake, maybe for the first time ever. I wasn't messing anything up. I wasn't making mistakes. I wasn't overthinking everything to the point of paralysis. I was doing everything the opposite of the way Esme Pearl usually did things, and yet I'd never felt more like myself.

Unpinning it from the palm, I yanked the sheet creature into the air, spinning it around and around to disorient it as I took it toward the Portal. Then, with one last swing, I let it go and sent it shooting back into the hole. Again, the flushing sound signaled a job well done.

Just as I was appreciating my Return, a smell worse than melting plastic palm hit my nose. The source of the stench looked like a mummy and smelled like a rotting can of sardines. I choked back my retching, and was wishing I had the platinum trash grabber I'd used on Kevin, when the demon burst into flames and started writhing and howling in pain.

A similar sound erupted behind me, and I turned to see Cassandra with her hand held out, palm up and spitting sparks. Twenty feet from her, a creature that looked like a scaly badger dissolved into a pile of flames. When an octopus–baby doll plopped out of the Portal and onto the floor beside me, I didn't think twice before tying several of its legs in a knot. Everywhere I looked, there was another demon—flying, crawling, slithering, running, hopping, heading straight for the crowd that was just on the other side of the mall. Still, I didn't care about those hundreds of people as much as I cared about one person right now: MacKenzie. My babysitting charge. My responsibility.

I screamed for Cassandra and ran toward her at the same time that she ran toward me, using her dagger to stab something in the neck along the way. "MacKenzie," I wailed. "She's in the Negative. What are we going to do?" I was sweating rivers, but my teeth were chattering like my feet were in ice. MacKenzie was a tough kid. I bet she hadn't even been scared when Dion had kidnapped her. She'd probably just looked at him and said, "Okay. Do I need my shoes?" But now she was trapped in a place more horrible than anything I could even imagine.

Cassandra looked at me, and then at the Portal. "I'm going in," she said.

"What?" I screamed, but she had already turned and was hoisting herself up onto the Dippin' Dots cart.

"I'm going in after her," she yelled. "When I jump, you grab on to me and throw me in."

Maybe I should have protested, told her that she was insane and we didn't know what was waiting on the other side of that interdimensional toilet. But instead I just nodded. "On the count of three," I yelled. "One!"

"Twothree!" she yelled back, and jumped.

The force of Cassandra's jump sent the Dippin' Dots cart crashing onto its side, and I held my palms out and caught her midair with my powers. I'd barely moved her a foot, though, when the force of the Portal grabbed her and started to suck her up. Just being close to it felt like being in the sticky undertow of a million tiny tentacles, so I couldn't begin to imagine what it felt like to actually go through it. It swallowed Cassandra up like she was no more than a piece of popcorn. I'd never prayed before, and I didn't even really know who I was praying to, but in that moment, I made a small ask that God—or whoever was in charge of these sorts of things—would help Cassandra find MacKenzie as quickly as possible and get them both back here fast. Like, five minutes ago would have been nice.

I braced myself for whatever was coming next. With Cassandra gone, I was on my own. I fixed my sights on the nearest demon and was preparing to grab it, when it was yanked upward like someone had grabbed the collar of its invisible shirt. I spun, and all around me, demons were zooming through the air like shooting stars, but up instead of down. The now-familiar flushing sound yanked my attention upward again, and the Portal started to swirl, the demons disappearing right into the middle. Instead of quickly returning to the same size, as it had with every Return we'd done tonight, it grew progressively smaller, and smaller, until it disappeared right before my eyes.

I blinked, thinking, wishing, hoping for a second that maybe the light had shifted and I just couldn't see the Portal now. But no. It was gone. It had taken everything with it, and that included Cassandra and MacKenzie. I screamed.

At the sound of footsteps, I spun around, hands raised and palms out, ready to kinetically blast whoever or whatever was coming for me.

It was Janis, holding a glowing blue object in her hand. "Esme," she said, breathlessly, "it's for you!" She thrust the object out at me.

"It's for you," she repeated. The glowing object was my phone. "It kept ringing, so I answered it." I reached out and took it from her, reeling from the fact that MacKenzie was gone, Cassandra was gone, a hole to another dimension had opened, and demons had flown out, yet something as normal as Janis answering my phone could still happen.

Then she said, "It's your mom."

"What?"

"It's your mom."

Mom? *Mom? MOM?* Mom had never called before. As far as I knew, she had no idea what to *do* with a phone. "Who?" I asked again.

"Your mom!" Janis was yelling now, joined by another voice, this one far away and filtering through the phone, that was screaming my name.

I put the phone to my ear. "Hello?"

"Esme?" said a shaky voice on the other end. "It's Mom."

"Mom? What?" I choked out. "Where are you calling from? Are you okay?"

"Esme, we don't have much time," she said. "But I need you to listen to me. Did you open the Portal?"

"Well, *I* didn't open it, but it opened, yes," I said, still in shock that she was talking. And making sense. "How did you know? What happened to you?"

"I can't explain right now," she answered, "but you need to listen carefully. It is very important that you do not let Erebus leave. Keep him here. Or there."

"Keep who where?" I asked. "Keep Dion in the mall?"

"No. Who's Dion? Erebus. Keep him wherever you are."

"Erebus?" I asked. "Who's Erebus?"

A few feet away, someone cleared his throat. "That would be me," he said.

Without hanging up, I lowered the phone to my side. "Okay," I said. I squinted in the dim light and could see that this man Erebus, whoever he was, looked familiar. He looked like he was probably in his late twenties or early thirties and was dressed like he'd come straight out of a time warp.

Retro, but not in a good way. He was wearing an oxblood leather jacket and a ball-chain necklace, with three days of beard scruff and hair that fell someplace between longish and shortish. He also looked human, totally and completely human.

"What are you doing here?" I asked. "Did you come over from the haunted house?"

"Oh, so that's what you're calling it these days," he said, and laughed. Or, more precisely, he said, "Hahaha," exactly like Dion Vader had a few minutes before.

"I don't understand," I said.

"Of course you don't," he said. "I came from there." He pointed a finger up, but I didn't look. What if it was a trick? And I didn't need to look, really, because with a dawning chill, I knew exactly what he was talking about.

"You came from the Portal," I said. "When we were fighting all the demons."

He grinned. "Ding, ding, ding, ding. I'm the whole reason the Portal was opened. Though I had hoped to bring a lot more friends with me when I came, but you know, nothing closes up a Portal like the passage of a Sitter." He took a step toward me, and I took a step back. "I guess we should be formally introduced," he said. "My name is Erebus. I'm Cassandra and Dion's father."

That was why he looked familiar. He hadn't aged a day from the photo that Dion had showed me. I swallowed, not wanting to let him know his words had shocked me. I found my voice.

"You're why Dion wanted to open the Portal?" I asked.

"Correction," he said, and sniffed. "I opened the Portal. Dion merely helped. I tried leaving it up to him, but he couldn't even successfully kidnap a tot on his own. I kept telling him he should take one from the parents, not a babysitter, but nooo, he had to mess with his sister's friends and do things his own way." Erebus shook his head, just like Dad did every time he talked about the driver's ed car. "I stepped in, because there's no way he could have handled a Red Magic ritual," he continued, like it was the most natural thing in the world.

I was wondering what he was talking about, when the pile of black plastic that was lying on the floor behind him groaned and sat up. It was Dion.

"Dad?" I heard his voice croak. "Oh my God, did it work?" He struggled to get to his feet, and stumbled over the cape, putting a big rip in the plastic. "Where's Cassandra? Does she know?"

"What? Are you stupid? Your sister got sucked up!" I shouted at him.

"What do you mean? Sucked up where into what?"

Dion wasn't playing dumb, I realized. He really was dumb. He had no clue what was going on, and I wasn't going to waste any more words on him. At least not right then.

I turned back to Erebus. "You have to help get your daughter back," I said.

He shook his head. "I don't think so," he said. "It's better for me if she stays where she is. I hadn't planned it, but what a happy accident. I needed you here for the ritual so we could siphon a little magic off the top, but there's no way I could have handled two Sitters, as I'm not up to speed yet." He started to dust off the sleeves of his jacket. "Which is lucky for you," he continued. "Because if I were, you wouldn't be standing here right now." He paused, as if he were thinking about something. "I could try to take you out now, because you don't look like much," he said. "But I'd rather save my strength and come back for you later."

He turned, then turned again, and again, before finally ending up right back where he'd started, staring straight at me. "Now, sweetie, if you could be a dear, I'll be on my way just as soon as you tell me where the exit is."

"It's up your butt," I said. Real mature, I know, but it just came out. Janis was standing behind me, and I heard her make a small snicker that warmed my heart.

Erebus, on the other hand, laughed like he'd never heard anything so funny, and that made my blood run cold. He was actually slapping his knee. "Aw, Esme Pearl," he said, and hearing my name come out of his mouth felt like slime in my ears. How did he know who I was? "No, we haven't met," he added, registering the look on my face. "But I can tell from the annoying voice and odd outfit that you are most definitely Theresa's daughter."

Odd outfit? Who the hell was he to talk? "Excuse me," I snapped. "This is my costume! And how many Denny's booths did you have to slaughter to make that jacket?"

Erebus threw his head back and laughed again, this time

opening his mouth so wide I could see his molars. "That was a great one," he said. "I've always said that if a woman can't be beautiful, she should at least be witty. So tell me, how is your mother these days?"

Through the phone, Mom was screaming my name again, as if she'd heard him talking about her. I put the phone back up to my ear.

"Esme," she was saying, "don't let him leave. Keep him there. Don't let him out of your sight."

"Okay," I said, and raised my hand, palm out, intending to use my powers to knock him to the floor and pin him there. He looked at me, smiled, and disappeared.

Into nothing. Poof. Like a firework.

"Esme?" Mom said after a few seconds had passed in silence.

I found my voice. "He left," I said. "He just vanished."

"Dammit," she said, letting out a tense breath. "You and Cassandra are going to have to split up. One of you should—"

"Cassandra's not here," I interrupted.

"What?" My mom sounded surprised. And not in a good way. "Did he take her with him?"

My voice went up a notch. "She went into the Portal after MacKenzie, and it closed behind her," I explained.

"Who's MacKenzie? Another Sitter?"

"No—" I was getting frustrated. "She's a little girl. Erebus, who was Dion, kidnapped her and put her in the middle of this circle. It was drawn with chalk, and then he flicked a match and she shot up into the air, and there was a Magic 8 Ball . . ." My voice trailed off. I didn't know how I was going to explain all this. It was certifiable. Though if anyone could understand certifiable, it was Mom.

"Slow down," she said. "Take a deep breath. Who's Dion?"

"Cassandra's brother."

Mom was quiet for a second. When she finally spoke, all she said was "Darn." I felt like my legs were made of paper and were about to fold underneath me. Then she said a very Mom thing, the first Mom thing I'd heard her say in my entire life. "Well, I'm sure you did your best. We'll fix this."

I swallowed, the lump in my throat growing bigger by the second. "Where are you?" I asked.

"I'm in my room. But I think someone should be coming in soon."

I started to do what she'd told me, and take deep breaths. We had to get MacKenzie back, and Cassandra. Mom could help me—she clearly knew what was going on—but I needed more. My mind flashed back to Brian's Bat Cave. His wall of sharp objects and his shelves of old books. That was what I needed. That was where I needed to go. No matter what I was going to do, I didn't have much time.

Janis stood a foot away from me, looking at me intently and listening to my conversation. Dion, still looking lost, was trying—mostly in vain—to take off his costume.

"Mom," I said. "There's something called an Uber. I'm sending you one."

"What is it?"

"It's like a ride you pay for."

"Like a taxi?"

"Yes, but people use their own—" I stopped myself, because now was not the time to try to explain the sharing economy to someone who'd been, for all intents and purposes, in a coma for the last decade and a half. "Okay, listen, Mom, we can talk about that later. Go to your window. You see that alley down there? I need you to go there and wait for your Uber."

I could hear her put the phone down, and then she was back two seconds later. "I see the alley," she said, "but the window won't open."

"You're going to have to break it," I said. "Can you do that?"

"Can I do that?" she scoffed. "My own daughter talking to me like I've never broken a window before."

I found myself smiling for the first time since I'd gone into MacKenzie's room and found her missing. "I'm glad you're back," I said. "And I'll see you soon."

I opened the Uber app on my phone and crossed my fingers that Dad wouldn't get a notification as soon as I ordered a ride. I typed in the facility's address for the pickup, and then the address for the drop-off. It was prime time on Halloween, so it might take forever to get a ride, but I breathed a sigh of relief as soon as I could see that Jeffrey in a Toyota Prius had accepted.

Then I called him. "Hi, Jeffrey," I said. "When you pick up, I actually need you to go around back, to the alley. Your passenger should be waiting there. Her name's Theresa. And, like, you don't even need to stop. Just slow down, and she'll jump in."

"What? That's not even legal." Jeffrey did not sound convinced.

"Five stars if you do, Jeffrey," I said. "And a big tip. Like, huge."

"What is this place I'm picking up from, anyway?"

Next to me, Dion started to cough.

"Gotta go, Jeffrey," I said. "I'll see you soon. With Theresa. Remember, big tip!" I hung up, then turned to Janis.

"Janis," I said, "I need one more ride, then you can go home."

"No way," she said, shaking her head. "I'm not leaving you."

"I won't be alone," I said. "My mom will be there." Something about those words made me stand up a little straighter.

"I'm still not leaving," Janis said. "I'm too far down this rabbit hole to turn back now. This night is too insane to even be scary." Part of me remembered what Brian had said, about keeping normies out of Sitter business for their own good, and this part of me knew that I should get her out of there and away from me immediately.

The other part of me, the bigger part of me, was happy that she was there. I mean, she'd hit Dion with a food court chair. Janis was the real MVP in this nightmare. "Okay," I said, smiling at her, "but if anything comes after you, you run, okay?"

"Got it, boss," she said, then pointed behind me. "But what about him?"

Dion was sitting in a chair now, his elbows on a table and his head in his hands. I walked over to him, and when he looked up at me, he looked confused. And scared.

"Esme, where are we? What's going on?"

"Do you seriously not remember?"

He shook his head, and I could tell it was the truth.

"Do you know what all this stuff is?" I gestured at the chalk lines, then picked up the teddy-bear head and held it out to him. He took it from me, turned it over, and pulled a clump of stuffing from its lacerated throat. He shook his head again.

"It was part of a ritual," I said. "You did a ritual to open up a hole that ate a kid and your little sister!"

"I swear, I don't know," he said, looking more confused than before. "I don't even remember coming here. Where's Cassandra?"

"She's gone! Because of what you did!" I was getting frantic and desperate. Janis had come over and was standing next to me, and when Dion looked at her, recognition washed over his face for the first time that night.

"The 8 Ball!" he said, taking it from her and giving it a hard shake. "Dad," he said to it, "did it work? Where are you?"

"Oh my God," I said. "You think a Magic 8 Ball is your dad!"

Now he looked at me as if I were the one whose brain was

cracked. "No. I talk to my dad through it." Of course. That was why he'd been reading off it earlier. It was how Erebus told him what to say.

He shook it again. "Dad, where are you? Did it work?"

The triangle that floated to the top just said, "As I see it, yes." I grabbed it from him, then used my powers to yank him up and onto his feet. I still didn't know what Dion had thought was going to happen, but in this moment, it didn't really matter. All I knew was that I wasn't leaving him behind. Not because I cared what happened to him, but because I didn't trust him for a second.

I led us back through the mall, marching Dion in front of me, with Janis right by my side. I'd given her the 8 Ball to carry, and as we walked, she shook it. Suddenly she stopped dead in her tracks.

"Janis!" I couldn't hide the annoyance in my voice. "Keep going."

"I think you should see this," she said, and passed me the 8 Ball.

I looked down, and the little blue triangle didn't say "Signs point to yes" or "Cannot predict now." Instead it said "Esme?"

In my shock, I almost dropped it. "Cassandra?" I said, then gave it a furious shake.

The triangle floated to the top again, surrounded by a froth of blue bubbles. "Yes," it said. I shook it again. "I'm with MacKenzie," the triangle said.

"Is she okay?"

"I think so." I shook it again, in case she had more to say. "Her eyes are open, but it's like she's asleep."

"Are you okay?" I asked.

"For now."

"What's it like in there?"

"It's grim. I don't know if I can hold out much longer. I am running out of positive things to think about." Her sentences were broken up by what could fit on a triangle, and I had to keep shaking the ball to refresh. I didn't want to think too much about what Cassandra and MacKenzie were enduring, because I was sure that anything I could imagine wouldn't even come close to their reality, and the thought was overwhelming. They were counting on me to get them out.

"You can do it," I said. "Think of bunnies, and free samples, and babies dancing to hip-hop. Just hold on. We're going to get you out."

I looked up from the triangle to see Dion staring at me intently. "Is it my dad?"

"Shut up," I said.

CHAPTER 21

The Mall of Terror was still raging, and we walked silently through the crowd and out into the parking lot, me keeping a tight grip on the back of Dion's neck with my powers. I shoved him into the back seat of Janis's car and turned on the child locks, since I knew all about them now. I punched the address into Janis's GPS and told her to drive carefully. "Not like you normally drive," I said. "We do not want to get pulled over."

"Got it," she said. "Nine miles an hour over the limit."

"Five," I said.

"Seven," she said.

"Deal." She put the car in drive and pulled out of the parking lot with minimal squealing.

"Where are we going?" she asked.

"Brian Davis's house."

"Who's that?"

"The football coach."

The car squealed to a stop. "The pervert coach?" Janis screeched, right along with her brakes.

"He's not a pervert," I said. "He's my and Cassandra's Counsel."

"What is that?"

"It's like a Watcher, but for Sitters," I said.

"A what for what?" Janis swerved to avoid a papier-mâché cow head that had been dumped in the street, a sad remnant of someone's costume.

"He's the Giles to our Buffy," I explained. "Though he claims he's never seen the show. He's supposed to teach us everything we need to know, and we think someone"—I pointed to the back seat—"got him out of the way so he couldn't help us tonight."

"And your Buffy is?"

"We're Sitters," I said. "We're supposed to protect the innocent and save the world from evil."

"Oh," Janis said, sounding very blasé for having just heard such a pronouncement. "It's gonna take me some time to process that," she added.

"Me too," I said. "We just found out this week."

"So far, it seems like you're doing a real crap job," Janis said. I knew Janis well enough to know that this wasn't an insult. She was just telling it like it is.

"We're still learning," I said. Janis nodded and sped up through a yellow light. I could see her speedometer. She was doing eight miles over the limit. I could always count on

Janis. I turned back to Dion, who was buckling his seat belt. "You need to start talking," I said. "And now."

"Where's my sister?" he asked. "Did she go with my dad?"

"Your sister," I said, "is trapped in the Negative after she went in there to rescue the little girl you kidnapped and sacrificed to the demon underworld. Do you even know what you did?"

He started to nod, then seemed to change his mind and started shaking his head back and forth.

"I helped my dad," he said. "So he could come back from that purgatory. He left his journal and the 8 Ball in the house so I would find them and help him. I just had to follow his directions so he could come back." He swallowed and looked out the window.

"What did your dad say you had to do?"

"He wanted me to kidnap a kid. I tried, but I couldn't do it. I mean, it's a kid. But he was okay with that. He said there were other ways. He gave me a spell, like the ones that you and Cass do. But I don't think it worked. There's a lot I can't remember after I did the spell."

"Dion! He possessed you! And he kidnapped a kid while he was you. Why did you trust a spell that a Magic 8 Ball gave you? How is that possibly okay?"

"Esme, my sister throws fire with her hands, and I just met a girl who can move things with her mind. I don't even know what normal is anymore."

I sighed. He had a point.

"What did you think was going to happen if you opened

the Portal?" I asked. "That you and your dad were going to go play catch?"

He sighed and pushed his hair off his forehead in a way that would have made me swoon just twenty-four hours earlier.

"He was going to come back. We were going to be a family again." Beside me, Janis lay on the horn and cursed at someone who was clearly texting and driving.

"OMG, we have a kid to save here, people!" she yelled.

I twisted back to Dion. There was no way the I-love-my-dad yarn was the whole story. "And?" I said. He hesitated. "Seriously, dude? I'm, like, your sister's only chance right now, and if something else happens to her, I will dedicate the rest of my life to making sure your life is every bit the hell that Cassandra is in right now."

He nodded. "My dad said he'd been wronged, and that it was a mistake that he was trapped in that place. He said he was just as powerful as my mom, but that your kind wouldn't recognize that."

"Keep going," I said.

"If I helped him come back, he could finally get what he deserved, and he would share it with me."

"And what was that?"

"Power. And respect." I couldn't help it—I laughed, spraying a mist of spit onto Janis's dash.

"And he told you all this through the Eight Ball?" I asked. "A plastic toy that seventh graders play with at slumber parties?" He nodded. I picked up the 8 Ball and shook it. Since it was now basically an interdimensional walkie-talkie, I figured I might as well use it. "Your brother is an idiot," I said to it.

"You're telling me," the triangle said in response.

We had made it to Brian's, and Janis parked the car on the street, a few doors down from his house. "You never park right in front of the house you're breaking into," she said.

"We're not breaking in," I said, climbing out of the car after her.

"Well, is Coach Davis here?"

I shook my head.

"Did he give you a key?"

I shook my head again.

"Then we are definitely breaking in," she said. "What are you going to do with pretty boy here?"

Because of the child locks, Dion was still sitting in the back seat of the car, looking up expectantly at us.

I walked over and opened the door so that he could get out. Janis gasped. "He's coming with us?"

"No freakin' way," I said. "He's getting into the trunk."

Janis smiled, and then beeped it open.

Anger apparently made my kinesis stronger, and getting Dion into the trunk was no more difficult than loading a sack of groceries. We were heading up the sidewalk when my phone started to ring again. I'd had more calls in one night than I'd ever gotten before in my life. I held it up to see who it was. It was Dad. I debated for a second, then hit decline. He called again. I hit decline again, then thought he was probably calling to tell me about Mom. I took a deep breath and answered it, trying to sound calm. "Hey, what's up?" I said.

"Where are you?"

"I'm babysitting. I told you this morning," I said, even though I hadn't told him anything. "What's wrong? You sound upset."

"Your mom's facility just called," he sighed. "Apparently, she went missing. She broke a window and climbed out."

I tried to muster up sounds of panic in my voice.

"Oh my God, Dad, where is she? I can call MacKenzie's parents, and they'll come home early. I'll get an Uber—"

"No, Es, stay where you are," he said, just like I'd known he would. "I'm going to go help look for her, and I'll keep you posted. The last thing we need is you running around on a night like tonight." I pretended to hesitate for a few moments.

"Okay," I said. "If you're sure there's nothing I can do."

"I'm sure," he said. Then, just as I was about to hang up, he stopped me. "Have you, uh, heard anything about Brian?"

I played dumb. "No. Is there a football game?"

"No. I was just wondering." He paused again. "Did he ever, uh, say or do anything weird to you?" I could tell how hard the words were for him to get out.

"No way," I said, scrambling to think of what I could say that might soothe Dad's worries. "I don't talk to him at school. Being buddy-buddy with the football coach would be bad for my rep. You know that. But I don't think he's offended. He gets it."

Dad sighed with relief. "Okay. Thanks, kid," he said. "I'll let you know if I hear anything about Mom."

"I hope she's okay," I said, then hung up, a smile spreading across my face as I saw her getting out of an Uber across the street.

"Thank you, Jeffrey," I called to the driver, running toward Mom as she was running to me. When we met in the middle of the street, we hugged just like a couple of people in a deodorant commercial. I didn't want to let go, and I could tell that she didn't either, but I finally pulled away. Brian's neighborhood was fortunately a quiet one, and the streets were empty except for a couple of smashed pumpkins.

"Where are we?" she asked. "Is this where you live? Is your dad here?"

I shook my head. "This is Brian's house. Brian Davis." I suddenly realized that Brian's name might not actually be "Brian" or "Davis" or anything involving those letters. "Our Counsel," I clarified, "though he's not here. He got arrested." Mom had been nodding, but her eyes widened at this. "I think someone wanted to get him out of the way."

"But he has the supplies for a Return?" she asked, and I nodded. It was just a simple question, but her words were balm to my chapped heart. She knew what to do, and I wasn't alone with this. I took her hand, and we started toward Brian's house.

I stopped after a few feet. "Mom," I said, "how are you here and not . . ."

I didn't want to use the word I'd been using, but Mom smiled and supplied it for me. "Crazy?" she asked, making air quotes, and I nodded.

"I never lost my mind," she went on. "I was cursed. It's complicated, and I'll tell you the whole story later. Right now we have to find Erebus. Him running around up here isn't good for anyone."

"I met him earlier," I said. "He certainly seemed like a d-bag extreme."

"Someday when we have more time, you'll have to explain to me what a d-bag is," she said, "but for now, I need you to tell me what happened tonight. My release from the curse depended on his release from the Negative. Since I'm here, I can assume that someone let him out. Was it you?"

I shook my head. "I wouldn't even know where to begin to do that. It's football season, so we haven't really started training."

"What does football season have to do with training?"

"Never mind," I said, trying to stick to what was relevant. "But yeah, he got his son to let him out. It looked like there was some sort of ritual? There was a big drawing and stuff, like what we use to cast a spell, but different. And a kid, Mom. MacKenzie. She's gone. She got flushed!"

Somehow Mom had followed what I was saying. "Red Magic," she said. "Red Magic is what normies use to acquire Sitters' powers. It's never good, and it's what got Erebus flushed in the first place. The Red Magic spell to open the Portal requires the sacrifice of a child. If we're going to get the little girl back, we don't have much time."

I took her hand and pulled her up the sidewalk. She was right. There was so much I wanted to know, ten billion questions I wanted to ask her, but all of that could wait until we had MacKenzie and Cassandra back. "Mom," I said, "this is my best friend, Janis. You've actually met before."

Mom smiled. "Oh yes," she said. "I remember. You had on that darling ochre cable-knit and those cute checkerboard slip-ons."

"Esme, your mom has good taste," Janis said.

I figured we should go in through the back, just in case someone was watching, even though, if someone was watching, they had already seen us shove a guy into the trunk. As we rounded the corner, something in what Mom had said clicked, and I stopped and turned toward her.

"Wait," I said. "So all this time, all we had to do to get you back was release Erebus from the Negative?"

Mom smiled, though it seemed a little forced. "It's not that simple. Everything about Red Magic is complex and dangerous, and this is about a lot more than just Erebus." I said nothing. She reached out and squeezed my hand but didn't meet my eyes. "Now come on. Let's get Cassandra back."

Standing on Brian's back porch, I pressed my face against the window to look inside. There wasn't a light on in the entire house. Janis jiggled the doorknob. "It's locked," she said, and before I could offer my services, she leaned down, picked up a garden gnome, and smashed the window. With her elbow, she knocked out the rest of the glass; then she reached in and unlocked the door. My mouth dropped open, and I saw Mom biting her lip. "I saw it in a movie," Janis said with a shrug, then tossed the orb into the bushes.

I walked into the kitchen and flipped on a small light above the stove. What I saw was a shock. It looked like a crime scene, though I guess that's because it was. The place had obviously been searched. Cabinets hung open, and Brian's tall vase of flowers, which I'd admired so much the first time we'd been there, now lay on its side, petals scattered on the floor and water pooling in the grooves between the counter tiles.

I led the way into the bedroom, where the mattress was shoved off the bed frame onto the floor and all the pillows had been split open.

"Dang," Janis said, looking around. "This looks like crap now, but I have to say that I like the coach's style."

"He's actually an interior decorator, not a football coach."

Janis nodded. "Of all the wild things I've heard tonight," she said, "that might be the wildest."

I picked up a few pillows and tossed them back onto the bed. "Brian told us the Portal had been sealed, and that we didn't have anything to worry about for a while. That's why we barely trained."

"Red Magic doesn't play by the rules," Mom said. "And

Erebus was, or is, tricky. To his credit, he mastered more magic than most Sitters. It just isn't good magic." She sighed. "This should have been expected. You shouldn't have been so unprepared." She looked around the room at the mess. "This just looks like normal stuff. Where are all the goods?"

Ugh. I hadn't thought that far ahead. My kinesis could handle a regular lock, but the Bat Cave had probably been built with that in mind. I went over to the closet. The tracksuits had all been cleaned out and tossed onto the floor as well, but I was relieved that the door was barely visible, camouflaged so that it looked like seams in the wall. I was about to give it a good hard kick when I heard Janis behind me.

"Dang," she said. "I had Coach pegged as more Jesus-on-the-cross, but this is wild." I spun around to see her about to put Brian's gold key necklace on over her head. I yelped and leapt over to rip it out of her hands.

"Sure, you can see it," she said, giving me a look.

"Janis," I said, "I love you so much. Where did you find that?"

"It was on the floor, under some stuff." I was sure Brian had left it on purpose, and I sent a mental thank-you to whatever weird holding cell he was sitting in right then. I swiped the pendant out of her hand, then held it flat against the wall and moved it around. When it hit the right spot, it started to glow, and then the wall silently slid open behind it.

Thankfully, everything in the Bat Cave was still in perfect

order. Mom started to laugh. "This is more like it," she said. She walked straight to the wall of tools and grabbed the razor barbell Brian had tossed at me that night in the gym. It was in her hand for just a second before it crashed to the floor, and she was barely able to jump back in time to keep it from crushing her foot and slicing it to bits at the same time.

"Oh no, Esme," she said. "This is not good."

She bent to pick it up. I could see the strain on her face, but the barbell didn't budge. I was next to her in two steps, and bent down and picked it up for her. "You're just rusty," I said, holding it out to her. "You'll get used to it again in no time."

She shook her head. "No, it's not that," she said. "My powers are gone."

I felt like I'd been thumped in the stomach with a soccer ball, and all the air went out of me. "What?"

"You're going to have to get MacKenzie and Cassandra back on your own."

"Mom, I'm not trained," I said as soon as I got my breath back. "I can't do that!"

"You don't have a choice," she said. "You're going to have to."

Mom knew that the Portal flushed automatically when Sitters were doing a Return, but to open it and pull something out rather than send something in required a spell. Part of

Mom's powers being gone meant that she had absolutely no idea what that spell was.

Mom was sitting in Brian's chair when she told me this, and for a second, I had an out-of-body experience where all I could focus on was her sweatpants, so large that they pooled around her ankles. I could feel myself getting hot and my breath quickening, sure signs of a panic attack coming my way. "Oh God," I moaned. "There's got to be someone who knows. If Brian's in jail, he gets one phone call, right? Does that mean we can call him?"

"Why don't you look the spell up?" Janis asked.

"Janis!" I snapped, my panic getting the better of me. "It's not like it's going to be on Wikipedia or anything."

"I mean in a book," she clapped back. "Dude's got a whole medieval library here." She pointed behind me. I spun around, then practically yelped with joy. There were Brian's books, all of which were massive, dusty tomes that looked like they'd been pulled straight out of the Jim Henson props department. We hadn't touched them in our training, but Janis was right: if there was a spell to open the Portal, this would be the best place to find it.

It was also an intimidating place to start. Each book was as thick as my thigh, and there were dozens of them. Think, I said to myself. What did I know I could do? I could move things with my mind. I'd unlocked doors, dangled humans, wrecked cars, and thrown dodgeballs. Some of that hadn't been intentional (sorry, baby birch tree), but when it had been, I'd just thought about the end result, and it had happened.

So maybe that would work here? If I wanted to use kinesis to open the book to the Portal page, maybe I could do that, even if I didn't know which page that was. Except Brian had said that our powers wouldn't work in the cave.

"Come on," I said to Janis and Mom. "Help me move them into the bedroom."

"I've reached a point in the night when I'm just going to stop asking questions," Janis said, and she hefted a book off the shelf, carried it back through the closet, and dropped it onto the bed, before returning to get another one. Mom and I did the same, and soon every surface in Brian's bedroom was covered with books. At any other library, we would have been sneezing and coughing from dust, but these books, like everything else at Brian's, were spotless.

When we'd moved the last book, I climbed onto the bed—silently apologizing to Brian's sheets for my shoes, though that was the least of his worries—to position myself in the middle of the room. I held my hands up and let everything else drain from my mind, thinking only, Portal spell, Portal spell, Portal spell, like a scratched record. All around me, the books flopped open and the pages riffled through the air, filling the room with the sound of rustling paper and a slight breeze. Then, just as suddenly, every book except one slapped shut. I held my breath as I jumped off the bed and walked over to the open book. I scanned the pages top to bottom, and my heart sank. There were spells to control blood, manipulate magnetic force, and read emotions through inanimate objects. But nothing about the Portal.

Then I saw it, in the upper left corner: a half line of text running over from the previous spread. I flipped the page.

As my eyes settled on it, the lettering changed from black to red. I'd found what I needed, and was so excited that I squealed out loud. Mom was next to me in an instant, looking at the book over my shoulder.

"Does this seem right?" I asked. She squinted, rubbed her eyes, and looked again.

"I have no idea," she said. "I don't think I'd know the difference between a spell and a recipe for beef stew anymore. The spells have to evolve with the times. They have to always involve modern ingredients that are easy enough to obtain. Otherwise, Sitters would spend all their time in the woods, digging for roots with names that no one can pronounce." She looked at the book again. "What's a vape cartridge?"

"It's . . . Never mind," I said. "But you wouldn't put it in a stew. So someone has to update all those books every time the spells change?"

She shook her head. "The books write the spells, so they just update themselves periodically."

That seemed both totally insane, and totally practical.

We split the spell ingredients three ways and started searching the house. There was a loud clatter, and the sound of falling plastic from the kitchen. Then Janis called out that she'd found cinnamon. It felt weird going through all Brian's stuff, but if anyone ever asked us, we'd be great character witnesses, because aside from a tube of Preparation H hidden behind some eye cream in the bathroom, we didn't find a single thing that hinted at the inner life, much less any shadiness, of the man behind the tracksuit. He was clean.

In spite of the orderliness of his house, Brian was a bit of a hoarder, which I was starting to think was a Sitter trait, and we eventually had everything we needed for the Portal spell, which took a lot more ingredients than anything I'd ever done before. I took a shibori-dyed pillowcase from the bedroom and used it as a sack, dumping everything in it and tying off the top. Finally, I whipped out my phone to take a picture of the spell, but as soon as I held the phone over the book, the words scrambled themselves. I put the phone down, and they straightened out. I raised it, and they jumbled. I hefted the book against my stomach to take it with us, and we were as ready as we were going to be.

CHAPTER 22

I let Mom have shotgun, and I sat in the back. I kept the book open on my lap as Janis drove, trying to commit everything to memory and double-check that we had what we needed. Then, at the bottom of the page, I saw something that I'd missed at Coach's house.

"Crap!" I yelled, the word coming out in a screech. "We're screwed!"

Janis swerved, and Mom stuck her arm out to brace herself on the dash. "It takes a whole coven," I said, pointing to a line on the page, even though there was no way Mom could see it in the dark. "A Sitter can't open or close the Portal on her own. She has to do it with her *coven*."

"Do you have a coven?" Mom asked.

"I didn't even know Sitters *had* covens! I thought that was just for witches!" I slammed the book closed. Damn Brian and his freaking football team!

Opening the book and looking at it again only increased my despair. "It doesn't even say how many Sitters are *in* a coven!" I slammed it closed for the second time.

"It's four," Janis said, and I vaulted forward between the seats to look at her. She continued, almost apologetically. "Like in *The Craft*, there were four of them, because that's balance. It represents the four elements, and the four directions and all that stuff." She rolled her eyes. "I guess you never Googled 'witchcraft' before. . . ."

"We don't have four Sitters," I moaned. "We don't even have four people." At that moment, it felt like the only people I even knew were in the car with me right then. Cassandra and MacKenzie were in hell, Brian was in jail, Dion was an idiot and in the trunk, Dad thought his best friend was a perv, and Erebus was goddess-knows-where, plotting something more horrible than anything I could imagine.

Then, in my despair, an idea clicked into place, and I read the spell again. It was a long shot, but it was still a shot.

"Actually, I know someone," I said. "We just have to pick her up, because she can't drive either."

"Who?" asked Janis, who knew better than Mom that I didn't have any other friends.

"Someone I trust a lot," I said. "She's loyal, obedient, and a very good girl."

The house was totally dark, and Dad's car wasn't in the driveway. Janis parked, and I jumped out. I ran down the sidewalk and around to the back of my house and let myself into the kitchen. I let out a low whistle, and could hear Pig jangle herself out of her bed in the living room so she could come to meet me. After a few slobbery kisses, I grabbed her Tupperware of food from the pantry and stepped out onto the back porch. Pig looked confused, glancing at her bowl, which was still empty, and back at me, the ruler of the food, standing outside. It wasn't much of a contest, though, and she obediently trotted after me and waited while I locked the door.

I hadn't grabbed her leash, but the dog food rattling under my arm was all I needed to keep her close at my heels. Mom had gotten out of the car and was leaning against it. Pig charged as soon as she saw her.

"Pig, no!" I shouted, but Mom bent down before I could grab Pig's collar, and Pig was covering her face in kisses, the opposite of the reaction she'd had the first time they met.

"I think she's glad I'm me again," Mom said, laughing, before standing up and opening the rear door so that Pig could jump in.

"I thought this might be what you were talking about," Janis said. "But then I told myself, 'Nah, Esme couldn't be talking about her dog.' But here you are, with your dog."

"She's a living, breathing creature," I said, giving her a shove so she'd move over to the other side of the seat. "She knows how to sit and stay, and she won't tell anyone what we're doing, which makes her superior to ninety-nine percent of the humans out there."

"I'm not arguing," Janis said. "But I am going to pre-emptively crack the windows."

I wasn't going to argue with that, because from the back seat, I could already tell there was nothing preemptive about it.

Pig nuzzled into me as I buckled my seat belt and cracked my own window. Janis pulled away, taking a corner too sharply, and the Magic 8 Ball rolled out from under the passenger seat. I picked it up and gave it a shake. "We're coming," I said to it. "Just hold on."

"Hurry," it said back.

When Janis pulled into the mall parking lot, it felt like decades had passed since we'd first been there. The Mall of Terror was starting to wind down, and the parking lot had fewer people and more piles of trash, though I wasn't sure there was that much difference between the two.

Janis killed the engine, and Mom rubbed her ears. "I think I'm hearing things," she said. "Like a pounding and a distant shouting."

"Oh crap!" I said, suddenly remembering Dion in the trunk. I jumped out and raced around to open it. As much as I hated Dion, I didn't want to kill him, at least not accidentally by asphyxiation. He sat up as soon as I opened the trunk, and I bit my lip to keep from smiling when he whacked his head on the lid.

"Ouch!" he said, rubbing his forehead. "I thought you forgot about me." He sounded annoyed, which I figured he had no right to feel. I used my kinesis to push him back down and keep him in place.

"Not so fast," I said.

Mom had let Pig out of the back seat, and now all four of us stood around the trunk, looking at him.

"Mom," I said, "this is Dion, who let the spirit of his evil undead father possess him so that he could kidnap a kid and use her as part of a ritual that also got his sister flushed up into the Negative." I paused. "And I'm also pretty sure he accused our Counsel of having inappropriate relationships with underage students." Dion looked just as confused as ever, but I figured that couldn't be taken as a denial or an admission. "What do we do with him?"

Janis walked over and slammed the trunk shut. "It's past his bedtime," she said, and that seemed to be the end of that.

The haunted house was still going, and no one bothered to stop two teen girls, a grown woman, and a dog from slipping through the barricades into the empty part of the mall.

We paused for a second to let our eyes adjust to the darkness. Pig was interested in the smells in a way that made my stomach turn.

"God," Mom said. "What happened to this place?"

"Amazon," I said.

"What? Like the river?"

"Never mind," I said, and added online shopping to my list of things I was going to have to explain as soon as we had the time.

Mom was having trouble keeping up with us, and after looking more closely, I could see that her pants weren't just baggy. They were about five sizes too big.

"Oh God, Mom, those pants."

"I know," she said, grabbing a handful of the waistband to keep them up. "You tried, and I appreciate that."

I was stunned. "You know I tried to get them to dress you in outfits?"

She nodded. "Esme, I knew everything. I was always there. I just couldn't do or say anything to let you know."

Hearing that made my eyes grow hot, and I wished I could climb into her lap and have a good long cry. But there was no time for that. A low, lingering growl from Pig announced that we were back at the food court, and we had a ritual to do.

I cleared away the Red Magic circle Dion had set up. I scuffed the chalk lines into the ground, their power gone now, and kicked the objects off into the dark. The wilting smiley-face balloon was tied to a ribbon, and when I kicked at it, it wrapped around my foot and then floated right into my face. I punched the balloon in the nose, then used my teeth to tear a hole in it. The helium hissed out, and it crumpled up like a plastic bag.

After I had destroyed everything from the Red Magic

ritual, I started to set up the one for Sitter Magic. Unlike the other spells Cassandra and I had done, which had just required that the objects be there, for this one, everything had to be performed precisely, and in a certain order. I took out a piece of rainbow sidewalk chalk and started drawing. First a five-pointed star, and then a circle around it. My lines were wobbly, and I hoped it wouldn't matter that it was drawn in three different colors. Then, in each section made by the points of the star, I drew in a different symbol, circles and lines with crosses and diamonds and stars. Finally I arranged the objects in a circle in the middle of the star: a Do Not Disturb sign, a dried-up wrist corsage, seven hot-pink plastic army men, a rose quartz crystal, a bottle of vanilla body spray, a stained glass candle, a playbill from *Wicked*, cinnamon sticks, cloves, a clementine, and a mango vape cartridge.

Mom had come over and was standing next to me as I put the last item into play. She reached out, grabbed my hand, and gave my fingers a squeeze. "I do remember this," she said. "I don't remember *how* to do it, but I definitely remember doing it."

In a weird way, I wasn't worried about MacKenzie having spent time in the Negative. There were spells for this, and as much as I hated the idea, I knew I could just erase her mind and she'd have no memory of her Halloween hellscape. But Cassandra—she wouldn't be able to forget. "Do you think Cassandra will be okay?" I asked Mom.

Mom was wearing socks and the generic slide sandals that were de rigueur, and she toed a tile with one of them. "She's going to need you when she comes back. Especially since it doesn't seem like she has anyone else."

"So if her horrible father is out there running around right now," I said, "then that whole thing about her parents dying in a car wreck is just made-up?"

Mom nodded. "I do remember some of that," she said. "Trash like Erebus is hard to forget. Circe looked the other way when he started dabbling in Red Magic. I knew about it too, but we didn't think he'd be able to do much. We were wrong. I know he got very powerful, very fast, and Circe called in the Synod." She paused and swallowed. I could tell it was hard for her, but she went on. "Everything is fuzzy after that."

"So Cassandra and Dion were just tossed aside and the Synod let your brain rot?"

"I don't think it was that simple, Esme," she said, "Circe said Cassandra didn't have the Sitter gene, so the Synod must have assumed it would be safer for her and her brother to be raised by normies. Bringing those without power into the fold is never safe." Her eyes flickered to Janis, who was standing just out of earshot with Pig. "For them," Mom added.

I had a trillion more things I wanted to know and learn, but the clock was ticking and Cassandra couldn't keep up her positive mental attitude forever. Still, there was one question I had to ask, even though I wasn't sure I wanted the answer to it. "Why didn't someone just call Erebus back and then, like, exterminate him?" I asked. "It doesn't seem like it would have been that much of a loss, and it would have lifted your curse."

She squeezed my fingers again. "It's not that easy, Esme. Sitters don't kill. We have a code," she said. "And you had better be ready to follow it."

I nodded, even though 20 percent of me was saying no.

Brian had talked about instinct and intuition, but the words hadn't meant that much to me. Second-guessing myself was kind of my thing; I had doubts about everything from the efficacy of my deodorant to the way I said the word "magazine." But now, for Cassandra's and MacKenzie's sakes, I had to trust myself. Even more than that, I had to be the leader. I felt like a camp counselor when I clapped my hands to call everyone together to get them into position. We stood spaced evenly, ninety degrees apart, around the edge of the circle, to represent the four directions. Pig was south. She gave me a pleading look, surely in relation to the dog food, but stayed put.

The last thing I told everyone to do was think of Cassandra. With everyone thinking of her, it would be like an interdimensional group text—insistent and impossible to ignore. We would pull her out, and something told me that her Sitter instinct meant that she would bring MacKenzie with her. I extended my hands, palms facing the center, fingers spread, and Mom and Janis followed my lead. Pig licked her nose and grunted. Janis looked nervous. I locked eyes with Mom, and she gave me a nod that was barely noticeable. "Diastasikinesis," I said, softly at first, then more loudly, and finally, a third time, shouting. My voice echoed in the big, empty building, and then it died into silence. We were about to save a kid and a Sitter, or destroy the world. Either was a likely possibility.

All the spells I had done before had felt like chugging a Red Bull first thing in the morning. A jolt, but nothing that would knock me off my feet. This time I felt like I'd dropped a hair dryer into the bathtub and was holding on for dear life. I could feel the spell run through me, in my veins, in my brain, in my heart, down to the tips of my eyelashes. It was every caffeinated beverage I'd ever drunk, every ride I'd ever been on at the fair, every first kiss I'd ever imagined, all rolled into one.

My vision blurred, and when the world came back into focus, I expected things to look different, but it was just the same as it had been thirty seconds before—dust and dirt and decay. I gnashed my teeth, and the electrified feeling faded from my gums. My mom cracked her neck. Janis's eyes were wide, but she didn't move. Pig scratched an itch. I spun in a complete circle, looking for the Portal, and when I didn't see it anywhere, the panic bubbled up like barf. I ran over to where it had been before, and still, nothing. A wave of weakness washed over me. We had no Plan B. I'd have to find other Sitters, and without Brian, I had no idea how long that would take. My head swam with possibilities, all of which carried the price tag of Cassandra and MacKenzie staying right where they were.

Then I saw it, finally, looming right above PandaSub.

After what Dion/Erebus had opened earlier, the Portal that hovered above us now was hardly impressive. It was barely the size of a hot tub, and the whole outer half trembled, like a mirage that could vanish any minute. Mom walked up and stood next to me.

"You did it," she said.

"Barely. It's piddly. It's for baby demons only. How can Cassandra and MacKenzie even come through that?" I gasped as something that definitely did look like a baby demon started to crawl through. I gave it a sharp shove back in with my mind, and had to strain to hear the flush.

I took a few steps closer, until I was standing right under it and could feel the Negative energy it generated moving around me in gross little whispers. I focused all my energy on Cassandra and let everything else drain away. Then I sent my mind in.

The trek was slow and uncomfortable, like moving through slushy water, and I inched along, growing more uncomfortable the deeper I got. It didn't feel cold; it didn't feel hot; it just felt . . . Negative. Icky. Like going down an hours-long social media scroll hole, or reading too much news. I felt jealous, bitter, angry, ashamed, bored—the kind of emotions that breed hate and apathy and violence.

I pushed deeper, sending mental signals out after Cassandra like I was reaching for her. When I hit something that felt like color after swimming through so much gray, I knew I'd found them. I started to retreat, pulling the energy with me, until my mind was back in my body. There was still no Cassandra, but then a blank spot became visible in the middle of the Portal, and it slowly grew bigger. When we'd opened the Portal before, everything had sailed through, but she was crawling, and I could hear her grunts as she pulled herself forward. When one of her hands finally emerged, I sprinted to her and grabbed it, with my own hands and with my kinesis, and I started to pull as hard as I could with both. Cassandra's hand clawed up my arm. It was like she was drowning in concrete, and rather than me pulling her out, she was pulling me in.

Then I felt arms grip me from behind and start dragging us away from the Portal. I glanced over my shoulder to see that a train had formed: Janis had a hold of me, Mom had a hold of Janis, and Pig had the waistband of Mom's pants clamped in her jaws. I threw my weight against Janis, and all four of us pulled with everything we had, until Cassandra, with MacKenzie clasped under her arm, was dislodged with a sucking sound and then a sudden pop that sent us all tumbling backward onto the ground.

I was on my feet first, having realized that while I had looked up how to open the Portal, I hadn't learned anything about closing it. In a panic, I held out my hand, the same way I'd done with all my other spells, and screamed the spell backward. To my relief, my piddly Portal sputtered, then disappeared. I raced back to Cassandra and MacKenzie, who were still lying on the ground. Cassandra's face was pale, and I panicked, thinking that maybe I would have learned adult CPR if I'd ever actually taken gym. I was only prepped for a kid choking on a Cheerio.

She moaned slightly, and her eyes fluttered open. She blinked a few times, as if she wasn't entirely sure where she was. Then, to my relief, she opened her mouth and started laughing.

The sound woke MacKenzie, who erupted in peals of her own laughter. We pulled them to their feet and gathered them up in a five-person group hug, with Pig butting her head in between our knees. Cassandra didn't stop laughing until we let her go. Then she took a step back to catch her breath.

"How are you?" I asked, worried that maybe her laughter was a sign that her mind hadn't come back with her.

"Okay," she said. "It just feels so good to feel good again." She looked around, then asked, "Where's Dion?"

"In Janis's trunk." This news threw Cassandra into another fit of laughter.

"And what about my supreme a-hole of a father?"

I gasped. "How'd you know about him?"

Her eyebrows knitted in concentration. "He's pretty famous down there," she said. "And not in a good way."

"You talked to people down there?"

"Not people," she said. "But yeah. And they knew who I was. . . ." Cassandra had a faraway look on her face, and it was actually one of the scariest things I'd seen all night.

She looked . . . worried. She reached out and grabbed my sleeve.

"Do you have a pen?" she asked.

"What?"

"Or a pencil." She looked around. "And paper. Ugh. I need to write this stuff down before I forget it. Where is my dad, anyway?"

"He got away," I said. "He's out there somewhere."

"So we get the kid home safe, and then find his sorry ass," she said, "and find out what this is all about." I promised that we would find her a pen, and I was so happy to have her back that I threw my arms around her to hug her again. What I saw over her shoulder made me scream like a prom queen in a slasher flick.

Erebus. His stupid face, less than a foot from mine, with that horrible smile smeared across it.

"Apologies for interrupting your moment, darlings, but it sounded like you were talking about me."

Without even thinking about it, I grabbed a handful of his hair, yanked his head every which way, and then spun around Cassandra and twisted his arm behind his back. Knowing he could disappear at any moment, I gave him everything I had. Cassandra was right beside me, brandishing the stolen dagger, which she had somehow managed to hold on to.

As the blade was just inches from connecting with him, he vanished again, and the momentum of swinging through nothing but air sent Cassandra stumbling forward.

Erebus reappeared behind us, and now he bent over with laughter. I went to grab him again. This time I was going for the fleshy parts of his face, his nose and his lips, where it would hurt the most. He sensed what I was about to do and held his hand up in my direction. Suddenly it felt like I had slammed into a plate-glass window, a head-to-toe sting that was, I realized, the feeling of my kinesis being thrown right back at me. It made my ears ring, which made the sound of his laughing again turn into an evil echo. Behind me, I could hear voices screaming my name. I tried to block them out and focus on Erebus, but I was wired to listen for children in distress, and MacKenzie's voice cut through the commotion. "Esme, look up! Look up!" she screamed.

So I did.

What I saw almost knocked me out. The Portal was back, and bigger than ever. It swirled above us like the sun, big enough for a monster truck to careen right through the middle, and it was darker and deeper than before. I saw Cassandra look up too, and it had a stunning effect on both of us as we stood there and stared. There was no doubt it was beautiful. There was no doubt it was terrifying.

It made Erebus scream, and that was when I realized we were no longer alone.

Without me even noticing, four other people had joined us, all adults, no one I had ever seen before. There was a middle-aged woman with dreads who wore a wax print dress that wouldn't have looked out of place on Solange, and another, in a tweed suit, who could have played the evil stepmother in a telenovela. The third wore all black, including a black headscarf, and the fourth made me do a double take. I'd seen her before, many, many times. It was Laurie Strode herself, now with a classic I-love-aging short haircut, but overall looking just as badass as ever.

They were positioned around us, and when they simultaneously raised their right hands to the center, palm out, I knew who they were.

The Synod.

And they were pissed.

I felt a crackle of magic go by me, and it hit Erebus from all directions at once, flashing around him like lightning. He rose into the air, and for a second I thought he was getting away. Then I realized that he wasn't in control at all. They were.

His body zoomed through the air, straight into the middle of the Portal. The flushing sound roared through my ears, and then, poof. Just like that, the Portal was gone. I turned to the nearest member of the Synod, the woman with dreads, and was starting to run toward her, ten million questions on the tip of my tongue, when her image burst like a balloon in front of me. I spun in a circle as the same thing happened to the next two. Laurie was the last one, and as I caught her eye, she gave me a quick wink. "Nice cardigan," she said, and then she vanished too. As suddenly as they had come, they were gone.

$\bullet$ $\bullet$ $\bullet$

I could tell she was gone, too, before I'd even gotten to her. The smart, funny, engaged Mom I'd just been getting to know had evaporated, right along with Erebus. In her place was the old one, the one I was too familiar with. I could tell by her face, the way the skin around her mouth was slack, the way her eyes looked like they were focused on something off in the distance.

I asked if she was okay.

For a few seconds she didn't respond. Then she muttered something about foosball.

As the adrenaline drained out of me, I felt myself start to shake. Cassandra came over. I tried to stop the shaking, but that just made my leg jump like it was having a seizure.

"What happened?" she whispered.

"As long as he's in there," I said, pointing to the spot above us where the Portal had appeared, "she's like this." My voice trailed off in despair. "There's nothing we can do," I said finally. "At least, not right now."

Cassandra put a hand on my shoulder and squeezed. "We'll figure it out," she said. "But right now, we gotta get that kid back to her house and take care of her before you get fired from babysitting."

I looked over. Janis and Pig were both standing protectively next to MacKenzie. MacKenzie had one hand on the dog and was rubbing her ear. I went up to her. If it was another kid, I would have hugged them or held their hand, but MacKenzie had boundaries, so I just stood next to her.

"Hey," I said, "are you okay?"

"Esme, this is all very strange," she said. "Where was I? Where am I now?"

I couldn't believe she wasn't crying or freaking out. What she'd been through would have been enough to make Wonder Woman cry, but I guess MacKenzie McAllister was one tough elementary school B.

"You're in a mall now, and before . . . well . . . Let's get you home." I'd look up Coach's mind-melting spell as soon as we got to the car, and if I needed any ingredients we didn't have, I'd make Janis stop for them on the way.

I raised my hand to the remains of the ritual and mumbled a cleaning spell. The chalk lines scrubbed themselves off the floor, and the ingredients put themselves back into the pillowcase before the chairs and tables scattered themselves around in the haphazard way we'd found them. I hefted the spell book onto my hip, and then we headed for the door, me holding Mom's hand and leading her along like she was a child.

The mall parking lot was still home to a few revelers, and everything was already tinted with regret and shame. Instinctively I went to shield MacKenzie's eyes, but then I remembered that a guy dirty dancing with a blow-up duck was far from the worst thing she had seen tonight.

At Janis's car, I helped Mom into the front seat, then helped MacKenzie and Pig into the back. Cassandra and I walked around the car, and I gave Dion a reassuring pound on the lid of the trunk. "Don't worry," I said into it. "We got her back. No thanks to you, of course."

"I'm so sorry, Cass," he said, his voice muffled. "I'm so sorry. Can you let me out of here now?" Both of us pretended not to hear him.

"What should we do with him?" I asked Cassandra as we squeezed into the back seat of the Honda. It was her decision, and I couldn't imagine what she was going through. I mean, I felt betrayed by Dion in my own way, but that was barely beans. He was her brother, and no matter how much he claimed to have been a pawn in this whole Halloween disaster, he had still made the decision to make himself a pawn.

And that sucked.

Cassandra looked away and wiped some steam off the window. "I'm going to sleep on it," she said. "Or to be precise, I'm going to lock him up in a closet, make sure there's no freakin' way he can get out, and then sleep on it."

We were racing against the clock to get MacKenzie home before her parents, stopping to let Cassandra and Dion out at a corner along the way. I wondered if Cassandra needed my help with him, but as soon as we popped the trunk to let Dion out, she landed a punch right in the middle of his nose, and I figured she could handle herself.

Mom was a different story. We left her two blocks from the home, and then Janis made a call to report what looked like a resident standing on the corner. Thankfully, whoever answered the phone believed Janis and didn't ask how she knew the difference between a resident and someone who'd just eaten too much candy.

Pulling away and leaving her like that was the hardest thing I'd done all night.

Janis drove like a bat out of hell—which meant she drove like she normally did—to get to MacKenzie's, while I sat in the back seat, using my powers to find the right spell in the book. Janis, bless her, kept up a steady stream of chatter, trying to convince MacKenzie that we'd just gone to a haunted house. It was futile, as MacKenzie was too smart to be swayed, but for the moment, she still appeared to be somewhat stunned, and that was buying me some time. Janis swung into a gas station, where I bought a pine tree air freshener and a bottle of Benadryl, crossing my fingers that the McAllisters had herbal tea and eye cream back at the house. As soon as I got her home, I was going to erase her memories of the night and replace them with ones spent downloading apps and going to bed early.

I was having a hard time concentrating, though, thinking of how I'd gotten flashes of what my life would have been like with Mom in it, and how those flashes already were starting to seem like a dream. I also dreaded returning home to Dad, who now thought his best friend was . . . Ugh. It was too much.

Janis took the back way to MacKenzie's house and parked in the alley. I had just let MacKenzie and myself in through the back kitchen door when lights from her parents' Uber swung into the driveway. "Get in bed, now," I whispered to MacKenzie, and went straight to the kitchen. I rifled through the cabinet, grabbed a Sleepytime tea bag, and made a detour into the master bathroom as MacKenzie shuffled down the hall. In her room, MacKenzie was already under the covers, her blanket pulled up to her chin, and her eyes were looking disconcertingly clear.

"Esme, what happened tonight?" she asked. "Who was that who kidnapped me? Where did I go? It was awful. . . . Where's my phone?"

She deserved an honest answer to that question, at least. "It got broken," I said. "And it was my fault. I'll buy you a new one." A new phone like the one she'd had was probably going to cost me more than the driver's ed Corolla. Any ceremony that I'd had planned for the spell went right out the window, and I just dumped the items onto her bed and held up my hand.

"What are you doing?" she asked.

"Cerebrumkinesis," I said. She blinked a few times and kept staring at me.

"What'd we do tonight?" I asked quickly.

"Your friend came over," she said. "And I set up my phone. Where is my phone?"

"It got broken," I said again, "and it was my fault. I'll buy you a new one." Then I raced out to meet her parents in the kitchen.

I could hear her mom's laugh as the keys jangled in the door, and seconds later, Mr. and Mrs. McAllister appeared in their now slightly rumpled Leia and Han Solo costumes. One of Mrs. McAllister's buns had come undone, and she was trying to pin it back up, with little success. They both seemed slightly drunk, which was good for me, because tipsy parents asked fewer questions.

"Whoa," Mr. McAllister said. "Is that what they're giving you guys for textbooks now? Looks like the schools are going back in time."

With horror, I realized he was talking about the spell book, which I had stupidly left sitting out in the open on the counter, for everyone to see.

"Oh, haha," I laughed, sliding it into my lap. "This is a prop for a play. It helps me practice my lines." Before I'd even finished my lie, he had turned and was rummaging through the fridge, my weird occultish drama club artifact already long forgotten.

I took the opportunity to tell Mrs. McAllister about the phone. "I dropped it, and it broke," I said. "I'm so sorry. I'll pay for it. I know it was brand-new."

"I won't hear of that, Esme," she said. "Phones break all the time. Where is it? If it's just the screen, I'm sure we can get it fixed."

Crap. I hadn't thought of that. The phone was at the mall, cracked screen and battery slowly dying somewhere in the food court. "I'm taking it with me," I said. "I'm going to take it to that place. That phone place." I said a silent prayer that she didn't ask to see it, but she was distracted by her husband squirting whipped cream directly into his mouth.

Through the kitchen window, I could see Janis's head-lights in the alley. "My ride is actually outside waiting for me," I said.

"Thanks for everything, Esme," Mrs. M. said, thrusting some bills at me with one hand while she used the other to try to wrest a bottle of chocolate sauce from her husband, causing him to miss his mouth and fill his ear canal with Hershey's. "You're such a good babysitter."

I swallowed. Tonight, that was definitely up for debate.

Janis dropped Pig and me off, and my phone rang as I was letting us into the house. I could hear the relief in Dad's voice as soon as I answered. "We found her," he said. "She was only a couple of blocks from the home. Someone called because they saw her sitting on a corner, but she's here now and she's fine."

The reality of that was sinking in. We had gone back to the way things had been for as long as I could remember. But just because I was used to it didn't mean it didn't suck. How could I accept that that was the way things were, when I'd seen how much better they could be?

"Okay, Dad. That's great," I said into the phone, ending my night with a lie. "I'm so happy."

I fell back onto my bed and tried half-heartedly to take off my shoes. Maybe tomorrow I'd cry, but tonight I was too tired.

CHAPTER 23

I woke up still dressed like Laurie Strode, a cardigan pattern embossed into my cheek. I had an Uber notification, alerting me to the fact that Jeffrey had given me a one-star review. I sighed and typed in his promised big tip anyway. Apparently, good customers did not ask their drivers to transport escaped mental patients.

I stood under the hot shower for about seven years. Pig was definitely sleeping in. She opened her eyes just enough to give me a death glare when I tried to nudge her off my laundry. I got dressed in my weekend casual, which was loosely dubbed "No Doubt roadie," then went downstairs. I hadn't heard Dad come home, but when I finally stumbled into the kitchen, coffee was made and I could tell he'd been at the crossword for a while, since he'd already rubbed one hole in the paper. He looked like crap, but since I looked like crap too, it certainly wasn't my place to say anything.

"Hey, kiddo," he said. "Eight letters across, meaning 'a lot, by sea.'" His casual approach to the events of the night before caught me off guard, but I thought for a second. "Fourth letter *t*, fifth letter *l*," he continued.

"Boatload," I said. Dad licked the tip of the pencil, like he always did when he was satisfied, and filled the puzzle in.

I poured myself some coffee and sat down, waiting for details of what had happened to Mom the night before— details from the official version—or for Dad to bring up Brian. Instead he kept working on the crossword, slurping his coffee in a way I was sure was louder than necessary. Every once in a while, he even hummed. Finally he put his pencil down, pinching the bridge of his nose and knitting his eyebrows.

"You know, it's crazy," he said. "I feel so tired, even though I was in bed by ten last night." I started to point out that this was most definitely not true, then decided to keep my mouth shut. He looked up at me and smiled. "I guess this is what they call getting old. Enjoy your youth while you can, all you kids and your crazy staying up until midnight." He chuckled to himself.

"Can I see the paper?" I asked, wanting to see if Brian's arrest had made the front page.

Dad shot me a look. "What side of the bed did you get up on today?" he asked. Then he made a big show of folding the paper in half and handing it to me dramatically. "Imagine that—my daughter being interested in the news." I rolled my eyes in response.

There was nothing on the front, so I flipped to each page, scanning from top to bottom, yet still nothing. Brian was practically a celebrity. Football coach was right up there with mayor in Spring River. There was no way news of his arrest wouldn't get coverage. I folded the paper and pushed it back toward Dad.

My phone dinged with a text from Janis.

> U up?
> mom wants me and this candy outta the house.
> I'll come get u?

Huh. Janis was acting like everything was normal, but I still considered my words carefully before responding.

> cool. How you feeling?
> crazy night last night

The bubble popped up, then finally filled in.

> IDK, maybe for you?
> the most exciting thing that happened over here
> was my bro losing a tooth to a piece of caramel
> omw
> cool, c u soon

I stared at the phone for a second, and then looked up at Dad, who was now slicing a banana into his cornflakes.

I was about to text Cassandra, then got a message from her first.

> dion doesn't remember last night
> he's even dumber than before

Wow. Had the Synod zapped the whole town? It was impressive, and chilling. Dad sat back down, his bowl clinking on the table. "So how was your night last night?" he asked.

"Oh, you know, just another night of babysitting," I said, adding another pour to my coffee to warm it up. "How exciting can that be, really?"

I grabbed my stuff and went to wait for Janis on the porch, and my phone started buzzing as I was closing the door behind me. It was a local number I didn't recognize, but I answered it as quickly as I could, thinking, hoping, that maybe it was Mom.

"Hello, Esme?" My heart started to slow at the male voice, then picked up again as soon as I realized what male.

"Brian," I said. "Don't worry. Cassandra and I were fine without you. How was jail?"

He groaned. "That place . . . The aesthetics alone. I mean, there were no aesthetics. But I digress. I'm calling because—"

"You were wrong AF and owe us, like, the world's hugest, most heartfelt apology?"

He cleared his throat. "Yes," he said, "I was wrong AF, and now I am sorry AF."

"If that Portal used to be sealed," I said, "it definitely is not now."

"Yes, I know," he said.

I took a deep breath. It wasn't a question that I wanted to ask, but one I had to ask. And anyway, last night I'd flushed monsters, so I could ask the hard questions. "How much do you know about my mom, Brian?" I said. "Be one hundred percent honest with me."

He paused for a second. "I only know what the Synod told me."

"And that is?"

Another pause. "I'm not supposed to tell you. They thought it would be too upsetting to know the truth."

I groaned. "Well, too late for that. I'm already upset."

I heard a rustle of nylon through the phone. "There's no mental illness," he said finally. "Erebus cursed her. There are ways to remove the curse, but it's . . . complicated."

"I know we have to help her, Brian," I said. "I have to help her."

I looked down the street to see Janis rounding the corner.

"I'll see what I can find out," he said. "We have a lot of work to do."

"Yep," I said. I was about to hang up when he said my name again.

"One more thing—the Synod was able to take care of everything from last night, which extends to all of your and Cassandra's magical activities over the past couple of weeks. All has been reversed."

I stood on the sidewalk, the impact of that slowly washing over me. "So you mean I did not wreck the driver's ed car?"

"You did not."

I let out a little yelp.

"But you know what else that means?"

I swallowed. "I do not."

"It means I'll see you in gym. So we really should discuss indepen—"

"Crackle, hiss," I said into the phone. "You're breaking up. I think I'm losing service."

I hung up on him right as Janis's hubcaps scraped the curb.

THE BABYSITTERS ARE BACK

FALL 2020

ACKNOWLEDGMENTS

Serious shout-outs go to:

Krista Marino, my patron saint of YA dreams coming true. This collaboration was ten years in the making, and I can't thank you enough for your patience, insight, and sense of humor.

Kerry Sparks, my incredible agent. Thank you for seeing the potential in this book when it was just a rough sketch with a good boner joke, and for helping me clean up puke that one time in Portland.

Regina Flath, for lending your witchy ways to this cover.

The entire team at Delacorte Press—I still can't believe I can sit with you. It's such an honor.

Amy, for both your legal and your knitting expertise.

Mojo, for all the reservoir walks and lunch dates. May the gods of freelance forever favor us both.

Daria, our Russian witch, for bringing your care and creativity into our lives, and for attempting to tame the Underbeast.

Carolyn, for being my IRL Janis for the past twenty years, and to Witch Baby and bad 420 parties for bringing us together.

Poppy, for being the coolest big cousin a baby could ever hope to have. Anybody want a waffle cold?

Molly, my ride-or-die. Even if we weren't sisters, you'd be my best friend.

Joe and Diane, for raising me in a house full of love, laughs, and books. To say I really lucked out in the parent department is an understatement.

To the Arroyo boys. I love you more than all the stars in the sky and all the waves in the ocean. You're the reason for it all.

And to Star Luz, we love you always. Shine on.

ABOUT THE AUTHOR

Kate Williams has written for *Seventeen,* NYLON, *Cosmopolitan, Bustle,* Urban Outfitters, Vans, Calvin Klein, and many other brands and magazines. She lives in California, but still calls Kansas home. *The Babysitters Coven* is her first novel. To read more about her work, go to heykatewilliams.com or follow @heykatewilliams on Twitter or Instagram.